I0746405

Stories of Crime & Detection

Volume Six

Cross Marks the Spot

James Ronald

Edited by Chris Verner

Moonstone Press

This edition published in 2024 by Moonstone Press
www.moonstonepress.co.uk

Introduction and About the Author © 2023 Chris Verner

Cross Marks the Spot originally published in 1933 by Hodder and
Stoughton
The Sundial Drug Mystery published in 1934 by Gramol

Stories of Crime and Detection, Vol VI: Cross Marks the Spot © 2024 the
Estate of James Ronald.
The right of James Ronald to be identified as author of this work has been
asserted in accordance with the Copyright, Designs and Patents Act 1988

ISBN 978-1-899000-82-1
eISBN 978-1-899000-83-8

A CIP catalogue record for this book is available from the British Library
Text designed and typeset by Moonstone Press
Cover illustration by Jason Anscomb

Royalties from the sale of this book will be donated to MND Scotland,
who fund ground-breaking MND (motor neurone disease) research and
world-class clinical trials to combat an uncommon condition that affects
the brain and nerves, and causes weakness that gets worse over time,
eventually resulting in death.

Contents

INTRODUCTION

This sixth volume of *James Ronald, Stories of Crime and Detection* is the first of three consecutive volumes to feature James Ronald's six stories about fictional crime reporter Julian Mendoza of the *London Morning World*. Mendoza is neither young nor good-looking, nor blue-blooded, nor in love with anybody at any point. In actual fact, he smokes a filthy pipe, has a marvellous landlady from Scotland, walks with a limp, is kind to down-and-outs but unkind to policemen, is rude to Society ladies; and is quite prepared to do anything to ensure his reputation as the greatest crime reporter in Fleet Street.

The volume contains a full-length novel and a novelette. The novel is an impossible crime/locked room murder story, *Cross Marks the Spot*. Actress Cicely Foster, has been invited by movie mogul Jacob Singerman to call at his flat to discuss a role in a 'talkie'. He says he is too busy during the day to see her and this is the only way. He makes inappropriate advances towards her and shocked and angry she fights him off, striking him on the head in a struggle.

Reporter Julian Mendoza, 'the bloodhound of Fleet Street,' sees Cicely Foster flee the building in which Jacob Singerman lives, looking distressed and frightened. When he discovers the movie mogul has been murdered and her blood-spattered glove and opened purse found at the scene of the crime, he tracks her down, telling her that Singerman was found dead shortly after her departure. It looks bleak…but for the small matter of the corpse having been found with a bullet between his eyes.

Mendoza starts in earnest to reveal the truth behind the killing which takes him into the studios of Colossal Pictures where he meets the obnoxious world-famous film director Gustav Von Blon. He ingeniously begins to piece together the identity of the murderer, how the murder was committed, and the reason why.

Dorothy L. Sayers reviewed mysteries on a weekly basis for *The Sunday Times* from 25 June 1933 through 18 August 1935. On 20th August 1933, she reviewed *Cross Marks the Spot*:

"Jolly mystery yarn… Julian Mendoza is a detective who will appeal to every woman's heart, as he does to that of his nice Scotch landlady. He is shabby and lame and occasionally takes one over the eight, but he is exceedingly lovable, and, moreover, does his detecting efficiently. Beginning with the shooting of a film magnate in an actress's flat [sic] the tale leads on, through sentiment and sensation, to the oft-told but always effective episode of the actor who is really killed in a stage fight. It is humorously and agreeably written, with good light entertainment on every page."

Cross Marks the Spot was James Ronald's second book for Hodder and Stoughton published August 1933 (the first being *Six Were To Die* in January 1933, republished in *Stories of Crime and Detection Volume One*).

An abridged and rewritten version of *Cross Marks the Spot* was republished in 1941 as *The Frightened Girl* under Ronald's nom de plume Michael Crombie. It was published by Mystery House—an affiliate of Arcadia House Inc.,70 Fifth Avenue, New York. Alex Hillman and Samuel Curl were co-founders of the Hillman-Curl and Arcadia House imprints in the mid-1930s. After the partnership ended in 1939, Curl went into business for himself. He retained the AH imprint, using it primarily for westerns and romances, and started the Mystery House line in 1940. *The Frightened Girl* was also published in paperback in abridged form as a Prize Mystery Novel No.11, in 1944 by Crestwood Publishing Co., Inc. The names of some of the characters have been changed in these editions. The murdered man, film magnet Mr. Jacob Singerman becomes Mr. James Surlin and his brother, managing director of the Colossal Film Company, originally Mr. Hyman Singerman is now Mr. John Surlin. John Surlin's brother-in-law Sam Finklebaum becomes Mr. Sam Ranker. The world-famous film director Gustav Von Blon becomes a less impressive named Stephen Billman. The version in this volume is the unabridged Hodder and Stoughton publication with original character names.

Not a Mendoza story, the novelette, *The Sundial Drug Mystery* completes this volume. During a stormy night, three members of the acting profession, a married couple and a girl, are travelling by motorcar to Norwich to appear in a play 'All for Love' at the Norwich Theatre. Their car breaks down. Lashed by driving rain, they struggle to find help. They arrive outside a deserted mansion and force their way in. A series of mysterious events ratchets up the tension, as they become aware they have trespassed into a hornet's nest of mystery and intrigue. There is never a dull moment in this fast-moving adventure, climaxing to an action-packed conclusion. We meet another character with the surname von Blon, this time not a film director but a famous flying ace during the war who has become a murderous drug smuggler.

The Sundial Drug Mystery was published in January,1934 by Gramol (Mystery Novels No.30) but likely to have been written much earlier. It is hard to believe that out of choice James Ronald began as a pulp writer for a prolific publisher of cheap fiction between the wars, Gramol Publications, 3 Duke Street, Adelphi, London W.C.2. The name Gramol was extracted from Arthur

Gray (1889-1960) and Frederick Matthew Mowl (1887-1949), who ran the outfit. They were regarded as the worst-paying publishers of the period. They had begun publishing in the 1920s, originally as the Federation Press, operating since about 1926, from Gramol House, Farringdon Avenue.

ABOUT THE AUTHOR

James Jack Ronald, to give his full name, was born 11 May 1905, in North Kelvinside, Glasgow, Scotland. He was the son of James Jack Ronald, a Chartered Public Accountant, and Katherine Hamilton Ronald. He was educated at Hillhead High School, Glasgow, established in 1885.

Until he was five, James Ronald says he was chubby, happy, and irresponsible; but in 1911, his sixth year, he was run over by an automobile causing a very real morbidity to creep in. For ten years following the accident he suffered recurrent dreams about a wheel that became larger and larger as it turned faster and faster. He was invalided over a long period during which, with his mother Catherine's encouragement, he enjoyed a prodigious amount of reading. He later claimed he owed his literary gift and resultant career to this near-fatal automobile accident, which caused him to change from a sunny little extrovert to a cloudy introvert.

When he was fourteen he wrote an account of the accident, setting down all the details in a somewhat light vein, not forgetting to note that the candy he had purchased with such delight on that foggy morning was found sticking to the wheels of the car as he was being carried off. The piece won him first prize for composition and congratulations from the masters at the school and even the headmaster wished him well, but that did not prevent corporal punishment for his appalling handwriting. He was called into the headmaster's office, but kept waiting so that everybody knew that he, James Ronald, was going to receive a beating from the headmaster. This injustice obviously affected him very deeply, because it remained with him all his life, and crops up in interview after interview:

> After all, I taught myself to read before going to school and could see no reason for accepting a beating because they failed to teach me how to write, so I bolted.

In a spirit of rebellion against repeated punishments for bad handwriting for compositions for which he invariably got an 'A', Ronald came home from school one day announcing he would never return. It was time to leave. His mother Catherine was understandably distressed, concerned her elder son leaving school at such a young age would diminish his career prospects. Aware of the scarcity of jobs just then in Glasgow, she told him he could only stay away from school if he remained active in some useful employment, making it clear she would not condone an idler in the family.

Within three days James Ronald was an errand boy for the *Glasgow Evening News*, a paper into which he had smuggled a poem some months earlier. But there was 'no writing, nothing editorial' in his set up and he thoroughly disliked it and lost the job. He found another post immediately with the *Glasgow Sunday Mail* and kept this one until he printed his own rival paper on the office mimeograph. He broke the machine and, failing to cover his tracks by leaving a sheet in the copier, he was fired. Then came a dozen jobs, including one with an art dealer for whom he gilded statues and washed windows. His mother told him, 'It is no disgrace to wash windows, James, but it is a disgrace to wash them like that.'

By the age of seventeen, James Ronald had run through all prospective employers in Glasgow, including every newspaper.

He felt the need of open space—'a lot of it'—and after various and sundry abortive departures, finally won grudging permission to seek his fortune in the New World.

For some reason, Chicago stuck in the mind of the young Ronald as a magic word. He became determined to travel to the United States of America. The main method of crossing the Atlantic Ocean in the 1920s was by steamship and ocean liner. The passengers aboard the *SS Saturnia* included seventeen-year-old James Ronald, who arrived at his destination on 6 December 1922, at the Port of Québec, an inland port located in Québec, Canada. From there he continued his journey across the Great Lakes to Chicago, Illinois, United States. He managed to survive in Chicago; the fastest-growing city in world history, with a flourishing economy approaching three million people, attracting huge numbers of new immigrants from Eastern and Central Europe. Ronald stayed in Chicago for five years, wanting to write, but unable to afford the time because he was forced to earn money to live. He was taken on and fired from a variety of jobs with monotonous regularity. Like his experiences in Glasgow, he exhausted all potential employers, dabbling in some forty jobs ranging from short-order cook and dishwasher to muslin salesman; from dance promoter and theatre manager to washing dishes again in a Greek restaurant. He edited ten trade journals at one time for a Chicago publisher; and gave new life to a women's religious magazine. A chain-smoker, he confessed slyly to have worked for the Anti-Cigarette League, his excuse being 'a man must eat don't you know'—at that time eating being the only philosophy he could afford to practise. It was in the Windy City that he learned about life.

Working in the U.S. as 'a visitor' to avoid immigration may have caught up with Ronald because, in 1927, he returned to Britain on a more permanent basis, and secured a well-paid job with an English newspaper chain, and a promise of future advancement. However, during his first holiday in the job, a car accident disrupted this promising career trajectory. Whilst driving a small open two-seater Rover 8, Ronald was struck by a two-ton truck and thrown out against the radiator of another vehicle. Left with a broken hip and temporarily crippled (and without the newly acquired job), he settled down to write.

Ronald's writing developed in three stages. First, he hammered out serializations and short stories which were syndicated in newspapers, both at home and abroad; and a number were also published in obscure pulp magazines. Some stories then became lost and forgotten and this has unfortunately contributed to a lack of recognition for an impressive body of work. These early narratives were very difficult to track down, but searching has provided me with an enjoyable and rewarding task—a treasure hunt for lost tales. This was not made any easier because many of these stories were published under pseudonyms; Peter Gale, Mark Ellison, Kenneth Streeter, Alan Napier, and even women; Cynthia Priestley and Norah Banning—in addition to known pseudonyms Michael Crombie and Kirk Wales. Those I have discovered have all been gathered together for republication in this series.

A second writing stage followed; the full-length mystery stories which have made him so popular with Golden Age of Detection aficionados. They are out-of-print, elusive to find, and first editions are very expensive.

Finally, late in life, James Ronald embarked on his Dickensian-style life drama novels. He received enthusiastic praise for his ingenuity, freshness, and sharp sense of humour by many critics and writers of the time, such as August Derleth. Orville Prescott, the main book reviewer for *The New York Times* for 24 years, called James Ronald 'a born novelist', and that he 'has in full measure the two basic drives which inspire a writer of fiction—the urge to create characters and to tell stories about them. Mr. Ronald does both naturally, directly and well.' His work received praise and has been compared to William de Morgan, H. G. Wells, Rudyard Kipling, J. M. Barrie, and Somerset Maugham.

James Ronald is a writer who has not gained the long-term recognition he deserves. His work has received high praise for his ingenuity, freshness, and sharp sense of humour by many critics and writers of the time and current enthusiasts, highlighting him as one of the leading storytellers of the day, yet barely anything has been republished since his death in 1972. I hope the reader will enjoy these imaginative and entertainingly written stories as much as I have collecting them.

Chris Verner

Berkhamsted, Buckinghamshire, UK

April 2023

CROSS MARKS THE SPOT

A Landlady and a Lodger

An appetising aroma preceded Mrs. MacDougal up the stairs from her basement kitchen as she ascended carefully, bearing a tray covered with a spotless teacloth and laden with a steaming bowl of broth, an immaculately clean spoon and a 'doorstep' of bread. An aroma to tempt the most jaded palate, it did Mrs. MacDougal's broth—rich, luscious, full-flavored, such as only a Scotswoman with her heart in her kitchen range can make—less than justice.

In the hall she paused with her head on one side, like a speculative bird, and listened, frowning, to a sound which came from one of the upper rooms.

A widow of sixty, Mrs. MacDougal had the small sleek head, the lean active body, the alert bright eyes and perky air of a sparrow. Her work-worn hands and nails were scrupulously clean, if unmanicured, and the honest soap and water which she vigorously applied to her face night and morning had not robbed her thin cheeks of their apple-redness. There were firm, almost hard lines at the corners of her mouth, the legacy of thirty years of coping with the whims and vagaries of boarders.

Her lips pursed as she listened. A thump. Mr. Mendoza! She might have known that he wouldn't obey the doctor's orders! He would cut his own throat if it would spite someone in authority.

She placed the tray on the hall table and tiptoed up the stairs to the landing above. For a moment she stood there, her ear to a door, then, with the light of battle in her eyes, she burst into the room.

"I thocht so!" she exclaimed, grimly surveying the large man, clad only in a shirt, who stood on one hairy leg in the middle of the room, trying to coax his other leg—a pitifully scarred and shrunken limb—into his trousers.

A smile softened the harsh contours of Julian Mendoza's face; there was a curious affinity between this huge, barbaric man and the trim little woman—but it changed to a scowl as he looked down at his recalcitrant member. A huge-bowled, blackened pipe was between his teeth; the atmosphere was hazy with the pungent smoke of his outlandish black tobacco.

"This weather's playing merry hell with my leg. I can't do anything with it."

"Are ye daft?" Mrs. MacDougal demanded. "Did ye no' hear the doctor sayin' ye were to keep your bed for a week?"

"All doctors are fools. 'Flu or no 'flu, I'm going out. If I don't I'll go mad and start climbing the walls."

"Ye're mair than a bit cracked already, I'm thinkin'," said Mrs. MacDougal flatly. "I'll be losing a lodger if you as much as put a foot over the door this night. Do ye no' hear the wind? It's rainin' cats and dogs. Ye'll catch y'r death of cold."

"No such luck," grunted Julian morosely. "Death only comes to those who want to live. Crocks like me go on forever."

She gave him a shrewd glance.

"That's the mood ye're in, is it? Then I'll say nae mair. It's a waste of breath talkin' to ye when ye've one o' these fits on. Awa' oot an' get drunk, ye thrawn deevil, and maybe ye'll have mair sense in the mornin'. Here—sit doon an' I'll help ye on with y'r breeches."

Mrs. MacDougal had borne three lusty sons; bathed them in infancy; nursed them through illness; wielded a strap when they merited chastisement; buried two of them. A man to her was simply a rather helpless creature on two legs, a being not quite all there who had to be handled patiently but firmly. She had no time for mock modesty.

Her lodger obediently sat on the edge of the bed and raised his feet from the floor. One of her hands touched his maimed leg as she drew his trousers up to his knees and he winced. Roughly, he thrust her aside and stood up. He could not bear the thought that she might be pitying him for his deformity. It was three years since a lion in West Africa had mauled his right leg and he still hated the crippled limb like a mortal enemy.

"I've made ye some broth," said Mrs. MacDougal unresentfully. "If ye're set on gaen oot ye may as well drink it first."

She returned with the tray when he was buttoning his waistcoat, set it on a table beside the fire, and withdrew in silence. She could not spank him and put him back in bed, but she could and did make him entirely aware of her disapproval.

Julian drew up a chair and ate in his shirtsleeves. To him, food was a necessity, not a ceremony. Since youth he had tramped, sailed, worked, loafed, starved, feasted, sung, cursed, fought, bled, suffered, swaggered, loved, hated, wherever suns were warm and life was elemental and one cannot do that without losing some of the niceties of civilized observance.

He had a rough, masculine ugliness which is often more attractive in a man than beauty. A large head, which might have been hewn out of a block of stone, topped with a shock of iron-grey hair; a long, blunt nose; a wide, thin-lipped mouth, almost like a knife gash, which yet had a pleasant boyish twist when he was pleased or amused. His eyes, set well apart, were dark and alive. They glowed black when his right to follow his own course was challenged; flamed red with the sudden explosion of his fiery temper, softened to brown in his moods of rare gentleness. Nicotine had stained yellow his large, even teeth. For all his size, his muscular body had a sinuous grace of movement. His massive shoulders tapered to a slim waist and lean hips.

He might have been any age between thirty-five and fifty. Actually, he was thirty-seven.

His clothes always looked as though he had acquired them

in the unredeemed pledge department of a pawnshop. Hot ash was constantly falling unnoticed from his pipe and burning small holes in them. The trousers were baggy. The jacket and waistcoat were wrinkled. At times when soap and water were not available, he was quite capable of wiping inky or greasy hands on them.

The restless Portuguese blood that was in him, having slumbered through four generations of sedate, respectable, Anglicised, wine-importing Mendozas, had come awake in him as a lad and made him the reckless adventurer he was—or had been until the encounter with the lion. That had changed everything. Six months after that drastic encounter he had landed in England with black emptiness in his heart and twenty pounds in his pocket. He would have faced Benguella or Parnanyba or Tahiti sooner with twenty pence. His only friend in London had been the managing editor of a morning paper, whom he had met years before in Bolivia and, since he always tackled his friends and acquaintances when he wanted something he could not reach out and take, Julian went to him. He had an idea, he explained, that he would make a good reporter.

"But, my dear fellow," his friend had said, running his fingers awkwardly through his thin yellow hair (he owed Julian a good turn, but hardly saw what he could do about it), "newspaper work is highly specialised. A reporter must be an expert at tracking down news."

"I can track down anything," declared Julian.

"I dare say—in the jungle—but this is London—and news and wild beasts are vastly different things."

Julian slapped an incredibly large hand, mahogany brown and thatched with golden hairs, down on the managing editor's desk.

"Half the stuff you print is about crime. Criminals are merely men with the instincts of animals. Wild beasts, or human animals—where's the difference? Know one species and you know the other. Besides, from Portuguese West Africa to the Bund and back I've played poker and matched wits with crooks who would make your city-bred variety look like Sunday school teachers. A crime reporter—that's it. I was made to be a crime reporter!"

(In the same spirit, six years before, when he was down and out in a tiny republic in the Andes, Julian had decided that he was made to be a president, and had made himself one and kept the job, with a revolver and his two fists, for twenty-three eventful days.)

"My dear fellow, it's impossible!"

"Why?" Julian insisted. "Don't tell me that it takes a college professor to get news. That yarn you got in Bolivia—you told me it earned you the best job you've ever had—where did all your training and experience come in there? But for me, you'd never have smelled it."

"Granted, but—"

"If you're thinking of my leg," growled Julian, "forget it. In a civilized city half a man is as good as a whole one. That's why I'm here."

No one could withstand the overwhelming personality of Julian Mendoza when he cared to exert it. Besides, the managing editor had a feeling that Julian with only one sound leg was worth three of most men with two. He sighed.

"Very well. I'll give you a month's trial."

To his amazement, Julian made good. In some ways he was the best reporter the *Morning World* had ever employed. He was slipshod, erratic, and his handwriting was the despair of compositors, but when he went after a news story, he had the eager tenacity of a bloodhound. In spite of his physical handicap, he was tireless and unsparing of himself—and the doorkeeper or secretary who could deny him admittance to whomsoever he wished to interview was yet to be born.

And yet, after two and a half years of reporting, he still suffered a nostalgia for the old free savage life; an aching which was briefly lulled when there was real news to be pursued but gnawed afresh under the strain of humdrum daily routine…

Having finished the broth, he crammed his pipe with the tarry black rope he was pleased to call tobacco and lit it with a glowing coal from the crumbling fire. Crossing to the window, he threw up the blind and looked out. The rain had slowed to a drizzle. The night was dark. He consulted his watch. Ten o'clock. Things happen in London between ten o'clock and the dawn. In the dark, Roguery and Vice stalk the streets. Murder raises its head. The dark beckoned to him.

When last he had undressed, he had taken off jacket and overcoat together, slipping his arms out of both simultaneously and leaving them mated. He put them on together and drew an ancient felt hat down over his forehead. The coat was as shapeless as his other garments; the collar was permanently turned up. When he bought a new overcoat, he invariably turned up the collar when he first tried it on and it remained like that, rain or shine, as long as he wore it. Mrs. MacDougal was not in evidence when he came downstairs, but as he opened the door, he heard a characteristic 'humph' from the nether regions, the good lady's final expression of disapproval.

On the pavement he halted and seemed to sniff the air.

Night hung before him like a velvet curtain.

Behind the curtain lay—what?

The Frightened Girl

After he fell the girl stood for a moment looking down at him; then, with an inarticulate cry, she let the weapon she had snatched up in desperation drop from her trembling fingers and stumbled to the door of the flat. Sobbing breathlessly, she tore it open and almost fell into the deserted corridor. As she slammed the door behind her, she heard a clock chiming. Automatically, she counted the strokes. Ten o'clock.

Her hand reached out to the lift-button, but she drew it back. She was in no condition to face the inquisitive eyes of the liftboy. She leant against the grill gates, shuddering with fright, sobbing hysterically, fighting desperately to regain control of herself. For the first time in her twenty-one years of life she almost fainted.

The reflection of her white face and wide eyes in a long mirror brought her to her senses. What a fright she looked! Instinctively she felt for her handkerchief and powderpuff and realized that she had left her handbag in the flat. She could not go back for it. Even if the closing of the door had not automatically locked her out, she could not have found the courage to enter the flat again. She raised her hand to her hair and gasped at what she saw reflected in the mirror. Uttering a little cry, she snatched off her right glove and crumpled it into a shapeless ball.

With fingers that still trembled she tidied her hair, straightened her hat; drew her coat more closely about her to hide the torn shoulder strap of her frock. Then, clutching the glove tightly in her hand, she began the long winding descent of the stairs. Halfway to the landing below she came upon a little man, sallow-faced and spectacled, in a shabby coat and bowler hat, who was tiptoeing up. They stopped and stared at each other, his pale lips parted as though he were about to speak, then she pushed past him and hurried on.

He hesitated. "Here! Wait a moment!" he called in a hoarse whisper, and started down the stairs after her.

She had never seen him before and had not the slightest idea who he might be, but not for words would she have stopped. She took the succeeding flights at a breakneck run, the little man hard at her heels. He sent no further summons after her, but saved his breath for the race. Down flight after flight they clattered, skidding through the corridors, with one or two hairbreadth escapes from accident, and he was gaining when they reached the ground floor. Sedately, if a little unsteadily, she crossed the carpeted hall to the revolving doors, looking neither to right or left of her; the pursuer also slowed down and sauntered casually a few paces in the rear.

The uniformed night porter on duty in the hall scratched his head and stared after the incongruous couple.

"Wasn't that the young lady you took up to the eighth floor an hour ago, Joe?"

"That's 'er," agreed the liftboy. "Looks as though she's been through the mill since then!"

"Judging by the gentleman she was visiting," said the porter judicially, "I shouldn't wonder if you were right."

A grin creased the boy's round, freckled face. "'E knows 'ow to pick 'em! Shouldn't mind takin' a few liberties with that bit o' stuff meself!"

Outside, the girl turned south and hurried toward the corner of the street, where the lights of Piccadilly glowed with diffused radiance through the thinning rain, but before she had taken half-a-dozen paces she heard pattering footsteps at her heels. Angrily, she wheeled round and found the strange little man at her elbow, squinting up into her face.

"Why are you following me?"

He blinked nervously and backed away a pace or two; ventured the mere ghost of a placating smile, which, awaking no response on the face of the girl, dissolved into a hesitant frown.

"I—I—"

"Yes?" she challenged, although her heart was thumping wildly. "Yes?"

He did not speak, only looked at her slyly, with an odd side glance, as though he were trying to sum her up; but when she turned impatiently away, he grasped her arm. "Look here—"

"If you've something to say to me, why don't you say it?" she snapped, shaking him off.

Again, the furtive stocktaking… He moistened his lips, but did not speak.

A tall man, muffled in a greatcoat, smoking a pipe, a shabby felt hat drooping over his eyes, appeared between them; a man who leaned heavily on a stout stick and looked keenly, with dark, alert eyes, from one to the other.

"Is he annoying you?" he asked softly.

The girl reflected. "No," she said, then she turned on her heel and disappeared round the corner into Piccadilly. Simultaneously the little man scuttled like a startled rabbit in the opposite direction. Julian Mendoza shrugged his shoulders. That was that! An odd pair. He had been watching them since they came out of Dorian House. The girl was smartly enough dressed, but her bearing hardly suggested wealth in keeping with that palatial block of service flats, while the man, apparently a clerk or bookkeeper, looked more like Brixton than Mayfair.

About to continue his walk, Julian noticed something lying at his feet. He picked it up. A crumpled cotton glove, worth, perhaps, two shillings the pair; certainly not worth the exertion that would be required to restore it to its hastening owner. Reaching out to place it on the railings of one of the proud old mansions which were being elbowed out of the street by the towering bulk of Dorian House, he paused and uttered a low whistle. The palm was smeared with a reddish-brown substance remarkably like blood. Under a street lamp he examined it more closely. It was blood!

He hesitated. There were other reasons than criminal ones for bloodstains on a glove. And yet...the girl had looked so frightened. The little man had been so queer. And why had she said that he was not annoying her, when he so obviously was?

Julian smelled news. And news with blood in it is the public's favourite reading. In a moment he had rounded the corner and was hurrying toward Piccadilly Circus as fast as his dragging right leg would let him. If only she hadn't taken a bus or taxi... His luck was in. A couple of hundred yards ahead he saw her weaving among the other pedestrians. He signalled a crawling taxi and told the driver to go as slowly as possible, but to keep her in sight. Three streets further on the vehicle was gradually overhauling her when it was involved in a traffic jam. Julian got out, gave the driver a shilling, and limped after his quarry, oblivious to the pain of his crippled leg. Once he slipped and almost fell, for the pavement was like shining black glass.

More than one pair of appraising, speculative eyes was turned on the girl as she dodged skilfully in and out among the surging traffic of Regent Street where it pours into Piccadilly Circus. But if her eyes flickered to right or left, it was to gauge the nearness of an oncoming vehicle, and not in response to tacit invitations.

Along Shaftesbury Avenue she hurried, with the grace of a flower in motion; a slender, shapely figure, in a tailored fawn coat, with slim legs sheathed in silk and silky bronze curls peeping from under a smart cloche hat.

Street lamps were strung along the bustling thoroughfare like a necklace of amber beads and here and there a theatre or restaurant sported a blazing adornment. Above, the purple, starless sky hung low, seeming almost to brush the tops of the buildings. The rumble of traffic followed her like the hoarse growling of an angry beast as she turned into the maze of mean streets that is Soho.

From a discreet distance, Julian watched her being admitted to a house in Angelus Row, a narrow offshoot from Old Compton Street. After the door closed behind her he crossed over and looked up at the drab, down-at-heels fabric of the house. It was no more in keeping with the girl than the splendour of Dorian House. A chipped iron railing, which surrounded an area littered with scraps of paper in the midst of which stood a battered dustbin with its lid at a rakish angle, mounted at one end with a flight of worn stone steps to the front door and at the other descended with a shorter, more muddy flight to the basement entrance. The ground floor was shrouded in darkness but for a flicker of light through a dusty pane above the door, but light shone through dingy curtains from the windows of upper rooms. A card, showing through the bars protecting the basement window, proclaimed that unfurnished rooms were to let within.

Julian went up to the front door and knocked. After a period of waiting that seemed interminable, he heard shuffling footsteps and the door was opened slightly by a tiny wisp of a woman with straggling grey hair who looked at him suspiciously. He smiled pleasantly and removed his hat.

"I wish to see the young lady who just came in."

"Miss Foster?"

"Yes. She's expecting me," he improvised. "I'm her cousin."

The woman opened the door wider, revealing a gas-lit hall, the dark green distemper of which did not quite conceal the gaudy flowered paper over which it had been applied, floored with threadbare red-and-green linoleum; with doors on each side, and, toward the rear, a flight of stairs covered with a carpet which had known too many feet.

"Wish I 'ad as many quid notes as these actresses 'ave cousins," she grunted wearily.

"Come in. Know the way up?"

"Yes," lied Julian. "First on the left at the head of the stairs, isn't it?"

"No. Second on the right. Mind findin' it yourself? My rheumatics is somethin' cruel."

She waited until he started to climb the stairs, then closed the door and shuffled off; hiccoughing, to the regions below stairs.

At the second door on the right on the first-floor landing, Julian halted and knocked. He heard movements within and a girlish voice called "Who is it?"

"It's me," he replied noncommittally.

After a pause a key grated in the lock and the door opened. The girl stood on the threshold. Recognising him, she uttered a gasp. Julian stood looking curiously at her for a moment, then held out the glove with the bloodstain uppermost.

"Yours, I think?"

Her eyes darted from his face to the outstretched hand and she drew in her breath sharply.

"No," she said hoarsely. "No. It isn't."

The door slammed to in his face.

He was standing there, undecided on his next move, when it opened as suddenly as it had closed. A hand snatched the glove from him, the door shut again, and the key was turned in the lock.

Julian raised his eyebrows. "Good night, Miss Foster," he called softly.

There was no answer.

Humming to himself, as he always did when pleased or interested, he went downstairs and let himself out.

"Her name is Foster, she lives at 24, Angelus Row, she is an actress and a confoundedly pretty girl, and she has been through a frightening experience this evening; an adventure with blood in it," he said to himself. "H'm…"

He was still humming as he retraced his steps toward Dorian House.

Murder!

Mr. Hyman Singerman, managing director of the Colossal Film Company, looked like a dignified kewpie doll as he came out of the steam room of the Crescent Turkish Baths. Mr. Singerman was almost naked, and every part of his round chubby, pink person glistened with perspiration.

Two glasses of cold water gurgled down his thick throat, then he waddled across the tiled floor of the rubbing room into the equatorial atmosphere of the hottest room, lay back in a canvas chair, and closed his eyes. Waves of heat beat on him, soothing him into a sensuous lethargy. Streams of perspiration trickled down his face, dropped from his chin to his chest, rolled with gathering speed down his curved abdomen and dripped from his legs to the floor. An attendant came and clapped a bag of ice wrapped in a towel on his bald head. Around him reclined other men, equally naked, equally solemn, fellow-worshippers at the shrine of heat. The minutes passed drowsily as Mr. Singerman's too, too solid flesh slowly melted.

There was quite a lot of him left, however, when he came out of the hottest room and stretched himself submissively on a marble rubbing slab. A muscular attendant in a loincloth proceeded to knead his stomach and the small of his back, thump and rub his legs and arms, and play a tattoo up and down his spine. Mr. Singerman was spanked, pummelled, thwacked and pounded; a sight which would have astonished and delighted some two thousands of his employees in Regent Street and at his Turnham Green studios; soaped and washed from head to foot like a helpless baby, and finally stood in a glass-enclosed shower bath which started warm, became cooler, then cold, then colder, until he was choking and gasping and floundering in an icy, stinging spray.

For thirty seconds he wallowed in the cold, green pool, looking very much as a hippopotamus would have looked if hippopotami were pink, then the rubber wrapped him in towels until only his eyes and his nose were showing, bundled him upstairs into a curtained booth, and flattened him on a long couch. Left alone, Mr. Singerman uttered a weary sigh and fell asleep.

A couple of hours later he woke and rang a bell on a table at his elbow.

"A large whiskey-and-soda and an evening paper," he said to the boy in buttons who answered the summons.

He drew himself up, switched on a light behind his head, and fumbled in the inside pocket of his jacket, which was hanging on a hook above him, until he found his cigar-case. The boy padded softly into the cubicle and placed a brass tray on the table.

"Say 'when', sir."

Mr. Singerman said 'when' almost at once. He flattened the evening paper on his drawn-up knees, sipped the mellow whiskey and inhaled the fragrant blue cigar smoke of his cigar and began to feel the warm glow of wellbeing which follows a Turkish bath.

The news was so familiar that it might have been carried over piecemeal from the previous evening's issue. A demonstration of unemployed in the North; a woman summoning her husband at Willesden; a tariff debate in the House of Commons; a motorist fined for killing a pedestrian; a crisis in the affairs of Ireland; a broken Mayfair engagement…

He had read it all before—nightly, it seemed—and lost no time in turning to the film page, where his real interest lay. Tonight, it engrossed him even more than usual. His full lips tightened and his eyes narrowed as he read the sprawling headline:

'MAD' DIRECTOR CAUSES PANIC
IN BRITISH FILM WORLD
(BY OUR SPECIAL CORRESPONDENT)

Gustav Von Blon, the world-famous director, known as 'The Mad Genius of the Silver Screen,' is creating a flurry of fear in the breasts of the film magnates for whom he is making his first British picture, 'ILLICIT LOVES.' Although he has spent thousands of pounds on the film and it has been in the making for three months, he has decided to scrap the result and start all over again.

That's Von Blon! His pictures are more artistic, more realistic, more sensational than those of less temperamental directors; they are also many times more expensive. There is a thrill in every foot of film he makes—and a pain in the bank account for the company for which he makes it!

It is whispered that Von Blon's whole future rests on the success of this picture. It is virtually his last chance as a director. He is out of favour with the Hollywood Moguls, who have rarely been able to make a profit on his masterpieces, and he has already bankrupted himself twice making pictures on his own account.

There were almost two columns of the article, but he read no further. He crushed the paper into a mangled ball and tossed it on the floor. There was a scowl on his fleshy face as he lit a fresh cigar with the chewed stump of his first one. Still wrapped in towels like a mummy, he came out of his cubicle and glanced at the clock. It was a few minutes past ten. He had been in the baths for over three hours.

The pageboy reappeared almost as his fingers touched the bell. "Get my brother on the 'phone," said Mr. Singerman. "The number's Mayfair 64325."

"Yes, sir." The boy flitted noiselessly away.

Mr. Singerman was reentering his cubicle for his trousers when a smiling face, lean, long-nosed, sallow, like the face of a smiling vulture, appeared between the curtains of a neighbouring cubicle and an ingratiating voice said: "Nu, Hyman! Fancy seeing you here!"

"My bad luck seeing you," grunted Singerman uncordially. "All smiles as usual, you gonof! You're so crooked you can't even keep your face straight!"

"You don't seem pleased to see me."

"I couldn't be so deceitful. The day I'm pleased to see you, I'll have my head examined."

Mr. Sam Finklebaum came into the passage, his bony figure bisected by a red-checked cloth, and prodded the film producer's bulging abdomen with a thin finger.

"Getting fat, ain't you? That's bad. I was reading in the paper only the other day that fat slows up the brain. I ask you; how can a man think with a stomach like you've got?"

"Do I think with my stomach?" asked Singerman indignantly.

"Of course not," beamed Finklebaum, "or you wouldn't be the great man you are today. But you'd better watch yourself. You might drop down dead any minute."

"Maybe that would be a blessing. I wouldn't have you grinning at my elbow all the time, you—you—you beanpole!"

Mr. Finklebaum made clicking noises of reproof with his tongue and teeth. "Is that friendly?" He lowered his voice. "Listen, Hyman, I want you to do me a little favour. If you weren't my brother-in-law I wouldn't ask it."

"Then pretend I ain't your brother-in-law!"

"It ain't much I'm asking," said Finklebaum soothingly. "Say a hundred pounds. Business is slack, and—"

"With a loafer like you, business would always be slack," retorted Singerman, purpling with indignation. "What do you care about business anyway? Since I married your sister Leah, you've made a soft living out of me. Fifty pounds here, a hundred pounds there. Always the same story. But only so often can you take the cracked pitcher to the well, then you spill the milk. Not another penny would I give you, even if you were starving!"

He turned away with a snort of indignation and found the pageboy at his elbow.

"I 'phoned your brother, Mr. Singerman, but there was no answer."

Mr. Singerman grunted and disappeared into his cubicle. While he dressed, he brooded over his wrongs at the hands of Sam Finklebaum. Twelve years of 'loans' that never were repaid. Twelve years of having his appetite ruined by the presence of Sam and, not infrequently, Sam's wife and five voracious children, at his dinner table, for Sam had an overwhelming affection for his sister which made him spend more time at her house than at his own. "The schnorrer," muttered Singerman. "He borrows money from me to feed his starving children and then brings them to me to be fed."

He was buttoning his waistcoat when Sam, still smiling, looked into his cubicle. Mr. Singerman made an elaborate pretence of being unaware of the hated presence.

"I dropped in to see Leah this afternoon," said Finklebaum softly. "She was showing me her diamond necklace—"

Mr. Singerman stiffened.

"Maybe I'm wrong... I didn't say anything to her...but it didn't look like the necklace you gave her for your tenth anniversary...no matter how good it is, paste never does look like the real thing..."

The film producer turned and the demoniacal glitter in his

eyes, the livid fury in his face, made his oily-tongued brother-in-law falter for a moment.

"Not that it's any of my business," he added hastily. "You ain't the only one who's feeling the pinch, only most of us ain't got wives with diamond necklaces that can be turned into cash. If we had, we would. Why not?—if the wife knows, and don't mind wearing paste for a while until things get better? Only, Leah didn't seem to know. I guess she'd be pretty wild if she did…"

For a long time they looked each other in the eyes, then, without a word, Mr. Singerman produced his chequebook.

"Make it a hundred and fifty," purred Finklebaum, smiling…

Frowning, Mr. Singerman came out of the Crescent Turkish Baths into the bright lights of Coventry Street, hailed a taxi, and gave the driver the address of the luxurious block of service flats in Mayfair in which his brother Jacob lived. He was still frowning and chewing his cigar nervously when the vehicle drew up outside the wide main entrance of Dorian House. Something in his eye prevented the driver from uttering the caustic remarks which rose to his tongue as Mr. Singerman placed the exact fare in his broad palm.

Dorian House is a massive, tall, white structure of steel, concrete and Portland stone, with glittering gilt window frames, a gilt-framed revolving door, and a Renaissance entrance hall reminiscent of the lobby of a super-cinema. It is easier to get into heaven than to become a tenant of Dorian House, for while heaven demands only goodness and piety, Dorian House requires a minimum income of five-thousand pounds a year.

The gold-braided night-porter touched his peak cap as Mr. Singerman marched through the entrance hall.

"My brother in?" asked the film magnate brusquely.

"Yes, sir… Boy!"

The liftboy snapped to attention, followed Mr. Singerman

into the gilt-and-glass cage, closed the gilt grill and moved a lever. The lift ascended swiftly and smoothly to the eighth floor. Mr. Singerman stepped out and pressed the mother-of-pearl button which was let into the wall beside the door of his brother's flat. After a lengthy pause he rang again—and again—but there was no answer.

With an impatient exclamation, he rang for the lift. "Didn't the porter say my brother is in?" he snapped when the gates slid open.

"Yes, sir."

"Well, I've rung three times and he don't answer."

"That's funny, sir. I know he's in, for I took up a lady at nine and he admitted her himself. She only came downstairs ten or fifteen minutes ago and he ain't gone out since."

"A lady? What kind of a lady?"

The boy grinned—but Mr. Singerman's scowl wiped away the grin like magic. "A young lady, sir," he replied meekly.

Mr. Singerman stood for a moment in silent thought, tapping his foot on the marble floor.

"I suppose there's a passkey which will open the door?"

"Yes, sir."

"Go and fetch it."

He waited impatiently, listening to the soft whine as the lift descended and ascended, then the gates opened again and the boy reappeared with a number of keys on a huge metal ring. The boy inserted one in the lock, turned it, and swung the door open.

"There you are, sir—Oh, my Gawd!"

Pale and trembling, he reeled back against the wall. "Oh, my Gawd!" he stammered incoherently. "Oh, my Gawd!"

Mr. Singerman took a step forward and peered fearfully through the open door. His face went a sickly greenish colour and he put out a shaking hand and grasped the door-post.

"God of Israel!" he whispered.

A limp figure in a red and black silk smoking jacket and black, braided trousers was slumped grotesquely against the wall, with the legs sprawled on the floor, like a fantastic doll, a few paces from the door of the flat. There was a blue hole, crusted with congealing blood, in the grey forehead, and a scarlet stain down one side of the face. The lips were parted, showing the teeth in a ghastly grin…

"Boy…!" he muttered thickly, staggering back. "Boy…quick! Go and 'phone the police! The police—do you hear?—the police—quick! The police… This is…murder!"

The night porter replaced the telephone receiver on the hook. "They're sending someone right over," he said.

"Golly, I hope they hurry," muttered the liftboy, at his elbow. "Crikey, the bloke wot did it may still be in the building."

"Maybe you ought to go upstairs and remain with Mr. Singerman's brother until the police come."

"Maybe I ought," said the lad, with a fearful glance over his shoulder. "But I ain't."

The night porter sat down at the house telephone switchboard, put on the ear-phones, plugged in to one of the flats, and pressed a switch.

"Mr. Salman there?" he asked respectfully, after a brief pause. "This is the night porter, Ma'am…Out, is he? Can you reach him, Ma'am…? Very important, indeed, Ma'am… Thank you, Ma'am."

The liftboy and the porter were standing in the porter's cubbyhole when Julian pushed through the revolving doors into the vast hall at half-past ten. The porter had just turned from the switchboard, and the boy was huddling close to him, as though for comfort and protection. They looked uncertainly at Julian as he limped toward them.

The porter had the carriage of an old army man. Thin-lipped, lean-jawed, he looked like a hard nut to crack. It was going to be tricky work getting anything out of him, Julian decided, unless he gained his confidence from the beginning. Employees of luxury flats are cautioned above all things to avoid scandal attaching to the good name of the building. Something had happened—that was evident from the boy's white face and the tension of the atmosphere—but, whatever it was, the porter was unlikely to unburden himself to a newspaper man. Nor was a bribe likely to loosen his tongue. Julian allowed him a brief glimpse of his police pass, half-hidden in his huge hand. The ruse worked.

"You from Scotland Yard?" asked the porter.

"Yes."

"But I've only just 'phoned the Yard."

"I was in the neighbourhood," bluffed Julian. "Before you had finished telling your story they got through to me on the 'phone and told me to come here at once. There will be other officers along presently."

The man eyed him from head to foot. "You don't look like a detective," he said dubiously.

"A detective wouldn't be much good if he did."

"It…it's on the eighth floor, sir," the boy blurted out suddenly.

'It.' That must be a body.

"Who is it?" asked Julian.

"Mr. Jacob Singerman," replied the porter. "One of the tenants."

"Who found him?"

The porter jerked a large thumb over his shoulder. "The boy, here, and Mr. Singerman's brother."

Julian looked at the boy. "You didn't touch anything?"

"Oh no, sir. We saw the…the…It when we opened the door and Mr. Singerman sent me straight down to telephone the police."

"Isn't there a 'phone in the flat, then?"

"Three of 'em, sir," said the porter. "But from what the boy tells me, nobody would want to go in the flat to use 'em."

"Gor, no," shivered the boy. "With that—that thing lying against the wall…starin' at you…"

"Sure he's dead?" asked Julian.

The boy gulped. Julian patted his shoulder. "Brace up, sonny. There's nothing very terrible about death. It is a long, deep sleep, that is all." He motioned to the lift. "Take me up."

The porter followed them into the cage.

"If you don't mind, sir, I'll go up with you. I've been trying to get in touch with Mr. Salaman —the manager—he's playing bridge somewhere—and until I find him, I'm in charge, so to speak."

Julian nodded.

On the eighth floor landing they found Hyman Singerman sitting limply on a windowsill, looking rather sick and mopping his grey, twitching face with a large silk handkerchief. He appeared to be on the verge of collapse. His hands were shaking and there was a stricken look in his eyes as though until the end of his life they would be seeing the crumpled, lifeless corpse of his brother.

The porter nodded silently to a door which was slightly ajar. Julian opened it wider and looked in. His lips tightened at what he saw and the porter, who was looking over his shoulder, drew back with a shiver.

"Anyone hear a shot?" asked Julian.

"I don't think so," replied the porter. "I've made no enquiries, of course, as I didn't want to alarm the other tenants any sooner than is absolutely necessary, but no unusual sound has been reported. These flats are all soundproof, in any case. You could almost fire a cannon in one of them without disturbing the neighbours."

Julian turned to the film magnate. "You've seen the body?"

"My God! Yes!" whispered Singerman and a shudder ran through his short, fat body. "It was awful."

"You identify the dead man as your brother?"

Singerman nodded silently.

"Did you share the flat with him?"

"No, I live with my wife in Bayswater. Jake lived alone."

"A bachelor?"

"Well…" Singerman spread his fleshy palms. "Not exactly a bachelor, but when a man supports three wives and don't live with any of 'em, you couldn't call him a husband, either."

"I see," said Julian dryly. "Any servants?"

Singerman shook his head. "The staff of the place did everything for him."

"Then, unless he had a visitor, he would be alone when this happened?"

"Except for the murderer," replied Singerman.

"He had a visitor tonight, sir," chimed in the liftboy, his eagerness to tell what he knew overcoming his terror. "A young lady. I brought her up about nine and she came downstairs—walked down all the way—at ten. She looked scared to death."

"That's right, sir, she did," said the porter. "The lad commented on it at the time. And there was a man following her. An odd little chap in a bowler hat. He didn't appear to be with her; walked a little behind. Funny thing… I didn't notice him come into the building."

"The girl was the only visitor who was taken up to this floor during the evening?"

"Yes, sir," said the boy positively.

"I suppose there's a rear entrance to the building? If the 'odd little chap' wasn't noticed coming in it may have been because he entered that way?"

"It's possible, sir. The kitchens are near the back door, but things get a bit slack after nine o'clock and the night chef might be having a quiet smoke and not notice anyone coming in."

Julian felt the quickening of the pulses he always experienced when hot on the trail of news. And dead men make live news! For the first time in his career as a reporter he had a virginal scent to follow, unsullied even by the police. But the police would arrive at any moment and he would be elbowed into the background. He would have to cover the ground quickly before they came, or this golden opportunity would be lost.

Putting on a pair of incredibly stained and ancient kid gloves, he went into the flat and knelt beside the body. His face was expressionless. He had looked too many times on the faces of the dead for death—even violent death—to hold any horrors for him. The wound in the pale, waxen forehead told its own story. It had been inflicted by a bullet of high calibre. Death must have come to Jacob Singerman as suddenly as the blowing out of a burning match in a high wind. He took the limp head between capable hands, turned it sideways, and submitted an ugly bruise on the left temple to a prolonged scrutiny. It interested him. He went over the body from head to foot, patiently, minutely, and returned again to the bruise. At last, he rose and dusted the knees of his trousers. Murder. Yes, it was murder. If it were suicide, the weapon would be lying within a few yards of the body, and he had found no weapon…

Above the sprawling corpse a large hole gouged in the plaster showed the course of the bullet after it had smashed through Singerman's head.

His eyes roved over the expensive, garish furnishings of the lounge hall. Here, at least, there were no signs of a struggle. Only the inert form of the dead man gave mute testimony to the grim tragedy which had been enacted. His eyes narrowed a little as they fell on a sedan chair (an incongruous thing to find in a service flat!), its panels outlined in gold and exquisitely painted by some long-dead artist, which stood against a wall. He opened the door and glanced inside. Some whimsical impulse had prompted the dead owner to have it fitted up as a telephone booth.

"Jake bought that a few months ago," Hyman Singerman croaked hoarsely from the door. "He got it at a bargain. It's three hundred years old. Jake was always picking up things like that.

He couldn't resist a bargain. We started in the junk business and Jake never seemed to forget it."

Julian opened the first door to the left of the hall and went into a long-panelled room, apparently the living-room of the flat. Near the door a small table lay on its side. It had evidently been thrown over violently: the things which had been on it—an embroidered silk cloth, a vase of red roses, an ashtray, a woman's photograph in a silver frame, and a bronze statuette of a dancing figure—were strewn about in wild confusion.

He picked up the dancing figure and held it to the light. His eyebrows went up. There was a dent on the base, smeared with some sticky substance, to which adhered a short dark hair. Julian replaced it as he had found it and crossed the room to a wide deep couch which was drawn up to a roaring fire. Beside it stood a low table on which were arrayed silver trays, half-filled with tiny square sandwiches, a gold-necked bottle, and an empty champagne glass. Another glass lay on the bearskin hearthrug, its stem snapped in the middle.

On the couch lay a leather handbag, secured with zip fasteners, more a pouch than anything else, of a kind that may be purchased for half-a-guinea or so at any large store. He opened it and examined the contents: a comb, a compact, a lipstick, a latchkey, a jade cigarette case containing three of a popular brand of 'gaspers,' a crumpled one-pound note and a few coins in a worn leather purse.

Julian looked troubled as he replaced it. Everything pointed to the girl he had followed home half an hour earlier and although feminine good looks seldom made any impression on him, there had been a fresh sweetness about her which he found difficult to reconcile with murder.

Frowning, he explored another room—a bedroom—and found it as neat and orderly as though the chambermaid had just left it, except for an evening dress coat which was draped over a chair, in the breast pocket of which he discovered a wallet bulging with five-pound notes, a folded programme, and a small notebook bound in red morocco.

He leafed over the pages slowly, glancing at the scores of names and addresses which were written on them. Muriels, Mabels, Gladyses, Mauds, Irmas, Violets, living in Chelsea, Bloomsburg, Paddington, Bayswater, Victoria, Kensington, and a dozen suburbs. Jacob Singerman had evidently been wholehearted in the pursuit of his hobby. Unfolding the programme, he found that it was of a play which had been taken off the previous night after less than a week's run. At the foot of a long list of the cast, he found the entry:

A Ladies' Maid...... Miss Cicely Foster.

The name was underlined in pencil.

Replacing everything as he had found it, he returned to the hall and, kneeling again beside the body of the murdered man, made a scientific search of his trousers and waistcoat pockets. They contained only the accessories a man in Jacob Singerman's position would be likely to carry: keys, loose change, a gold pocket-knife, fountain pen and pencil, a platinum watch, with the initials 'J.S.' in diamonds, and a gold cigarette case.

With a last look round the hall of the flat, Julian went out to the landing and drew Hyman Singerman out of earshot of the porter and the boy.

"This is a delicate question, Mr. Singerman, but I have a reason for asking it: Your brother was rather partial to feminine society, wasn't he? And perhaps inclined to go a little too far on insufficient excuse?"

Singerman frowned. "Jake always lost his head over a pretty

girl and he hadn't any judgment. We were continually losing typists until he found one who didn't object."

Every moment Julian lingered heightened the danger of being found by the police at the scene of the crime and he had a particular reason for not wishing to meet them. It would mean that he would be detained, if nothing worse, and it was imperative that he should get through to his night editor as quickly as possible. Here was news; red-hot news; the scoop which is every reporter's fondest hope and which he gets only once in a lifetime—if he's lucky! And deadlines are inflexible, they wait for no men, not even dead ones. Julian decided that it would not be a bad thing for the lift to remain where it was for the present. It would at least mean a brief delay when the police arrived. A good citizen would not have wished the police to be delayed, but Julian was not a good citizen. He turned to the porter.

"I'm going to have a look at some of the lower floors. You stay here."

Without waiting to discuss the point, he started down the stairs. At the bottom of the flight leading to the fifth floor landing he collided with someone who was stealthily creeping up. It was the sallow-faced little man who had been following the girl. He started back and took to his heels. Julian did his best to overtake him but the handicap of his crippled leg was too great and when he reached the ground floor the little man had vanished.

"Now where does he come in?" murmured Julian.

Through the glass panels of the revolving door, he saw a long-bonneted sports car drawing up to the kerb. Out of it climbed a Scotland Yard inspector of his acquaintance, followed by two other plainclothes officers, and the driver tilted his hat over his eyes, turned up his coat collar, and settled down in his seat for a long wait.

Julian went to look for the back door.

I Didn't Mean to Kill Him

When Cicely Foster had first come to look at a room in Angelus Row, she thought she would never be able to bear living in it. Philip Dressler, the friend who had suggested it, had warned her what it was like. "It isn't your sort of place," he had said, "but if you're really broke

and looking for somewhere dead cheap, you may care to give it a trial." She was broke. The nest-egg on which she had come to London, which had afforded her a pleasant bed-sitting-room during her two years at the Royal Academy of Dramatic Art, had shrunk almost to nothing and professional engagements were few and far between, but that awful first glimpse of dust and cobwebs was almost too much for her.

Mrs. Mould, the drab, tired-looking woman, smelling, even in the afternoon, of gin, who 'kept' the house for the Armenian owner of a dozen similar properties, had stood with folded arms, saying nothing, eyeing her with a dispirited air which implied that she might be mad enough to take it, but it wasn't likely. Cicely, looking at the grimy windows, the wide cracks between the floorboards, the discoloured patches on the faded wallpaper, the ghastly roses as big as saucers that rambled up it, the laths showing like unfleshed ribs through gaping holes in the plaster, felt an impulse to hand the woman a shilling and bolt. Instead, she thought of the terrifying fewness of her last pound notes and took the room.

Outside, breathing air like wine after the mingled odours which had assailed her nostrils in the cramped hall, she almost made up her mind to forfeit the ten shillings (a week's rent) she had left as a deposit. But ten shillings was a lot of money just then. Too much to throw away because one hadn't been brought up to accept filth and smells as a natural atmosphere. With sinking heart, she moved in.

And, like all bogies when inspected closely, the rickety old house was not nearly so fearsome as she had imagined. Arming herself with an array of paint-pots and brushes she had attacked the hideous walls, the blistered woodwork and the rusty grate. The ceiling and the upper part of the walls, down to a frieze of green leaves, she distempered a pale yellow; below the frieze the walls were apple green. She painted the fireplace dark green and the woodwork and mantelpiece a still darker green, relieved with gold; the effect was at once striking and restful. Putty in the cracks and a golden oak stain made the floor quite passable.

She had not been able to afford much furniture and what there was the product of ingenuity rather than craftsmanship— she had worked wonders with orange-boxes and contrived a plausible divan out of an old wooden bedstead by sawing off the head and foot rests and the greater part of the legs—but gay chintz curtains and chair covers and an armful of silk cushions brought two years before from home disguised most deficiencies and gave the room a pleasant cosiness.

There were some other quite human people in the house and she made friends with a few of them. Philip Dressler, of course, she already knew. She had been introduced to him a year before by a successful young actor with whom she had gone about for a time until his overpowering conceit got on her nerves. Philip was almost a household word. As a child she had worshipped a profile photograph of him, purchased for twopence in a postcard shop, and taken in the days when he was a matinee idol, before he had parted from his wife and started morosely drinking himself to death.

Miss Middleton, a faded spinster, with scant greying hair, skin the colour of the keys of a very old piano, and a pathetic gentility of speech, manner and ideas, had a room across the second-floor passage from Philip's. Cicely had said "Good morning" when she met her on the stairs a few days after she moved in. Miss Middleton had not been quite sure how to take that first salutation; she was doubtful whether a girl of Cicely's looks and youth living alone in such a place could be altogether nice to know; but she had ventured a guarded acknowledgment and with the passing of weeks, her suspicions allayed, had become almost affable. She, too, was poor. Only in the squalor of Angelus Row and by stinting herself of food almost to starvation point did she contrive to exist.

And Kenneth Archer, the motor-mad young man from the North, who had invented a carburettor and was wearing out his shoes tramping London in a vain endeavour to sell it… Kenneth. In a short time from their first meeting (a collision in the doorway of the poky bathroom) Kenneth had become a very special friend.

*

After she snatched her glove out of Julian Mendoza's hand and slammed the door in his face, Cicely stood listening with her heart pounding wildly. She heard him call: "Good night, Miss Foster!" but did not stir until she heard his receding footsteps on the stairs. When the front door closed, she darted to the window and, peering out between the drawn curtains, watched him pass through the yellow pool of light cast by a street lamp and merge with the shadows beyond. There was something vaguely sinister about the bulky, limping figure; something frightening about the glowing eyes that had seemed to look into her very brain as he held out the glove. Who was he? What did he want? Why had he followed her? How had he learned her name?

Nervously, she paced the room, twisting something in her restless fingers. With a spasm of revulsion, she realized that it was the bloodstained glove. Hastily, she threw it in the fire and poked it deep into the blazing coals, poked at it until the charred remnants disintegrated.

As she rose to her feet the mirror above the mantelpiece reminded her of her torn frock. Mending it would give her fingers something to do; would keep her mind from nagging her into hysteria. She drew it off over her head and slipped on a Japanese silk wrap. She was settling by the fire in her one comfortable chair when there was another knock at the door. She did not answer for a moment and the knock was repeated.

"Who is it?" she called doubtfully.

"Kenneth," replied a deep masculine voice.

Tucking the torn dress behind a cushion, Cicely rose and opened the door. A tall young man of about twenty-five, with a slimness acquired through missing many meals, was standing on the threshold. He had a lean dark face, the large-eyed, sombre face of a dreamer; and the thick, capable hands of a worker. The slightest of moustaches fringed his full, sensitive lips; 'I'm an eyebrow, really, if the truth were told,' it seemed to say: 'But the effect is rather droll, don't you think?'

He was wearing a wet raincoat and the grey soft hat in his hand dripped a puddle of water on the carpet. He stepped in quickly, closed the door, and took Cicely in his arms. She returned his kiss warmly, then disengaged herself and reopened the door. "Will you never learn?"

Kenneth cocked an eye at the door, open widely enough to permit a view of every part of the room from the landing, and smiled ruefully. "I don't know why you bother to pander to the old cat."

"Miss Middleton is a respectable middle-aged lady and it is

only good manners not to offend against her notions," Cicely replied. "Besides, it's taken me months to convince her that I'm not a fast young woman and I don't intend to have the effect spoiled. She doesn't think it's quite nice for me to entertain you alone in my room, in any case. She told me so yesterday."

"Why can't she mind her own business?" growled Kenneth truculently. "I should think anyone with half an eye could see that you ate the sweetest, purest—"

"You can't always judge the contents of the package by the outside wrapping. That's one of Miss Middleton's maxims. Don't be a sulky brute. What does it matter if she keeps an eye on us or not? I think it's rather nice of her to bother. Give me a cigarette and sit down. You can stay for five minutes, no longer."

Kenneth extended his cigarette case and struck a match for her. "Where have you been all evening? I knocked twice."

Cicely exhaled a puff of fragrant blue smoke.

"Out," she said, with a vague gesture.

"Out where?"

"Oh, just out."

Kenneth scrutinised her from beneath lowered lids.

"Not becoming secretive, are you?"

"No, darling. It wouldn't go with my type."

"Then where were you?"

"Kenneth," she sighed, "don't browbeat me. I've a headache."

"Did you see that film producer chap—the one you thought might give you a job?"

"Yes…No. Oh, don't let's talk about him. It isn't likely it'll come to anything, anyway. What about you? Is there anything fresh?"

"Not likely," he answered gloomily. "I've given up peddling my invention. What's the use? I've called on dozens of big motor firms and seen no one more important than office-boys.

Now I'm looking for a job, but there isn't much I can do except drive a car and tinker with engines. I'm not even a qualified mechanic. But I can drive. I've been trying today to persuade the Aero Six people to let me have a car for the big Italian road race. It would give me a chance to show what my carburettor can do. But d'you suppose they'd listen? Not they! Said they only use crack racing drivers."

"I know. It's the same in the show business. You've got to prove yourself before they'll let you do anything for them. As though you could show what you can do before you've had a chance to do it."

"It isn't as thought I were a raw beginner," Kenneth grumbled. "I've won races at Southport—amateur ones, of course." He scratched the toe of one shoe with the worn sole of the other. "I've about reached the end of my string. I daresay it'll mean crawling back to a job in Dad's office at Manchester before long. And won't that just be Hades! Dad will never stop doing the 'I-told-you-so-my-boy' stuff."

Cicely threw her cigarette in the fire and put a slim white hand on his shabby blue sleeve.

"Keep your chin up. There's always tomorrow—and another day after that. Your luck is bound to turn."

"I don't believe it," he said, putting an arm about her slender shoulders, "but it sounds nice when you say it. Give me a kiss."

She did. After a long time, he put a hand under her chin and looked down gravely at her face. "You're sweet. So sweet. And lovely. I've never known anyone half so lovely."

Even to less biased eyes, Cicely was good to look at. She had the clear complexion of a child; soft, curly hair, bronze-red in colour, streaked with gold; dark eyebrows and eye-lashes; candid blue eyes; and a small nose with a slight tip-tilt which war rather charming.

"I'm so glad you don't pluck your eyebrows and whitewash your face and generally make yourself look like a china egg, my sweet," he whispered. "It may not be fashionable for a girl to have a face, but I do so like yours."

"Idiot," she laughed.

He leaned back and blew smoke rings at her. "And now, where were you this evening?"

Cicely stared into the crumbling embers of the fire. "Kenneth, you're not starting that all over again!"

He studied her intently. "There's something funny about you tonight," he said.

"I told you I have a headache. I'm tired."

"It's more than that," he said slowly. "There's something wrong. What is it?"

"Imagination, my good boy."

"No, but there is," he insisted. "What is it? Why won't you tell me where you've been? What's the secret? Another man?"

"Jealous beast!" she retorted lightly. And then, overwhelmed by the strain from which she had been suffering all evening, she added bitterly. "Oh, all men are beasts!"

Kenneth stared. "Look here, what is it?" he demanded.

His eyes fell on her frock, partly visible above the cushion behind which she had stuffed it. He drew it out, a flimsy handful of lemon silk, and held it up to the light.

"Your dress… It's torn… I knew something had happened." Jumping up, he glowered down at her. "That film chap… Singerman…"

"Don't be an ass. I haven't seen Mr. Singerman."

"That's a lie. You have. I can see it in your eyes. You went to his flat."

"What do you think he is?" retorted Cicely wearily. "Directors of film companies don't invite young actresses to call on them.

They employ staffs of secretaries to keep them out."

"Then why won't you tell me where you were?"

Cicely was silent. She averted her face. Kenneth bent over her with a savage scowl and shook a clenched fist in midair.

In their preoccupation neither of them heard the dragging footsteps that were coming up the stairs.

"If I were sure that you've been to his flat—that he's insulted you—" said Kenneth, slowly, distinctly, "I'd—I'd kill him!"

"You're just a little late," remarked a quiet voice. "Someone has forestalled you."

Kenneth wheeled and stared at Julian Mendoza, who was standing passively in the doorway.

With a strangled gasp Cicely rose to her feet.

"My God!" she cried. "I didn't mean to kill him!"

The tense, suffocating silence that ensued seemed to swell until it filled the room. Moments passed while they stood immobile, as though the girl's wild outburst had robbed them of the power of speech and motion. Then, with a low moan, Cicely dropped into a chair. That broke the spell. Kenneth stared in stunned horror from the girl to the huge, disreputably-clad man lounging in the doorway and from him to the diaphanous garment in his hand.

"Who the devil are you?" he exploded suddenly.

Julian removed his shabby hat, came into the room, and closed the door. "Merely a reporter," he said. "Your best friend when you've done something you want to brag about; your worst enemy when there's something you want to hush up."

"How did you get in?"

"A slightly fuddled old woman admitted me."

"Mrs. Mould," said Cicely mechanically.

"The name fits. It might have been made to measure for her."

"This rot about killing Singerman…"

"It isn't rot," said Julian. "He's very dead."

Kenneth squared up to him fiercely.

"Well, Miss Foster didn't have anything to do with it. She has been with me all evening."

Julian said nothing. His eyes swung to Cicely, with a mocking glint in them. She shook her head wearily.

"Kenneth, it isn't any good. He saw me coming away."

"Then you were at Singerman's flat?"

"Yes."

The young man dropped to his knees at her feet and looked up at her with a dazed, wondering look.

"Darling, you didn't…didn't…"

Cicely stroked his hair, oddly like a mother comforting a distressed child. Only her eyes answered him. He groaned.

"Cicely, Cicely, what are we going to do?"

Like a tiger he sprang to his feet and glared at Julian. "Are the police with you?"

"No. But by this time they're looking for the girl who visited Singerman tonight and it won't be long before they find her. I had the advantage in knowing her identity and her address."

"I'd like to break every bone in your body," declared Kenneth fiercely.

"A highly commendable desire," said Julian dryly. "Thoroughly in keeping with the gentlemanly tradition of using one's fists when one's brain refuses to function."

To Cicely, he said: "Mind if I sit down? My leg, you know…"

She nodded silently. She was amazed at herself, at her calmness, her lack of fear. Perhaps it was because her brain refused to grasp the reality of her position. She had an odd, detached feeling as though it were all a dream from which she would presently waken.

"This is all rot," said Kenneth suddenly. "I can't believe it."

"Neither can I," said Julian quietly.

They stared at him. This calm pronouncement, the last thing she had expected to hear, did more than anything else to restore Cicely's sense of reality.

"But it's true," she said. Then, almost wildly: "But I swear I didn't mean to do it. It was all a ghastly accident. Oh, what on earth am I to do?"

Julian sucked at his empty pipe. Empty, it had more flavour than most full ones have.

"I'll be better able to advise you if you tell me the whole story from the beginning."

"So that you can print it in your rotten rag?" sneered Kenneth.

"Very likely," agreed Julian. "First, Miss Foster, I suggest a cigarette to steady your nerves. I don't smoke 'em, but perhaps our young friend will oblige."

Kenneth mechanically produced his case and offered it to Cicely. After a few puffs she felt better.

"And now?" suggested Julian.

"Don't!" said Kenneth. "Don't tell him anything. It's a trap. He'll twist anything you say and use it against you."

But there was something indefinable about the reporter which made Cicely decide to trust him.

"I'm an actress," she said slowly. "A rotten one, perhaps; at any rate, I haven't made much impression on the people who count. I've been playing small parts for a year, but the plays I've been in have been distinguished by nothing but the shortness of their runs. My last part was in 'Gypsy Romance,' which was taken off yesterday after five performances. Last night Mr. Singerman's card was brought to the dressing-room I shared with another girl. At first, I could hardly believe it. Jacob Singerman, the film magnate, to see me! I thought it was a mistake. I had never met him, of course, but who hasn't heard of him? I didn't dare think what it might mean. Naturally, I had him shown in at once. He told me he had admired my performance and thought I had distinct film possibilities, and asked me to ring him up at his office today. I did, but he said he was too busy to see me just then and asked me, quite casually, to run up to his flat about nine tonight. He was dining with a director, he said, and wanted him to meet me."

She took a long draw at her cigarette.

"He was so offhand in his manner that I didn't hesitate about going, and even when I arrived and found him alone, I didn't suspect anything. He explained that the director had been detained and would arrive presently. In the meantime, I could hardly refuse a glass of wine and a sandwich. We sat by the fire and talked about films. His hand slipped from the back of the couch, as though by accident, and I moved away. And then—Oh, it was awful!"

The cigarette between her fingers snapped and cascaded a stream of golden dust to the carpet.

"His manner changed. Even his face seemed to change. His hands were trembling. He kept telling me to be a 'smart little girl.' He said there wasn't anything he wouldn't do for me if I would be nice to him. You've got to be nice to people, he said, if you want to get on in the world. I could be a star if I were smart enough to see on which side my bread was buttered. I tried to rise, but he wouldn't let me. There was a struggle and I tore myself free and ran to the door. He darted after me and grasped me by the shoulders. I was terrified. His eyes—they were awful! Hardly knowing what I was doing, I picked up something and hit him with it as hard as I could. He gave an awful grunt and slowly sagged to the floor. I didn't dare stop to discover whether I'd hurt him badly. I was too frightened. I simply bolted as fast as I could."

Her voice trailed away and she covered her face with her hands.

"The swine," muttered Kenneth, who, while she was talking, had been clenching and unclenching his fists.

"And that was all that happened?" asked Julian, methodically filling his pipe.

She nodded.

"Then you didn't kill him." A match flared in his cupped hands. "He was shot."

It took a moment for his words to sink into her brain, then an overwhelming flood of relief surged over her. Not until that moment had she realized how great a weight was on her mind.

"I didn't kill him!" she repeated, savouring the words.

"You'll have to tell your story to the police," he went on. "I advise you to go to Scotland Yard at once and get it over. It's only a matter of time before they come here for you: you left your bag at the flat and there's a programme of 'Gypsy Romance' with your name underlined in Singerman's pocket; they'll trace you easily from the latter alone. It will make a more favourable impression if you don't wait to be fetched."

"Do you think they'll believe me?"

Julian shrugged his shoulders. "It isn't their business to be too credulous. They may. Unfortunately, Singerman was shot only a few minutes at most after you left the flat, and although I searched pretty thoroughly, I found no trace of another visitor. Perhaps they've been more successful."

"I'm afraid," she confessed.

"If it will make you any easier, I'll go with you. It may help to have someone present who believes your story—and I've more than half an idea that they'll want to have a word with me, too."

"If you would—"

"And I'm jolly well going, too!" said Kenneth.

Julian laid a paternal hand on his arm. "You're a nice young man, and all that, but you'd better not. You'd probably want to punch the head of anyone who ventured to doubt Miss Foster's story and nothing gets a policeman's back up so much as that kind of argument."

"Don't you think it would be nice if you minded your own business for a change?" retorted Kenneth truculently.

"Kenneth, please," begged Cicely.

"Oh, all right. But I'm going to wait outside for you. And if they keep you too long, I'll jolly well come in and fetch you."

The men waited in hostile silence in the corridor while Cicely dressed. Obeying Julian's instructions, she put on the frock and coat she had been wearing earlier in the evening.

On the doorstep they encountered a burly man in a fawn over-coat and bowler hat who was looking up at the house number.

"Smart work, Owen," said Julian approvingly. "I didn't expect you so soon. Miss Foster, may I present Sergeant Owen—the Human Bloodhound of Scotland Yard!"

Sir Basil Mumford, Deputy Commissioner of Scotland Yard, sat hunched up in his chair at his massive walnut desk with his elbows on the armrests and his hands pressed together under his chin. His bushy brows were drawn down over sunken grey eyes and his pale clean-shaven face had a thoughtful expression.

"You think, then, that this girl—" he paused and glanced across the desk at his subordinate; he had a trick of leaving certain sentences for others to finish.

Inspector Howells nodded. A tall, spare, angular man, between forty-five and fifty, neatly dressed, with a clipped grey moustache above a wide, thin-lipped mouth, he looked more like a successful accountant than the able detective he was.

"Everything points to the girl, Sir Basil. The divisional surgeon sets the time of death within twenty minutes of ten o'clock and she left the building almost on the stroke of ten. The porter states that she looked scared to death. I found no trace of another visitor. Every part of the flat was in perfect order, except the living-room, and there was no sign of an intruder having forced an entrance. It isn't hard to imagine what happened. They had a sandwich or two and a glass of wine and then Singerman got fresh. The girl wasn't having any. There was a struggle on the couch, a glass was broken, and she tore herself free, leaving her handbag behind.

"Singerman followed and there was another tussle. Cornered, she picked up a small bronze statuette and hit him on the head with it. He collapsed and she ran into the hall, but before she could open the door he was after her again. By that time, he would be crazy with rage and, in a frenzy of fear, she must have shot him."

Sir Basil had been listening with his eyes shut. Now he opened them and murmured: "And the revolver? Where did it come from?"

"She may have brought it with her. Singerman had an unsavoury reputation. Or perhaps it was lying about the flat and she picked it up."

"Thin, Howells, thin," Sir Basil commented. He glanced at an ormulu clock on the mantelpiece. "Ten past twelve. Why can't people do their murders at a reasonable hour? Even policemen have a right to a little undisturbed leisure. I was playing my first good hand of the evening when they got through to me on the 'phone. Nine trumps and two side aces, one of them backed with a king."

"Annoying to have to throw in a hand like that," said Howells patiently.

"Au contraire, I played it out and got a small slam. What are you doing to find the girl?"

Singerman's private directory of lady friends was in his coat pocket. I've sent Brown and the liftboy to make a round of the addresses and see whether the lad recognises the girl. Sergeant Owen is locating another girl whose name was underlined in a programme which was also in the pocket. I've left two more men at the flat to take fingerprints and a fifth to photograph the body and the living-room."

"This mysterious johnny who arrived on the scene shortly after the alarm was given and posed as a detective; better put someone on to find him."

"I shall, Sir Basil. He ought not to be difficult to trace from the description the porter gave me."

"H'm... Wonder what his game was? Oh, and Singerman's brother: what about him? Sure he didn't have anything to do with it?"

"Quite sure, Sir Basil. I've verified his alibi. He was at the Crescent Turkish Baths at the time of the murder and the liftboy was with him when he discovered the body."

"I suppose Singerman had enemies?"

"His brother can't think of any."

"He had a number of ex-wives," reflected Sir Basil. "What about them?"

"According to Mr. Hyman Singerman, they received their alimony cheques regularly on the first of every month, Sir Basil. They would hardly be likely to kill the goose that laid the golden eggs. However, I'll check up on them in the morning."

"Do. Frankly, I'm a little dubious about this girl. She must be a wench of character if she actually did perforate Singerman's greasy hide."

One of the ranked battery of telephones on the desk emitted a low buzzing note. Sir Basil sighed and lifted the receiver.

"No rest for the wicked," he said. "Hello, Basil Mumford speaking… Who…? Oh, send him up, please."

"Sergeant Owen," he said to Howells, replacing the receiver.

Shortly there was a knock at the door and Sergeant Owen entered. Saluting Sir Basil, he turned to Inspector Howells.

"I found the girl, sir. She's downstairs. She was going out when I reached her digs; said she was on her way here. There's someone with her."

"Who?" asked Howells swiftly.

"Mendoza, sir, of the *Morning World*."

The Inspector brought his hand down with a resounding thump on the desk. "That nosy reporter! So, he was the limping man! I might have guessed as much! By the Lord Harry, I like his nerve."

"Better have 'em both up," yawned Sir Basil. "You do the talking, Howells. I'm no good at conversation after dinner."

When Julian and Cicely were shown into the room, they found Inspector Howells facing them sternly from behind the Deputy Commissioner's desk. Sir Basil was sitting in the background, looking pensively at a cigar between his long fingers. In a corner sat a man in plainclothes with a notebook and pencil.

"Well, Mr. Mendoza," barked Howells, with an icy glare.

"'Evening, Inspector," responded Julian coolly. "You, too, Sir Basil? This is an unexpected pleasure." He nodded to a couple of chairs which were placed under the light. "These for us? Thanks. Won't you sit down, Miss Foster?"

Cicely took one of the chairs. Her bearing suggested a self-possession she was far from feeling. Rouge masked her pallor, but she had a sinking feeling and only the somehow comforting presence of this amazing, swaggering stranger who had so calmly shouldered his way into her life prevented her from showing it.

There was nothing intimidating about the room, at least. It was simply an unusually neat office, a little bare, walled at one end with a row of metal filing cabinets, with a thick rose-coloured carpet on the floor and a vivid, colourful daub of the impressionist school above the mantelpiece. To gain a brief respite from the time when she must look into the searching eyes of the man at the desk, she fixed her eyes on the painting and wondered whether it was a still life, a portrait, or a landscape. The other man looked rather friendly, she thought. He had the unpretentious smartness of the sort of cultured Englishman who seems to have been born wearing clothes.

"Look here, Mendoza," said Howells, leaning across the desk, "I have warned you before about obstructing the work of the police. You seem to imagine that the *Morning World* is a power above the Law and that you can get away with anything with it behind you. You can't! For two pins I'd clap you in the cells for impersonating an officer."

"Do, by all means," urged Julian cheerfully. "I've always wanted to find out from first-hand experience how English jails compare with those abroad. And think what a good story it would make! 'REPORTER ARRESTED FOR GETTING AHEAD OF THE FLYING SQUAD!' I shouldn't repeat that threat to my news editor, if I were you, or he'll make you carry it out. He'd jail his own mother for a couple of paragraphs, that man would. Mind if I smoke?"

Sir Basil, who had been listening with his eyelids drooping and a faint smile on his face produced a gold cigarette case and extended it to Cicely.

"No, thanks," she said quietly.

"Mr. Mendoza? Or would you prefer a cigar?"

Julian also declined and proceeded lovingly to fill with rank tobacco his foul ancient pipe. Inspector Howells favoured him with a glance expressive of many things and, consulting a slip of paper which Sergeant Owen had placed on the desk, turned to Cicely.

"You are Miss Cicely Foster, of 24, Angelus Row, Soho?"

"I am."

"An actress?"

"Yes."

"You wish to make a voluntary statement regarding the death of Jacob Singerman?"

"I do."

"Then I must first warn you that a charge may brought against you and that anything you say at this time may be used in evidence against you. Do you still wish to make a statement?"

She nodded jerkily. Out of the corner of her eye she could see the police clerk writing busily and that did not help her to keep her courage but, steeling herself, she repeated in a low even voice the story she had told Julian and Kenneth Archer. Only once did she falter and that was when she told of the sudden change that had come over Jacob Singerman while they sat together on the couch before the roaring fire. Talking about it made her live again through that nightmare moment in all its horror.

When she had finished there was a brief silence, then the Inspector said:

"You left the flat at ten?"

"Yes. I heard a clock striking as I let myself out."

"Then what would you say, Miss Foster"—he was watching her face keenly—"if I told you that the time of Jacob Singerman's death has been placed at approximately ten o'clock."

"I can only repeat what I have said already," she replied shakily. "I admit having struck him, but I did not shoot him."

The Inspector looked down his nose and toyed with a pencil on his desk.

"Frankly, your story is a little hard to believe."

"Isn't it?" murmured Julian, without removing his pipe. "The moment I heard it I said to myself: 'Howells will be too smart to believe this.'"

The Inspector was not amused. His jaw hardened and his eyes smouldered with suppressed anger, but he said nothing. He wrote a few words on a pad before him, tore off the top page, and passed it to Sir Basil, who read it silently, added a word or two, and returned it. Howells glanced at what his superior had written and nodded.

"Miss Foster," he said crisply. "I am by no means satisfied. On consideration, I have decided to—"

"Just a moment," interrupted Julian, rising to his feet. "Before you decide to detain Miss Foster, if that's what's in your mind, I've got something to say. I make no apologies for butting in, but I advise you to hear me out before you do anything rash."

"If it's anything of importance," snapped Howells, "say it."

"I've been over the ground, as you know, and you can't deny that the mute testimony of the disordered living-room of the dead man's flat bears out every particular of Miss Foster's story up to the point where she struck Singerman with the bronze statuette."

"Granted. Well?"

"I've examined the bruise on Singerman's forehead and I'm telling you straight that no man who received a blow like that could have come up for more before Miss Foster had time to be out of the flat—damn it, out of the building! Wait a moment!—there's more to follow. Supposing, for the sake of argument, that Singerman had been able to rise and overtake her, your only possible theory is that, having failed to stop him with the statuette, she became frantic and shot him. Have I got that right? Very well!"

Distinctly, bitingly, he spat out the following sentences, emphasising his points by jabbing across the desk at the other with his pipe: "Where did she get the gun? Out of the empty air? If she had been holding it in her hand all along, why didn't she hit him with it, instead of with the statuette? Why use it in the hall and not in the living-room? Singerman was shot in the hall and her handbag was on the couch in the living-room—and a woman who took a weapon to a rendezvous would take it in her handbag—women don't have pockets."

He wheeled suddenly and hauled Cicely to her feet.

"Take a good look at her! She's dressed exactly as she was when she left Dorian House tonight. Do you suggest that she could have concealed a weapon in that coat, or that frock?"

"It may not have been her own," objected Howells. "Singerman may have produced it in his blind rage—"

Julian threw back his leonine head and uttered a booming laugh. "That's rich! That's priceless! Does she look like the sort of Amazon who could wrest a revolver from a furious man? If she were, she would hardly be likely to appeal to a connoisseur of women. Besides, Singerman was obviously shot with a high-calibre gun: a man's gun; and it takes muscle and a certain knack to fire one of that type. Not one woman in ten thousand could do it and hit anything but the ceiling or the floor, far less a man—and square in the centre of the forehead! Think again, Howells!"

The Inspector thought again. He frowned.

Julian picked up his hat. "Sleep on it," he said mockingly. "And if you think of anything more you want to ask Miss Foster, send a bobby for her in the morning. She won't run away. Good night, Sir Basil. Good night, Inspector. Coming, Miss Foster?"

Cicely hesitated. Watching the Inspector's darkening face, she thought the reporter's cool effrontery was going to evoke a furious storm. But, obeying a signal from the Deputy Commissioner, Howells nodded curtly. "You can go."

As the door closed upon Julian and the girl, Howells wheeled in his chair and faced Sir Basil. "It was all I could do to keep my hands off him," he growled. "Did you ever hear such sauce?"

Sir Basil chuckled. "You must admit he talked a certain amount of hard sense. I told you the revolver was the weak part of your case."

"I'm not satisfied, sir. I have a feeling the girl knows more than she told. If Mendoza hadn't been with her, I might have wrung it out of her. Pity I didn't see them separately."

"Oh, no," murmured Sir Basil sleepily. "I wouldn't have missed the Wild Man of Fleet Street in action for the world."

"I'm going to put a man on to shadow her."

"I should. H'm. Neat legs, Howells… Shouldn't mind being the man. Lucky beggar, eh?"

Kenneth was stalking up and down outside Scotland Yard

when Julian and Cicely came out. He was blue with cold, although his coat collar was buttoned up and his hands were thrust deeply into his pockets. An icy wind from the sluggish black river was sweeping the Embankment.

"Well?" he demanded eagerly.

"They've decided to let me go for the present," replied Cicely with a catch in her voice. "Thanks to Mr. Mendoza. Kenneth, he was splendid!" She turned to Julian. "It was wonderful of you to take my part I don't know how to thank you."

"That's all right," grunted Julian. "I wanted to take a rise out of Howells as much as anything."

"Oh." Subdued and faint, that little: 'Oh.'

They walked along in silence for a few minutes, the girl's hand clasped in one of Kenneth's and tucked into his coat pocket; the reporter walking a little apart. Under a lamppost he stopped.

"If you'll excuse me, there's a telephone booth over there, and I'd better use it. I've got to put my night editor in touch with current developments."

"Then it'll all be in the papers in the morning? My name and everything?"

"Of course." The question surprised him. "What did you expect?"

She hadn't had time to consider the matter. On reflection, she did not like it. Her face clouded over.

"Mother! I'd forgotten her! She'll read it. Oh, she'll be terribly worried about me."

"Your mother?" Julian fired questions at her. How old was her mother? Where did she live? Was her father living? Dead? What had been his occupation when alive? Satisfied, he was turning away when she caught his arm.

"Why did you ask me all that? You're not going to print it? Oh, you mustn't."

The yellow glow overhead showed the harsh outlines of his face in sharp relief; gaunt, expressionless, like a death mask. His deep-set eyes were shadowed, unfathomable.

"Certainly I am. You are news. Your mother is news. Everything about you is news. I gather news. That's my job. Good night!"

He swung away and his scarecrow figure disappeared into the gloom, his stick tap, tap, tapping on the pavement, his right leg dragging…

A distant clock chimed. Deep, reverberating, the notes shattered the hush of a slumbering world, hung resonantly on the air, swelling like the circles that widen when a stone is thrown into a pool, echoing endlessly as though down a long corridor.

Cicely counted the strokes. One. Two. Three. For two hours she had been lying in bed, her eyes fixed hypnotically on the oblong patch of milky light thrown on the ceiling by the street light outside her window, too tired to sleep, too confused to think, ceaselessly pursuing uncertainty through the fretted maze of her mind. Faces… They crowded on her, smiling, leering, frowning, gaping; one face melting into another. The moist, leering face of Jacob Singerman; the fascinating ugliness of Julian Mendoza; Kenneth's sombre, lean features; the stern countenance of Inspector Howells; the prim austerity of Miss Middleton; the unhealthy pallor of the odd little man in the bowler hat; the vacant stare of Sarah Mould; and other unknown faces, faces without features, with only eyes, staring eyes; the faces of her fears.

The stillness seemed to lie heavily upon her chest. All she could hear was the hoarse, fitful whispering of the decaying house, like the tired voice of someone about to die.

And then, wavering, irregular footsteps on the pavement outside; uncertain feet climbing two steps and staggering back one; a key clattering all-round the lock before it found the key-hole; the door shutting with a bang. Philip Dressler was home!

Cicely could hear him blundering about below, then a loud thump made her head start from the pillow. She listened. Silence. No opening doors. No fretful inquiring voices. Silence. Even Philip, the noisy one, was silent. She pictured him groaning in the darkness with a broken leg.

Shivering, she crept out of bed, found a box of matches, struck one, and slipped on a wrap. Opening the door, she crept out to the dim, ghostly corridor. From the room opposite she heard Kenneth's deep regular breathing. Nothing could disturb him when once he had fallen asleep. The house might fall on him and he would slumber peacefully, she thought resentfully, trembling with cold.

The staircase was illuminated by a single flickering gas-jet, turned down low, and placed by design too high on the wall to be reached without aid. Mrs. Mould used an improvised metal arm to light and extinguish the tiny flame. Cicely groped her way down through dissolving masses of light and shadow.

A crumpled figure was lying in the hall. It lurched to its feet as she descended and she saw the waxen white face and staring eyes of Philip Dressler. He blinked at her. "A ghos'," he said owlishly. "A bootifu' lady ghos'!"

"Sh! You'll waken the whole house!"

Inclining forward, he gaped gravely at her. "'S not a ghos'! I's Shissley!"

Sweeping off his hat he made a low bow and had to wave his arms frantically to retain his balance. "Salutations, Fair Lady!" he exclaimed.

Cicely took his arm and coaxed him up the stairs.

"Exshelshior!" he cried, waving his hat, when they gained the first-floor landing; and almost tumbled backward. It took all her strength to save him and herself. Kenneth was still sleeping soundly, but as she struggled with the handle of Philip's door on the next landing—at the same time keeping a firm hand on that wavering young man—the door across the corridor opened and Miss Middleton's outraged face, topped with a headdress of curl-papers, appeared.

"Disgusting!" the spinster exclaimed, and slammed the door.

In his room, Cicely let Philip flop down on the bed while she struck a match and groped for the gas bracket. Her head hit against something and there was a jangling noise. The match flickered out. She lit another and, holding it above her head, found the bead-trimmed gas fixture which had scraped her brow. Her fingers fumbled with it, there was a 'pop' and a dull yellow glow filled the room.

"Disgustin'!" repeated Philip earnestly. "P'fec'ly disgustin'!"

At thirty-five, dissolute and heedless, in spite of the pouches under his grey eyes and the sagging lines of his mouth, he still retained much of the exquisite Grecian beauty that had made women rave about him, that had raised him to stardom as a youth, when most actors are struggling to reach the first rung of the ladder. That was the pity of it. It was like looking at a ghost.

"She's right!" Cicely flared. "You are disgusting! A filthy, depraved brute. Drowning your wits, deadening your sense of decency, destroying your talents! Oh, you ought to be ashamed of yourself!"

Her outburst sobered him momentarily, as though she had dashed cold water in his face. His twitching eyes dropped from hers to the frowsty bed, unmade for days, on which he was reclining. He drew himself up and looked round the drab room, at the stained walls, the dusty floor, the grease-spotted gas-ring on which stood a grimy frying pan containing a solitary scorched sausage in a bed of congealed lard, the chipped sink crowded with dirty crockery, the uncurtained windows, the rickety chest of drawers, the battered chairs, a tawdry picture or two that the last tenant had not thought enough of to remove and which he had not troubled to take down. And only a year or so ago he had lunched at the Savoy, dined at the Ritz, danced at the Embassy Club, lived like a millionaire, carried himself like a king, condescended to a legion of worshipping satellites…

His grey face was twisted with pain. For a moment she thought he was going to cry. But his mood changed. "Oh, what does it matter? Go on, nag me; just like my dear wife. I don't care. I don't care a hang for anyone or anything."

"Not for Norma?" asked Cicely.

"Norma? Why should I care for her? She left me. Ran away with Clayton. She's a no-good baggage." He wobbled about the room. "A—a—a trollop, that's what she is. A trollop!"

The word amused him. He repeated it over and over again: "A trollop, a trollop, a lolloping trollop!"

"Now you're talking nonsense. You know perfectly well that there's nothing between her and Russell Clayton. She left you because she couldn't stand your drinking."

"Why shoulden she stand it?" He waved an unsteady finger under her nose. "Ans'r me that: why shoulden she stand it? A man's got to have something to take'm out off'm self, hasn' he? 'Shpecially an actor. An actor's life is give, give, give. Tearing himself in little bits an' distributin' 'em about the theatre. Wringin' himself dry like a rag to pr'vide second-hand thrills for chocl't-guzzlin' ol' hens. Got to have somethin' to relieve the strain, has'n he?"

"He needn't make a pig of himself."

Philip looked shocked. "Never made a pig of m'self. Never. A drink or two, that's all. An' don' think I haven' been tempted. I've had women throw themselves at me. Crowds of 'em. Hungry women. You don' know what women can be like. But did I take 'em? I did not. I was true to my wife. Faithful; that's it; faithful."

"You love her, don't you? For her sake, why not try to make a man of yourself?"

Dismally, he gloomed into her eyes.

"'S the woman's place to make a man of a chap. Refining

influ'nce raisin' 'm from the dregs to nobl' heights. She never tried."

Cicely was shivering with cold. "Philip, if I leave you now, will you be good and go quietly to bed?"

"Don' go yet. Wan' tell you 'bout my job."

"You've found a job? Oh, I'm glad!"

"Sure I've found a job. When they wan' a real actor, they've gotta come to Ol' Philip. Got a job on th' films. Fifty quid a week. 'S a comedown, but a fella's got to live Tha's what I said to Von Blon. ''S an insult,' I said, 'but I'll take it'."

"Von Blon?"

"Tha's th' name. Film d'rector. Went down on his knees to m'. 'Dressler,' he said, 'you'll be th' bigges' draw th' talkies ever had'."

"But how splendid!"

"No." He shook his head and continued to shake it solemnly from side to side. "No. What's the good of it? Norma's gone. She's gone with Clayton."

He looked long and earnestly into Cicely's face. "You're a fren' o' mine?"

"You know I am. Would I be standing here with you at this time of the morning— catching my death of cold—if I weren't?"

"Then c'm 'ere. I wan' show you something."

Grasping her hand, like a small boy taking his mother for a walk, he led her across the room. He raised one of the garish pictures and a stream of letters dropped from behind it to the floor. Cicely fell on one knee and examined them. They were all addressed to: Miss Norma Lavery, Apollo Theatre, Shaftesbury Avenue, W.I.

"Letters," he said. "Bootiful poetic letters. Sometimes, when I'm drunk, I write them to her. W'en I'm sober, I tear 'em up. I haven't been sober very much lately—that's why there's so many."

"Why don't you send her one?"

"And let her laugh at me? She woulden read it. She loves Clayton." He gesticulated wildly and almost fell over. "'F I were a man, d'you know whar I'd do? I'd shoot Clayton. Shoor'm like a dog."

"Philip, don't talk such rot."

Ignoring the interruption, he maundered on with maudlin relish.

"I would! Shoor'm like a dog."

"You're drunk," she said. "You don't know what you're saying. Philip, I'm going to bed. I'm tired and it's bitterly cold. Promise you'll tumble in, like a good boy."

Dawn Interlude

Cicely turned to the door, but she hesitated. Somehow, she did not like to leave him. She had seen him drunk before; that was nothing unusual. But tonight, he was in the strangest of all the many vagrant moods of his erratic temperament.

"Philip—"

But he had already forgotten what he had said. The mood had passed. Now he was on his hands and knees beside the bed, prising up a loose floorboard. He produced a black bottle with a white label from the dusty space between two floor supports.

"Got to hide it there from Old Mouldy," he murmured, half to himself, as he rose, nursing it fondly in his arms.

"Philip, you're not going to have any more to drink."

"Oh, yes, I am! Goin' to drink an' drink an' drink. That's all that's left. Just drink."

He drew the cork and raised the bottle to his lips, but she snatched it from him and thrust it behind her. He laughed. This was a good game. Playfully, he tried to get at the hand which was holding his treasure. But it wasn't a game for long. When he realized that she was in earnest, his eyes reddened with anger and his hands, tightening on her arms, bit into her soft flesh.

"Give it to me. I want it. I must have it, I tell you. Hand it over, or, by God! I'll—"

Cicely tore herself free and ran across the room. The amber liquid gurgled out of the bottle neck and mingled with the greasy slops in the foul sink. A cry of rage and self-pity burst from Philip's lips, such a cry as a frantic mother might utter who saw her only child impaled upon a spear. He snatched the bottle from her hand and the last drop splashed upon the dusty floor. With an oath he tossed it aside. There was a crash of shattered glass and crockery. He took her by the shoulders and shook her fiercely.

"I could kill you for that! What right had you to do it? My last bottle—"

"Philip, you're hurting me! Philip! Please!"

He became a little calmer. His grip relaxed. "If you knew what that stuff means to me," he muttered. "I'm lonely, lost—oh, damned in hell without it."

Her hair, soft, silken as gossamer threads, the colour of autumn leaves, was tumbling about her flushed, lovely face in wild, enchanting profusion. The disorder of her wrap revealed the smooth, white texture of her flesh, a froth of lace, the curved firmness of her bosom. His hands, still on her shoulders, became caressingly gentle.

"Philip," she said steadily, "let me go."

He released her and went to the door. Before she could stop him, he had locked it and withdrawn the key.

"Don't be a fool," she said, less calmly. "Give me that key."

Laughing, he lurched over to the window. A broken pane tinkled as the key flew out into the night. He wheeled round and caught her in his arms. She could feel his warm breath on her cheek. Exerting all her strength, she thrust him away. He tripped and sprawled on the untidy bed.

Cicely darted to the door. About to hammer on one of the panels, she paused with her clenched hands in midair, realizing what that would mean. The whole house roused. A scene. Explanations that would not be easy to give. Miss Middleton's eyes staring at her with the intolerant scorn of one whose life has moved in narrow, sluggish channels, who suspects a freedom that she does not understand. Mrs. Mould, fuddled with gin—she was said to take a bottle to bed with her—wrapped in her ancient red-flannel dressing-gown, with her rats' tails of hair sticking out all over her head like a starfish, her bleary eyes saying: 'Tell me another, Dearie!' as plainly as the more refined orbs of the spinster. Kenneth, furious with Philip, believing in Cicely and yet somehow doubting her. The other lodgers, whom she had only encountered in hurried passing on the stairs, nudging one another and winking. How could she face them and make the truth, the lame truth, sound convincing? That she had helped Philip up to his room, stayed with him, wrestled with him for the whiskey bottle for no other reason than friendship: it wasn't, after all, a very plausible story. Could she blame them if they decided that a girl who went in night attire to a drunken man's room at three in the morning needn't be so fussy as to waken the whole house to protect her honour? Could she blame Kenneth for torturing himself with doubts, even while he tried to get at Philip and pound him to a pulp? No. Besides, she did not want Philip pounded to a pulp. Poor, tipsy fool, it was no more his fault than it was hers. Warm, soft flesh; propinquity; that was all a man needed to work himself into the passion he preferred to call love. She had exposed herself to this in the 'I-can-take-care-of-myself' spirit of the modern girl; she would get out of it alone.

In the stillness, small sounds were magnified. A mouse squeaking in the rotting walls; a heavy truck rumbling over cobblestones, streets away a distant motor-horn challenging the silence; and, like the beating of a drum, the sound of her own heart, loud in her ears.

She turned from the door. "Look here," she said, "don't be a silly ass."

But Philip did not answer. He was lying prone on the bed and uttering queer, guttural sounds. Cicely hesitated, then went a little nearer. She leant over him cautiously. Then she began to giggle. She simply couldn't help it. Here she was, trembling, expecting every moment to have to cope with an attempt at violent seduction—and there sprawled Philip, fast asleep, snoring!

Not much of a compliment, but what a relief!

She checked her mirth. Miss Middleton's room was across the corridor; and feminine giggling sounds rather bad, coming from a man's room in the early morning. Besides, it was all very well to laugh, but how was she to get out?

The window? No, it was hopeless. Two storeys up and no footholds; a sheer drop to the broken bottles, half-bricks and empty sardine-tins of the backyard.

It was cold. She drew her wrap closer about her throat and went over to the bed. Her sense of humour had robbed the dishevelled, whiskey-smelling actor of all power to frighten her.

"Philip!" she whispered, shaking his shoulder. "Wake up! You've got to help me to get out of here!"

Philip rolled over on his front and buried his face in the pillows. Asleep, he looked like a wilful schoolboy. She shook him again, but with no different result.

"That's a man for you!" she exclaimed. "Gets you into a mess by playing the fool and then snores his silly fat head off and lets you dig yourself out alone."

Next time he fell down in the hall he could lie there all night for all she cared. She would do as men do; cover her head with the blankets and snore into the pillow. Unreasonably, she began to think harsh thoughts of Kenneth, slumbering as soundly as Philip in the room below. Everyone was sleeping but her, and she was as tired as anyone. More. She had never felt so tired in all her life. Impossible that she could have lain in bed tonight for two whole hours without closing an eye! Every bone in her body ached for rest.

There were clever things one could do to locks with hairpins, but Cicely was of a generation that had never worn hairpins. The thought led naturally to seeing what she could do with a knife. Gingerly, she fished a greasy one out of the sink and inserted the buttery blade between the catch and the door-jamb. The lock yielded after surprisingly little resistance (no wonder Miss Middleton invariably put a chair under her door-handle!) and she pulled the door open with a sigh of relief, Free!

Reaching up to turn out the gas, her eyes fell on the litter of envelopes on the floor. She replaced them behind the picture, to protect them from the sacrilegious eyes of Mrs. Mould, who had acquired an avid taste for love letters through much reading of the juicier bits in the Sunday papers. On second thoughts, she slipped one into the pocket of her wrap.

As Cicely closed the door and tiptoed stealthily down the stairs, the door of Miss Middleton's room opened narrowly and the spinster's curl-papered head looked covertly out. She nodded to herself, with grim satisfaction.

Rat-a-tat-a-tat! Rat-a-tat-a-tat! The summons, at first low and insistent, gradually becoming loud and clamouring, penetrated irritatingly to Cicely's drowsy brain, seeming to come from afar off. Sighing, she turned over and burrowed her head deep into the blankets. Louder. Louder. To a thunderous crescendo, she woke with a start. Yawning, rebellious, she sat up in bed. Surely it could not be more than a few minutes since her tired body had yielded gratefully to sleep! But the room was flooded with the harsh light of day. The hands of the tinny pink clock on the dressing-table (it had cost three hundred cigarette coupons) pointed accusingly to half past nine. The clock might lie (it was a barefaced and inveterate liar), but not the sun.

Rat-a-tat-a-tat! Rat-a-tat-a-tat!

Above the furious knocking, voices. Mrs. Mould's thin, querulous grumble. Kenneth, angrily protesting. The cool, crisp tones of other men, polite, but persistent. Memory returned in a flood. Last night! The murder of Jacob Singerman! Scotland Yard! Perhaps the strangers who were arguing with Kenneth outside her door were policemen come to fetch her.

Out of bed she crept, shivering, donned a wrap and opened the door. In surged a platoon of young men, smartly dressed, some of them carrying rolled umbrellas. At their heels, Mrs. Mould in a bedraggled blue print dress and an incredibly dirty apron, whining:

"Don't go blamin' me, Miss. I couldn't do nothin' to stop 'em. They pushed right past me the moment I opened the front door—saucy young cubs!"

"I'm from the *Daily Cry*."..."the *Courier*."..."*Post*."..."the *Echo*."...

It was bewildering.

Kenneth shouldered his way through the knot of reporters into the room. "Look here, I've said she can't see you. She's got nothing to say. She knows nothing. If you don't clear out at once, I'll—I'll—"

The foremost of the young men smiled apologetically at Cicely. "Sorry to barge in on you like this, but it's most important that we should have a statement from you at once. There are all sorts of wild rumours afloat about your part in past night's—er—tragic affair—and it is only fair that your side of the story should be told without delay."

The invasion had rendered Cicely a little breathless. "Yes… Yes… Oh, Good Lord!" she gasped round the ring of alert faces. "I—This is rather overwhelming. I'm afraid—"

"We don't want to inconvenience you," said the spokesman pleasantly. "Supposing we wait downstairs until you dress?"

"Oh, if you would—"

The reporters filed out and she was left alone with Kenneth and Mrs. Mould, who, fearful for the security of her weekly tip, repeated morosely: Don't you go blaming me—"

"I'm not blaming you," said Cicely, pushing her to the door. "Only, for goodness' sake, get out!"

She flopped down on the bed. "Whew!" she exclaimed.

"Infernal cheek!" glowered Kenneth. "I wish I'd given one or two of them a black eye."

"It's their job, darling. Besides, they were quite decent."

"Take a look at the *Morning World*," he said, unfolding a newspaper. "Half a page about the murder. A whole column about you. Even a photograph—Lord knows where they got it."

Cicely glanced at the smiling face in the centre of the page.

"It's the one that photographic agency took when I was in 'The Secret Garden'."

"From the fuss they're making, anyone would think you shot Singerman. What are you going to tell them?"

"I'm hungry," said Cicely. "Let's have breakfast."

Crossing the room, she opened a door which concealed her larder, a gas stove, and a shiningly scoured sink.

"If I were you, I should refuse to tell them anything."

"Oh, dear! No eggs. Barely a teaspoonful of coffee. One rasher of bacon. And I'm simply famishing! I meant to do my shopping yesterday afternoon, but I forgot."

"We'll slip round to the 'Coffee Pot'," said Kenneth impatiently. "About these reporters—

Cicely remembered something else.

"Kenneth, I haven't a bean. My last pound was in the bag I left at Singerman's flat last night I expect the police have it. That's a blow. Have you any money?"

She asked the question as though it were the least likely thing in the world.

"Enough to pay for breakfast. Darling, we must have a serious talk. This is important…"

"Then talk to me while we're eating. I can't think on an empty tummy. Hop it and let me dress."

Cold water quickened her brain, and made her skin tingle and glow. She powdered her nose lightly, combed and brushed her hair, put on a green frock that looked like Bond Street, but had been 'run up' on a friend's sewing machine. As she opened the door she remembered the reporters, lying in wait for her in the hall. But Kenneth had a plan for evading them; he had used it once to dodge a bill collector.

"We'll go up to Long's room in the attic," he whispered. "He'll be out, but he never locks the door and the window opens to the roof. We'll slip over the roofs to Number Twelve—it's quite easy, really—and get in through Bill Hodge's window.

Bill's a pal of mine. An artist. Then, out by the front door of Number Twelve, and—"

"—the villains are foiled!" she exclaimed gaily. "Kenneth, what fun!"

Hand in hand, with the happy, guilty air of children out for a lark, they crept, giggling, up the stairs to the attics. Mr. Long's door, as Kenneth had prophesied, was unlocked. He opened the window, helped her out to the sloping slate roof, and joined her nimbly. Agile as cats they crossed the checkered grey expanse to a window five houses away. Kenneth knocked and a startled face, with round eyes goggling through horn-rimmed glasses and a mop of ginger hair, peered out at them. The window went up.

"Duns again?" asked Bill Hodge blithely, as they skipped into the room.

"Reporters," said Kenneth. "Bill, this is Miss Foster. She is ambushed by a gang of pressmen and I simply had to get her away by this route. As it is, the morning papers are full of her."

"Charmed to meet you," smiled Hodge admiringly. "'Fraid I don't read the papers. What have you done—killed someone?"

There was an awkward pause, then Kenneth grasped Cicely's arm and hustled her across the room.

"Silly ass!" he called back to the astonished artist.

They ran swiftly down the stairs. Kenneth opened the front door, went out on the steps, and looked carefully up and down the street.

"Coast's clear," he said.

Cicely joined him and they scudded round the corner into Old Compton Street. A minute's walk, then they entered a little restaurant, the front of which was done up as a huge brown coffeepot, with puffs of real steam coming from the spout. Gasping with suppressed laughter, they dropped into chairs at a small table covered with a spotless primrose-and-brown checked cloth and a waitress in primrose-and-coffee-brown came towards them. Her languid morning air evaporated at sight of Cicely.

"Waffles with maple syrup," ordered Cicely, consulting the menu, "and sausages. Oh, and a pot of coffee."

Even while she was writing on her pad the waitress could hardly keep her eyes off Cicely.

"I'll have the same," muttered Kenneth, fumbling with the coins in his trousers pocket and hoping that the two large ones were half-crowns and not, as he feared, a half-crown and a penny.

The waitress reluctantly tore herself away from the table. She went through a swing door at the rear and an excited whispering started in the kitchen; in a moment the flushed face of the female chef peered out at Cicely in morbid fascination. Kenneth scowled and it disappeared abruptly. More whispering.

"You see!" said Kenneth. "That's what Mr. Precious Mendoza and his rotten rag have done for you! Look at this."

He spread the paper in front of her and jabbed a finger at the headlines that sprawled across the top of the front page.

FILM MAGNATE MURDERED

IN MAYFAIR FLAT

WHO KILLED JACOB SINGERMAN?

'MYSTERY GIRL'S' OWN STORY

ALLEGES VIOLENT ATTACK

Cicely read a few lines of the heavily-leaded opening paragraph. It was difficult to realize that she, herself, had played a part in the sensational events it related; that she, herself, was the 'beautiful, glamorous actress,' the last known person to have seen the murdered man alive.

"There's a whole screed about your 'grey-haired widowed mother' in the third column," said Kenneth. "Thanks to Mr.

Mendoza. I told you not to trust him."

A little upset, Cicely thrust the paper aside.

"It's his job to give the public the sort of news it wants," she replied. "Besides, I'd probably be locked up at Scotland Yard now if he hadn't taken my part last night."

"That reminds me; you haven't yet told me exactly what transpired at that interview."

"There's nothing much to tell. I simply told my story, almost in the same words as I had told it to you and Mr. Mendoza."

"What did the detectives say?"

"I don't altogether remember," frowned Cicely wearily. "I was in rather a daze. They didn't entirely believe me."

"Well, try to think of all that was said. This is important. I can't help you very much unless you tell me everything."

"I'm afraid neither of us can do much in any case, except wait for the police to find the murderer of Singerman."

Kenneth leaned across the table and looked earnestly into her eyes. The waitress and the chef were interested onlookers from the obscurity of the barely-open kitchen door.

"Cicely, it may be months before they find him," he said. "You can't stay in London all that time, to be stared at and pointed out in the streets. Look here, I've thought it all out. I'm going to wire Dad for some money; fifty or sixty pounds should be enough—he'll let me have it if I say I'm coming home to go to work in his office. When it comes, I'll get my other suit out of pawn and we'll get married. Perhaps we can get a special licence and be married today—I'm not quite sure—at any rate, as soon as the ceremony's over, we'll go straight to the station and catch a train for Manchester. No one knows you there; there won't be staring and whispering wherever you go, as there's bound to be here—you can see that for yourself. Besides, our marriage will silence, once and for all, the scandal-mongers who are sure to insinuate there was more between you and Singerman than meets the eye."

Cecily leaned back in her chair and gasped. The approach of the waitress with a laden tray prevented her from making any reply for the moment, but as soon as the girl—all eyes—had withdrawn, she thanked him, a trifle satirically, for disposing of her future with so little need for mental effort on her own part.

"It's sweet of you to think of my reputation," she added, "but no one I care about would dream of believing that kind of gossip and I don't care what anyone else thinks. In any case, nothing ever silences scandal-mongers. And I can see your father's face if you turned up in Manchester with me on your arm and said: 'Dad, meet the wife—formerly Miss Cicely Foster—you've seen her picture in all the papers—you know, the girl in the Singerman Murder case—I've just married her to make an honest woman of her.'"

"Dad will love you at first sight," protested Kenneth stoutly. "I'll settle down to hard work, and forget my invention. It's a rotten invention anyway; only it took this to make me realize it."

"I've yet to meet the business man who would welcome into the bosom of his family an actress who was smeared all over the headlines as the 'mystery girl' in a murder case. No, Kenneth, it won't do. Besides, I've told you time and again that I won't dream of marrying you for years. After all the sacrifices Mother made to give me my chance—against her better judgment, too—I've simply to make good. I owe it to her. Oh, I know there's nothing she'd like better than to see me married to a nice young man of good family (she tried hard enough, when I was at home), but that isn't the point. I left home to make good as an actress and I've simply got to do it."

"Now, darling," said Kenneth patiently, "please don't be silly."

"I'll be as silly as I choose! If you ask me, it's you who's being silly. Returned prodigals have to eat humble pie, nowadays. They don't march in boldly with a suitcase full of soiled clothes in one hand and a wife in the other and challenge the family to take her or leave her. Not with any hope of a welcome, they don't. And I don't particularly want to meet my husband's family for the first time in such circumstances."

Kenneth threw up his hands. "Alright. Have it your own way! Be a free show wherever you go, if that's what you want. You know you're a rotten actress; you've said so yourself, many a time. You've been engaged to me for a month, but don't let that make any difference. Only, from now on, please don't pretend that you love me."

"I do love you and you know it; you spoiled baby! There's a big difference between loving you and rushing into matrimony with you. All the same, I think it's a jolly good idea for you to go back to Manchester and settle down."

"Oh, you do, eh? Well, if you think I'm going to go away and leave you on your own to get into heaven-knows-what-kind-of-a-mess, you're jolly well mistaken."

"You'll have to, sooner or later," she pointed out. "You know you haven't any money."

"I'll get a job." Furiously, he leafed over the newspaper until he came to the classified advertisement page. "There! I noticed that ad. this morning. It's just the job for me, but I was ready to chuck it and go home for your sake."

Following the direction of his finger, Cicely read this advertisement:

WANTED, by a film company, a stunt driver not over 30, for talkie now in production. Must be fearless, level-headed, and highly-experienced racing driver. Apply Colossal Film Company Studios, Turnham Green, W.4.

"There will be hundreds of applications for that job," she said. "And stunt driving is a profession for lunatics. It carries an expectation of life rather shorter than that of a Chicago gangster."

"Well, it doesn't matter to you whether I'm killed or not," Kenneth grumbled huffily, "so why worry about that?"

At that moment, Miss Middleton came in and went up to the counter that ran the full length of the restaurant for the daily bag of buns which constituted practically her entire nourishment. She smiled graciously at Kenneth Archer, then stiffened and glared through and beyond Cicely.

In astonishment, Kenneth glanced from the thin, acidulated spinster to the pale girl across the table from him.

"Well, I like that! Anyone would think that you were a—a—a—" He rose. "I'm jolly well going to tackle her about it!"

Before Cicely could stop him, he marched aggressively up to Miss Middleton.

"Will you be so kind as to tell me why you have seen fit to insult Miss Foster?" he demanded.

The spinster clasped her bag of buns like a shield to her thin bosom. "I do not like your tone, young man," she retorted, pursing her lips.

"I'm sorry, but I must insist on an answer. If your attitude is due to the lying reports in the morning papers—"

"I have no wish to make trouble," responded Miss Middleton loftily, "but if you wish to know the reason why I desire no further intercourse with Miss Foster, I recommend you to ask her where she spent the time between three and four o'clock this morning."

Turning on her heel, she marched out, expressing virtue triumphant in every line of her meagre body.

Cicely held her breath and waited for the storm. The waitress behind the counter and the female chef, gaping through an aperture in the kitchen door (the latter not quite gathering the full drift of what was going on, but realizing that Something Was Up), also waited in breathless expectancy.

The storm broke.

"What did she mean?" demanded Kenneth.

Dark and sullen, he towered over Cicely. "Where were you between three and four this morning?"

"Why pay any attention to her?" evaded Cicely. "You said yourself she is a nosy old cat."

"Answer me at once," he stormed. "Where were you?"

"Need we have a scene here?"

"I want to know where you were. Why don't you tell me? Are you ashamed to let me know?"

Cicely poured herself a cup of coffee, trying to appear cool and unconcerned—but the amber splash that stained the table cloth betrayed her.

"Why don't you ask Miss Middleton?" she retorted icily.

"Alright, I shall!" Wheeling abruptly, he dashed out of the restaurant. Cicely sipped her coffee, smouldering inwardly with not unreasonable anger. Why need he instantly jump to conclusions and take it for granted that she was where she shouldn't have been? Admitted, she was; but Kenneth should have laughed at the spinster's frigid manner and waited patiently for Cicely to explain; even been content if she had offered no explanation. If he loved her, that is what he would have done, she brooded. But she had a just nature and, even as she thought it, she realized with a sigh that men, even in love—especially in love—are jealous, unreasoning, suspicious creatures. She longed to rise and make a dignified exit, to depart out of range of the inquisitive eyes of the waitress, but that was impossible without a penny in her possession with which to pay for the cold sausages and forlorn waffle lying neglected on the plate before her. She was forced to sit and wait, fuming with exasperation, for Kenneth's return.

He came in like a tornado, slamming the door behind him, his brows in a straight line over his furious eyes, his face dark with anger, and strode up to the table. At a glance, Cicely could see that Miss Middleton had told him everything—all she suspected, as well as all she knew.

"What were you doing in Dressler's room?" he demanded, dropping into a chair and glaring at her.

"Can't you guess?" said Cicely coldly. "If you can't, I'm sure your friend, Miss Middleton, will be able to help you."

"Don't joke. I want the truth."

"How can you expect to hear it from a depraved creature like me?" She rose. "If you had asked me decently, I should have told you. Now, I'm dashed if I will."

"You refuse to explain?" he snapped.

"Put it that way, if you like. You can stew in your own juice until you're in a more reasonable frame of mind."

"Until you've had time to invent a plausible lie, you mean!"

Both of them knew that he didn't mean it. Words uttered in anger have a way of pouring themselves out almost without the volition of the speaker; but they are none the less difficult to forgive. Cicely left him. She was seething with indignation, but she held her head high as she returned to Angelus Row.

At first, she was not conscious of the crowd that had collected outside the house in which she lived. Errand boys with baskets on their arms; male and female idlers, with avid looks on their faces; every type of inquisitive humanity was staring up at the three stories of brick masked with cracked, grimy stucco, as though they had never seen its like before. A flower pot containing a solitary drooping geranium which someone had placed on the ledge of a second storey window, was the target of many pointing fingers. On Cicely's approach much of the attention was diverted to her, and nods, winks and nudges were rife as she pushed her way through to the steps of the house.

Her face was a frozen white mask. If she heard the whispered speculations that rippled through the crowd, she showed no signs of caring.

"Brazen 'ussy!" commented a woman, quite audibly. "I bet it's 'er all right. But 'er pictures flatter 'er!"

Her latchkey was in the bag she had left at Dorian House, so she was forced to ring the bell. The door was promptly opened by a reporter, whose eyes widened with surprise at sight of her.

"How did you get out without us seeing you? We were just about to go upstairs and give you a knock."

On the verge of breaking down, she brushed past him without answering and went up to her room. Mrs. Mould started as the door opened and put down a photograph of Cicely which she had been about to conceal under her apron.

"If one of these young fellows tells you 'e was goin' to give me five bob for this, miss, don't you believe him," she snuffled. "I 'opes you know me better than that. I only come up to bring you these"—she held out a pile of telegrams.

Cicely took them mechanically, and with a sly, gloating look at her pale, set face, the woman shuffled out. The girl locked the door before she sat down, dazed and bewildered, on the bed. Her restless fingers tore open the buff envelopes almost of their own volition. The first three telegrams were from theatrical agents.

…"See me without delay. Sam Mandel"…"Offer twenty-five

pounds a week for fifteen weeks provincial tour. Marcus Abrams"…"Can get you part in new Latour revue. Joe Steiner"…

Her fingers shredded them and littered them about the floor at her feet. Rending the fourth, which she had almost torn in half in her nervous preoccupation, she started to her feet with a cry, letting the rest slip unheeded from her lap.

"Arriving Waterloo 12.15. Love. Mother."

Knocking at the door…furious…repeated… She tore it open and faced the crowd of reporters in the corridor. They were not so pleasant now. Some of them had first editions shortly going to press and all of them had news editors who accepted no alibis. They came into the room and she backed, her head whirling with giddiness, to the window.

Questions beat mercilessly on her confused brain like waves dashing against a rock.

"How long had you known Mr. Singerman…?"

"…Is it true that you are still under suspicion at Scotland Yard…?"

"…They say that you and the deceased were frequently seen together at West End restaurants…"

"Have you ever owned a revolver…?"

Is this true? Is that true? Why did you do this? Why did you do that?

A circle of faces, keen, alert faces, with shrewd, dissecting eyes, eyes like sharp lancets, probing into her brain.

"Hold that pose, Miss Foster!"

Acrid fumes of flashlight powder; the click of a camera…

"Stop!" she cried hysterically. "Stop! Leave me alone. Why won't you leave me alone? I've done nothing. Nothing, I tell you!"

The floor seemed to rise up to meet her and she swam dizzily into enfolding blackness. She did not see Julian Mendoza entering the room, or the startled concern on his face and the faces of the other reporters; or feel his powerful arms catching her as she swayed forward. She knew nothing.

Tersely, blasphemously, Julian gave his opinion of his colleagues while he lifted the girl's limp form on to the bed. One of them handed him a handkerchief soaked in cold water and he snarled at the giver, even while he applied it to Cicely's forehead. There were times when he felt that news-gathering, his own trade, had a kinship to the nauseous means of livelihood of vultures. He said so.

"Tell that to my news editor," retorted one of the younger men; "he wants a column and a half by twelve o'clock and he doesn't care a damn how I get it."

"Tell him—" began Julian fiercely. "Oh, what's the use? He knows it already. Listen carefully, then get out. Here's the dope—"

He outlined concisely all he knew about the Singerman Murder Case, apart from the facts their respective new editors had already gleaned (with blasphemy, over the *Morning World's* scoop) from the columns of his own paper.

When Cicely opened her eyes the other reporters had gone and only Julian's harsh, gaunt face, curiously softened by the concern he felt, loomed over her. Her first conscious thought was of her mother and she sat up with an apprehensive cry.

"Take it easy," growled Julian. "Easy…"

And then, having swooned like any twittering miss of the period before women put behind them all that which is unmanly, Cicely completed her ignominious descent from the proud heights of twentieth century independence by melting into tears.

Julian Takes Command

Julian was unutterably relieved. Tears are a woman's natural safety valve. It is when her agony is voiceless that she is near to the breaking point. He let her cry. Lighting his pipe, he limped across to the window and scowled down at the gaping throng in front of the house. Presently he heard the divan bed creaking and found Cicely at his elbow.

"What do they want?" she asked, in a still, dry voice. "Why do they stand and stare? Haven't they anything else to do?"

"Oh, yes. Most of the women have sinks piled with dirty dishes awaiting them at home and children coming in from school for lunch—but they won't budge until the appetite for rubbernecking is glutted. It is a craving, like addiction to drugs.

"Your nose is shiny," he added.

Cicely went to her dressing-table and made herself look more presentable. A powdered nose did more to steady her nerves than anything else could have done. Julian discarded his shabby coat and hat and, with the explorer's unerring instinct, opened the door that concealed her kitchenette-larder, filled the kettle, and put it on a lighted gas-ring. He produced tea, a tea-pot, cups and saucers and spoons, as methodically as though he had been used to Cicely's housekeeping arrangements for years. Cicely sat by the grey ashes of the previous night's fire and watched him in subdued wonder. She had never before known such a man. The Lion and the Lamb lying down together in the same complex nature. He warmed the teapot with a little hot water, put in four spoonsful of tea (one for each of us, one for the pot, and one for luck, counted Cicely) and filled it at the precise moment that the kettle came to the boil.

When the tea had infused, he handed her a cup of the strong

amber liquid. "How did you know I don't take sugar or cream?" she asked curiously.

"Instinct," he replied, putting three large lumps in his own cup.

"Do you know, you're a remarkable man?"

"Yes," he said, quite naturally. "But we're not talking about me; we're talking about you. What's the trouble? Oh, I know you've been through enough during the last twelve hours to give an ordinary girl a fit of the vapours, but you're not an ordinary girl. And it isn't only the newspaper men, nor yet those halfwits outside. What is it?"

Cicely sipped her tea. "It's everything. Most of all, my mother. I've had a wire from her. She's coming here."

A single, expressive gesture embraced her entire surroundings.

"What will she think? Oh, I know my room's alright, but this awful house—the beastly street—that morbid crowd—She'll be shocked. Hurt. Horrified. I know she's been living in a daze ever since she read the papers this morning. I can see her stunned bewilderment as she realized that I am the girl in the headlines. Her first thought, of course, was to rush to me. You see—it's difficult to explain—I'm not just her daughter—even if I were, it would be bad enough; I'm her only child, all she's got in the world. I could hardly bear her eyes when I first came away to London; they looked as though she were being torn from limb to limb. She had saved a little money to give me my chance, but it was quite impossible for her to manage to come with me. Oh, I was cruel, heartless, to leave her! And now! Think what I've done to her! I'm a nice daughter for anyone to have. The 'mystery girl' in a murder case!"

Tears brimmed in her eyes. Her lips trembled. "She lives in a little village fifty miles from London and a hundred years from the twentieth century. Imagine her walk through the main street to the station this morning; every door a frame for curious faces. Whispers. Murmurs. Who was it said that each man kills the thing he loves? He should have added that every mother is crucified by her own child."

The words seemed to choke her. It was a long time before she could speak. "She'll find me here—in this ghastly place."

"She mustn't," said Julian quietly. "When she comes, she must find you cheerful in comfortable surroundings and you must treat the whole thing as a ghastly mistake. Tell her the newspapers have exaggerated your part in the story; she'll believe that; everybody is ready to believe anything of a newspaper. You're an actress. Here's your chance to show what's in you. Laugh at her fears. Convince her that everything is well with you."

"How can I?" protested Cicely, spreading her hands hopelessly. "I can't move from here. I haven't a cent. I've nothing left to pawn except a watch she gave me and she'd notice at once if that were missing."

Julian produced a worn leather wallet, stuffed with old envelopes, scraps of paper, bus tickets, and other rubbish of a similar nature, and, crumpled up with the rest, banknotes of various denominations, which he proceeded to sort out on his knee.

"How much do you need? Ten pounds? Twenty? Fifty? Don't hesitate to mention a figure. I'm filthy with money. Never spend any."

Cicely gasped. "Oh, I couldn't borrow from you. Thanks awfully, but I couldn't."

"Don't be a fool," he growled. "What's it matter who you borrow from? The money's just as good. Never hesitate to borrow when you need it. I know. I've been borrowing all my life. Everyone does it, when pressed, and you are too unimportant a cog to be allowed to throw the entire system out of gear. Shall we say twenty pounds?" Without waiting for an answer, he thrust the money into her hands and refused to listen to objections.

"There's one thing I want to ask you," he said suddenly. "I'm asking it not as a reporter, but as a friend—you don't happen to have a gun?"

Cicely shook her head.

"You're sure?" he insisted. "There isn't even one in the house to which you might have access?"

"Not to my knowledge. Why?"

"Then that's all right. Only I heard through a certain channel—which I keep well-oiled—that Inspector Howells has discovered that Jacob Singerman owned a revolver of large calibre which is now missing. Howells may come here with a search warrant to look for it."

"Then he still suspects me?"

"Howells suspects everyone. That's his job. A law court must keep an open mind, but a bobby must hold everyone guilty until they're proven innocent."

He ran his fingers through his hair, making it an even unrulier tangle than usual. "I have an idea," he said. "I'm going to take you to my landlady. She's a good soul, and though she wouldn't have a female lodger for all the gold in Egypt, I believe she'll help you. One of the other lodgers is away for a few days and he has rather a swagger room; we'll bag it to make a good impression on your mother."

"Do you really think—" Cicely began dubiously.

Julian rose and flourished his large, hairy hands impatiently. "Don't goggle at me, woman! When's your mother arriving? 12.15? We'll meet the train, after we've seen Mrs. MacDougal and set the stage."

A human tornado, he swept about the room, jerking his crippled limb after him like a hurrying child dragging a toy horse on a string; snatched up cushions, tore pictures from the walls, bundled up her toilet articles in a gay embroidered silk cover from the dressing-table; stacked them on the floor and looked about for more.

"We'll need these, for atmosphere. Trust a woman to tell a man's room from a woman's at a glance; but we'll fool her! Get your hat on—do you think we've got all day? Is there a 'phone in the house?"

"In the hall," she stammered numbly.

She enjoyed a brief respite while he went to telephone for a taxi; then he was back, spurring her to haste.

"It'll be here any minute. Got your things together? You may have to spend the night at Mrs. MacDougal's—perhaps a few days—so take everything you're likely to want. We'll try to persuade your mother to go home tonight—she'll be better out of the way—but if she won't you'll have to hang on until she does. Oh, for the love of heaven, hurry! I could pack a steamer trunk in the time you're taking over that tiny case."

"I daresay you could," Cicely was stung to retort. "The way you pack!"

The taxi appeared. "Come on," ordered Julian.

Imagine the hurrying small boy, bound for home and his favourite tea through the gathering dusk, with a wooden engine to drag after him (more often on its side than not) as well as the horse, and you can see Cicely, overwhelmed, breathless, carrying Julian's walking-stick and an attaché case, trailing after the huge reporter as, with arms heaped high with the spoils of this foray on her room, he hobbled swiftly down the stairs. Julian was like that. Arrived at a decision, he liked to arrive at the accomplished fact without red tape or ceremony.

The curiosity-seekers in the road and on the pavement were milling about the taxi, apparently regarding it—an ancient Beardmore—as a choice and engrossing exhibit in the Singerman Murder Case. Julian barged through them, using elbows and shoulders impartially with as much violence as his unwieldy burden would permit. Cicely kept close behind him. The searching eyes of the crowd reminded her of one of those dreams in which you are walking down a busy street with nothing on. Julian dumped his spoils into the back seat of the taxi and bundled her in after them.

"I'll tell you where to go after we're away from this nosy rabble," he called to the driver.

A grin spread over that worthy's fat red face. He touched his cap and the taxi moved off.

"Well!" said the onlookers to one another. "Well!"

The general opinion was that they had never seen or heard the like of it, no indeed, they never had.

An inconspicuously-dressed man detached himself from the crowd and followed the taxi. In Old Compton Street he hailed another, and ordered the driver to keep the first vehicle in sight.

Mrs. MacDougal's prim little house was in one of the less fashionable side-streets on the eastern fringe of Hyde Park. Julian opened the door with his latchkey (no inconsiderable feat of balancing was required to keep his burden from falling while he did so) and dropped the shapeless load on the hall floor. Looking at the shiningly clean blue-and-white checked linoleum, the gleaming paintwork, the unsullied cream wallpaper and the polished oak hall furniture, Cicely felt no forebodings about the woman she was shortly to meet.

Julian descended to the basement and interviewed Mrs. MacDougal alone. What he said to her, Cicely never knew, but in a few minutes the bustling little Scotswoman came upstairs with a welcoming beam on her rosy countenance.

"It's no' for just onybody that I'd tale the liberty o' makin' use o' a lodger's room when he's no there tae object, but if the half o' whit Mr. Mendoza's been tellin' me is true, my lamb, I'll dae everything in my power for ye," she declared.

Julian consulted his watch. "Good Lord! We'll have to hurry to meet that train. Good thing I kept the taxi waiting. Mrs. MacDougal"—pointing to the bundle on the floor—"will you scatter these things about Thackray's room—you know, the woman's touch, and all that—and tuck his pipes and brushes out of sight? Oh, and we'll want a roaring fire and hot lunch—and if you can arrange for some muffins at teatime—"

Mrs. MacDougal surveyed him scornfully with her hands on her hips.

"Are ye tryin' tae teach y'r granny?" she demanded witheringly.

Along shaft of sunlight, flecked with dancing specks of dust and wreathed with curling tendrils of steam fell slantwise across the booking-hall and in and out of it bobbed human beings scurrying like ants: porters wheeling hand-trucks piled high with luggage; stout fussy business men, consulting their watches; young men in plus-fours, carrying golf-bags; young women pausing to powder their noses at the mirrors on the weighing-machines; elderly women hurrying frantically to catch trains that were not yet due and trains that had already steamed out of the station; darting boys, leather-lunged, bawling, with trays of magazines (all the wrong ones), chocolates, cigarettes and fruit. In and out they weaved, barging into one another, stumbling over suitcases, stepping on each other's toes: mumbling, apologising, blaspheming…

Mind your eye… Watch your step… Oh, I'm so sorry I… Pray don't mention it…! Why the—don't you watch where you're going…? Who the—do you think you're talking to…? The stillness seemed to lie heavily upon her chest. All she could hear was the hoarse, fitful whispering of the decaying house, like the tired voice of someone dying.

Trains shunting. Whistles blowing. Stentorian voices shouting. A little girl, with a grubby knuckle to her eye, wailing: 'I've lorst my Ma!' A red-faced, burdened woman furiously exclaiming: 'Just wait till I get my hands on you, Emmeline Jane! I'll teach you to lose yourself!' (As though Emmeline Jane needed any teaching! she has had a positive genius for losing herself since the day she was born.)

In the midst of it all, with his Godforsaken felt hat low on his forehead, Julian Mendoza, eating salted peanuts.

"More chocolate?" suggested, chinking pennies in his hand.

"No, thanks," said Cicely absently, her eyes on the clock.

"Try your weight?"

Cicely frowned the length of the platform. "The train's late."

"Trains often are."

She looked at him with a puzzled expression. The more she saw of him the less she understood him. "You seem to have changed within the past ten minutes. You're not the man you were when you were rushing me off my feet to get here."

"I live up to a simple rule: never race your engine when your car is standing at the kerb. In other words, no amount of worrying will bring your mother's train in a second sooner, so why worry. Incidentally—here it is now!"

As the panting engine slowly approached the buffers and the doors of the gliding coaches began to be thrown open, Cicely started to run along the platform looking through the windows of each compartment until at last she saw the pale, sweet worried face for which she was looking.

"Mother!"

"Cicely!"

They kissed, then clung together, sobbing, muttering brokenly; hugging each other tightly. It was a long time before Mrs. Foster held her daughter at arm's-length and anxiously inspected her.

"Cicely, darling, it's so good to see you. I was afraid—oh, I can't tell you how worried I've been."

Her cue. Cicely forced a smile, conquering the longing to bury her head on her mother's bosom and sob out her troubles.

"Then you were a very foolish little mother," she retorted, with a catch in her voice. "There was nothing to worry about."

"But the newspapers—"

"All lies, mother dear. Newspapers have to print lies, to keep their readers interested. The truth is always too dull for words."

"But they said you—"

"I know, darling. They had the slightest of excuses for dragging me in and they made the most of it."

How difficult it was to face those grave trusting eyes and lie! Cicely began to doubt whether she could keep it up. It was a relief to have Julian Mendoza standing in the background (gazing with an expression of intense interest at a shampoo powder poster) to drag forward and present.

"Mother, this is Mr. Mendoza, a friend of mine."

Julian raised his hat and smiled down at the frail, faded little woman in grey, whose eyes had the wise, sad expression of one who had looked often on the face of Sorrow. It is not the least remarkable thing about him that, despite his slovenly apparel and vagabond air he greeted her with a gentle courtesy that won Mrs. Foster's instant trust.

"Have you a bag, mother?" asked Cicely.

"My dear child, I haven't. Wasn't it stupid of me? I came away in such a hurry that I forgot to bring a thing. I didn't think of it until I was in the train, and then it was too late."

Cicely's mind framed a tactful utterance about it being best, in any event, for her mother to go home that evening, but she suppressed it. Anxious as she was to have her mother at a discreet distance until she extricated herself from the mess she was in, she could hardly suggest her departure the moment she arrived.

There was an awkward pause, which Julian broke by announcing that he had bagged a taxi. Mrs. Foster talked about her garden, her cottage, and the life of the village in which she lived while the vehicle glided through thronged London streets, for which Cicely thanked her lucky stars. It was easy to appear natural and cheerful as long as the conversation remained out of treacherous channels.

But when Cicely and her mother were lunching together in the room Julian had commandeered for her, it was not so easy to pretend that all was well. Cicely had a frank, impetuous nature. Lying did not come easily to her. Several times she was on the point of blurting out the truth. And Mrs. Foster was not a gullible person. Mothers never are, where their children are concerned, although they sometimes pretend to be for reasons of their own.

All afternoon Cicely kept changing the subject—she talked of theatres, books, films, old friends, a hundred and one things, until she was wrung dry of small talk—and still it kept drifting back to the Singerman Murder Case. Cicely's head was beginning to ache when, at four o'clock, Julian knocked at the door and asked if he might come to tea.

"Oh, I hoped you would!" exclaimed Cicely gladly.

"That will be very nice," agreed her mother, politely.

Mrs. Foster had photographed the room in her mind when she first entered it. Now she made a more exhaustive survey of it and was agreeably impressed.

"You are really very comfortable here, my child," she said. "I was afraid I'd find you in some awful place. Soho—I didn't like the sound of it. I'm glad you moved. You must be doing quite well. By the way, what are you doing now? You tell me so little in your letters."

Cicely hesitated. What could she say? Not the truth, or her mother would insist on giving her some money, and she had little enough to live on herself. If she mentioned a current play and claimed to be in it, Mrs. Foster would want to see it that evening and she would promptly be discovered in a lie. Inspiration suggested a film. Films are often in the making for months—and within weeks she might have disentangled herself from the muddle she was in and be able to tell the whole truth…

"I have a part in a talkie," she replied.

"How nice! What is the name of the picture?"

"'Illicit Loves'," Cicely plunged boldly. "The great German director, Gustav Von Blon—you must have heard of him—is making it for the Colossal Film Company."

"Gustav Von Blon," repeated Mrs. Foster, wrinkling her brow. "But isn't he rather a horrid type of man? I read an article about him in one of the papers. It said he was quite brutal to the actors and actresses under his direction."

"Oh, that's just publicity," said Cicely quickly. "He's not a bit like that, really. He's most kind and considerate."

"I see…" Mrs. Foster frowned again. "The Colossal Film Company… The man who was shot—Mr. Singerman—wasn't he a director of that Company?"

"Yes," Cicely admitted, wishing she had thought of some other film company.

Her mother leaned forward and placed a worn, thin hand on her knee. "Cicely, I want you to tell me exactly how you came to be involved in that dreadful affair. You've evaded all my questions, and that's not like you." She turned to Julian. "Mr. Mendoza, I am her mother. Don't you think she ought to trust and confide in me?"

"But I do trust you, mother. It's only—"

"—only that there is so little to tell," said Julian smoothly. "You mustn't allow the newspaper reports to worry you, Mrs. Foster. Newspapers always make the worst of a bad job. The true facts are simple. Your daughter went to Mr. Singerman's flat the other night to discuss—er—a further contract after the present picture is completed. She found him worried and distraught, in no condition to talk business, so she left quite soon and came home. That was all her part in the affair. What happened after she left him remains a mystery, but I can tell you confidentially that Singerman was perplexed by business worries and there is a strong feeling that he shot himself. In any case, murder or suicide, the police are satisfied that your daughter had no connection with the sad affair. The papers dragged her in because sudden death with a beautiful girl in it is worth three columns, while the same death without the girl is hardly front-page news. They made up a story about Singerman having attacked her because that's the way a newspaperman's mind works." (He said it without a flicker of an eyelid.) "To us who knew him, the suggestion is ludicrous. A shyer, more retiring man would have been hard to find. A home-lover, married, and devoted to his wife."

He almost said 'wives.'

Mrs. Foster said it for him.

"I thought he had been through the divorce court more than once," she murmured diffidently.

"I refer to the present Mrs. Singerman," explained Julian hastily. "He was devoted to her. Previously he had been unfortunate in marriage—he was an idealist, and idealists in this material world are often hurt."

"I see," said Mrs. Foster doubtfully.

Her eyes rested fondly on Cicely. The dancing flames of the fire flickered on the girl's delicate oval face and lent it an ethereal beauty. The long eyelashes which drooped on her cheeks gave her an innocent, childlike appearance.

"My child is very precious to me," said Mrs. Foster, half to herself. "Anything that happened to her would hurt me very much."

Julian was silent for a moment, then: "I assure you nothing will happen to her," he said soberly.

Mrs. MacDougal bustled into the room carrying a tray on which her best silver tea-service was arrayed. She set it on a table near the fire and placed a huge dish of piping hot muffins on the hearth. As she went out of the room, she beckoned ominously to Julian who followed her to the landing.

"There's a young man to see you, Mr. Mendoza," she whispered. "A richt stubborn young fellow. I told him ye were busy, but he swore he'd pu' the hoose doon tae find ye."

Julian went downstairs and found Kenneth Archer pacing the narrow hall restlessly. He wheeled and glowered at the reporter.

"Where is she?" he demanded fiercely. "What have you done with her?"

"I should think you must have a diseased liver," replied Julian casually. "Nothing else accounts for your impossible temper."

"Never mind that. I'm told you took her away in a cab. Where is she?"

He raised his fist threateningly. Julian smiled softly and looked into his eyes.

"Calm down, my hasty young friend," he murmured. "I might think you meant it—and that would be just too bad."

For a moment they stared into each other's eyes, then Julian turned on his heel.

"Come," he said, "I'll take you to her."

He led the way upstairs and ushered Kenneth into the cheerful room in which the girl and her mother were sitting. Cicely rose.

"Oh," she said. "You."

"Yes," muttered Kenneth. "Me."

A pause. "I should have thought—" she began; then, recollecting the presence of her mother, she broke off hastily. "Mother, this is Kenneth Archer."

The expression on Kenneth's face was laughable. "How do you do?" he stammered.

Surely this sullen creature could not be the wonderful young man about whom Cicely had told her so much, thought Mrs. Foster, as she shook hands with him. She reflected with a sigh that a daughter's 'wonderful young men' are usually a disappointment to her mother.

"Tea?" suggested Cicely.

"No, thanks," sulked Kenneth. "I've had some."

His coming did nothing to relieve the tension of the atmosphere. Cicely was on tenterhooks wondering what he might say. But he said nothing. He simply sat and frowned at each of them in turn.

Cicely tried to think of a tactful way to suggest her mother's return home that evening, but after all, Mrs. Foster was the first to broach the subject, with a remark about the infrequent railway service to the village in which she lived. She had been in too much of a hurry that morning she said to ascertain the time of a suitable train on which to go back.

"There's a good one in an hour," said Julian glancing at his watch. "I looked it up at the station."

Mrs. Foster waited for Cicely to say that she wouldn't dream of letting her run away so soon. But Cicely said nothing.

"Very well," she said, a little sadly. "I'd better catch it."

Cicely threw her arms about the forlorn little woman. "Mother, I'd love to have you stay, only—"

"Darling, I understand." Mrs. Foster forced a smile. "But, of course, it's out of the question. Why, I haven't even a toothbrush! Never mind, perhaps in the early summer I'll come up for a week and we'll do all the sights and then you can come home with me for a nice long rest at the cottage."

It was not a particularly happy party that saw her off at the station. Cicely's conscience was pricking her as she looked at her mother's wistful expression. Kenneth skulked along behind, glaring at Julian. As they clustered round the door of a third-class compartment, Mrs. Foster pointed, with a frown, to an inconspicuously-dressed man who was lounging at the barrier.

"Do you know that man, my dear? I'm sure I saw him hanging about the station when I arrived, and when I glanced out of the window of your room someone very like him was looking up at the house."

"I don't know him from Adam, Mother darling," replied Cicely. "London's full of men who look like that."

Before the train went, Mrs. Foster had a private word with Julian. "I don't believe a word of what you told me, Mr. Mendoza," she said gravely. "I feel in my heart that Cicely is in terrible trouble. It hurts me to leave her. But I'm going to trust you to stand by her and help her."

"I'll do everything I can," he promised quietly.

"I feel an absolute pig," said Cicely, as the train steamed out of the station.

Julian nodded. "So do I."

Kenneth inserted his shoulder between them. "Cicely," he growled, "I want to talk to you."

"I'm not at all sure I want to talk to you," she answered aloofly. "In fact, I'm quite sure I don't."

They went out of the station in silence. Kenneth walked stiffly beside Cicely and Julian dropped into Kenneth's former position in the rear. The inconspicuously-dressed man drifted along a few yards behind. Julian turned and beckoned to him and he approached sheepishly.

"Miss Foster," said Julian. "May I present Detective Burke. He's going to be keeping you company quite a lot in the near future, so you might as well make his acquaintance."

It had snowed from midnight until dawn and the branches of the trees, bare and stark the previous day, were laden with fleecy foliage and the shrubs were nodding under their hoary burdens like sheep ripe for the shears and the grey slate roofs across the way were transformed into snow-capped peaks of enchanted mountains. The sun, shining on an alabaster world, cast a silvern sheen everywhere. But, as she let up the blinds with a rattle, Mrs. MacDougal had no eyes for the world's white splendour. She liked snow on Christmas cards but not on London's streets.

The harsh light of day streamed in on Julian's eyelids. He burrowed his tousled head into the rumpled pillow and clung to the skirts of fleeing sleep. Mrs. MacDougal shook his shoulder.

"I've brocht up your breakfast," she said.

"It's eleven o'clock."

Julian sat up. "Eleven o'clock! Why do you always wake me at eight when I want to sleep and let me doze half the day when I simply must get up?"

His landlady deftly inserted another pillow behind his head and plumped a tray on his lap.

"I thocht ye'd be all the better for the rest," she said placidly. "I lit the fire an hour ago,

But ye were dead tae the world. If ye tak' my advice ye'll spend the day in bed. Ye're no' ower the 'flu yet."

"Flu!" Julian bisected a sausage. "Pooh! It's gone. That's one for your book, Mrs. Mac. A sure cure for the 'flu: go out against all advice and run slap into a murder. In a word, Excitement; the cure for all ills."

Mrs. MacDougal picked up her lodger's trousers, which

had fallen to the floor from the chair on which he had uselessly tossed them, shook them, and folded them neatly.

"An awful business, that murder," she said casually.

Julian smiled. He was not deceived by her disinterested air. Mrs. MacDougal's one vice was a passion for the macabre. There was nothing she enjoyed more than the gruesome details of a murder case—the grimmer the better—and she believed that there was a story too awful to tell behind every violent death. She relied on her lodger to tell her that story. Julian liked to give his public what it wanted. Drawing boldly on his imagination between mouthfuls of sausage-and-egg he spun a tale that made her shiver with delicious horror. He plastered it on thickly: made her see the white, sapped corpse of Jacob Singerman lying in a welter of gore, riddled with countless bullets; the hall of his flat, blood-spattered like a slaughterhouse. In the middle of it, when Mrs. MacDougal's breath was coming in shocked gasps and her eyes were wide with excitement, a bell shrilled an imperative summons. The good woman jumped a yard.

"Only the front door bell," said Julian.

"Confound the bell!" cried Mrs. MacDougal, as she fled to answer it.

Shortly she returned and announced in an awed voice that Inspector Howells of the Criminal Investigation Department wished to see Julian.

"Howells!" murmured the reporter. "Wonder what he wants? Better show him up."

The Inspector's solemn lean face wore an uncertain expression when he entered the room. Julian waved a piece of toast at him, as cheerfully as though receiving a visitor in bed at eleven o'clock were the most natural thing in the world.

"Sit down, Inspector. You've breakfasted, no doubt?"

"Hours ago," said Howells pointedly.

He dropped heavily into a chair without removing his overcoat and glanced at Julian hesitantly as though he hardly knew how to express what he had come to say. Julian gave him no aid. He heaped marmalade on the toast and applied himself to it with evident relish.

The Scotland Yard man took stock of his surroundings, from habit rather than genuine interest, with a veiled glance that saw everything without appearing to look at anything. He muttered 'Good God!' under his breath. The room affected most people like that.

No Scotswoman of Mrs. MacDougal's class ever throws away anything. Mrs. MacDougal's own sitting-room was crowded with pictures and bric-a-brac, but it was not spacious enough to accommodate more than half of her treasures. The rest, rejected politely but firmly by her other lodgers, had found its way by degrees into Julian's room. The walls were crowded with pictures so closely that one could barely have inserted a fingertip between the neighbouring frames. In an idle hour Julian had counted seventy-two pictures and a hundred and four 'ornaments' before he gave up, with one wall and the dressing-table still to cata-logue.

Queen Victoria and her consort looked down with placid dignity from the place of honour above the mantelpiece, flanked on the left by King Edward and Queen Alexandra and on the right by King George and Queen Mary. There was a large coloured print of the present Royal family when children and half a dozen photographs of the Prince of Wales. For democracy's sweet sake, a country girl looking pensively at a basket of mauve flowers and the same country girl looking gaily at the same flowers. At least a dozen pictures of round blobby children in shorts too long and skirts too short, and studies of dogs with glassy eyes and dead fish with roguish expressions, and women with coy, fixed smiles and leg-of-mutton sleeves, and men with soup-strainer moustaches and large Adam's-apples.

Bric-a-brac littered the mantelpiece, the sideboard, the chest of drawers and the dressing-table. Presents From Everywhere. Mugs, jugs, vases, cups, china dogs, cats, babies, elephants, ducks, shepherds, shepherdesses; and one appalling large, fat, pink, nude female balancing a pot on her shoulder with one hand and modestly concealing her person from rude eyes with the other as effectively as a postage stamp would have concealed a mountain. It was a room to make an aesthete swoon and turn green, but Julian's was not an aesthetic soul.

There was a somewhat dazed look in the eyes of Inspector Howells when he concluded his survey of the room. He looked at Julian and coughed.

Julian went on eating. Howells coughed again. Still Julian said nothing and the Inspector was forced to break the silence.

"I've got a proposition to make you," he said awkwardly.

"Name it," replied Julian noncommittally.

The Inspector lit a cigarette and turned his eyes to the ceiling.

"We haven't hit it off in the past," he said, "and we aren't likely to get along any better in the future, but at present it happens that our interests are identical. You'd give your eyes to solve the Singerman Case. So would I. I'm prepared to do a deal with you and pool information, on the understanding, of course, that you play fair with me and don't print anything that might prejudice the case before it is solved."

"In other words," murmured Julian lazily, "you have a clue you think I can follow up more fruitfully than you can."

"Put it like that if you choose," frowned Howells. "I'll be frank. I don't like you. You know that. But I'll give you your due; you've got a knack of pushing yourself in wherever you wish to go—"

"Thanks," said Julian modestly.

"—and I can use the assistance of a man with that talent. This isn't regular, of course, but there are times when for expediency's sake regularity goes by the board. Yesterday I found a letter in Singerman's flat which I think has a bearing on the case. There is no indication who sent it, but I've a hunch the writer is employed by the Colossal Film Company. It isn't much use sending a plainclothes man to the studios; he'd probably discover nothing. But a reporter might have more luck. A reporter—you, for instance —would have the run of the place and be able to nose about as much he liked."

"Let's see the letter."

Howells handed him a soiled crumpled sheet of notepaper on which a few lines were written in pencil in block lettering. There was no date and it began abruptly:

SOMEONE YOU TRUST IS SWINDLING YOU. HE HAS ROBBED YOU OF THOUSANDS OF POUNDS. IF YOU ARE PREPARED TO PAY TWO HUNDRED POUNDS FOR DETAILED INFORMATION AND PROOF INSERT AN ADVERTISEMENT TO THAT EFFECT IN THE AGONY COLUMN OF THE 'EVENING GLOBE.'

Julian turned the letter over and examined it minutely. "Fingerprints?" he queried.

"Only Jacob Singerman's."

"I suppose you've gone over the files of the *Globe?*"

"The advertisement appeared a few days ago."

The Inspector produced a clipping and read it aloud: "'X.— Will pay if proof is satisfactory. J. S.'"

Julian placed the breakfast tray on the floor, lit his pipe, and lay back, his knees forming a mountain under the bedclothes.

"Why are you so sure that the writer is employed at the Colossal Film Company's studios? Jacob Singerman had no business interests apart from the film company; therefore, I assume that the person who 'robbed him of thousands of pounds' is associated with it. And who would have been more likely to have discovered the fact than an employee?"

"There's something in that. Where did you find the note?"

"In a pocket of one of the dead man's suits."

"Find anything else?"

"Nothing of importance."

Julian cocked an eye at him. "Quite sure? Don't hold out on me if you want me to help you."

Howells nodded irritably. "Certainly, I'm sure."

"Don't get huffy. I was only asking. I noted a safe in Singerman's bedroom: wasn't there anything in that?"

"Oh, some letters from women, a little over a hundred pounds in notes and some personal jewellery. Nothing else."

"When did you open the safe?"

"Hyman Singerman opened it for me yesterday afternoon. He has the combination."

"I see." Julian drew hard on his pipe. "Alright. I'll see what I can find out and let you know as soon as I have something. But I want my pound of flesh. Come on, out with it: what else have you discovered within the past twenty-four hours?"

"Not a great deal, although I did make one discovery that strengthens suspicion against your protegee, Miss Foster. Jacob Singerman owned a revolver—a large-calibre revolver—which he kept in a drawer in the living-room of his flat. It was noticed there less than a week ago by a valet employed at Dorian House and it is now missing."

He glanced keenly at Julian to mark the effect of his words.

"Yes, I heard about that," agreed the reporter complacently.

Howells jumped as though he had been stung. "You did? Who told you?"

"A little bird," replied Julian nonchalantly. "Even Scotland Yard has its little birds who will warble all they know for a handful of seed."

"When I catch your 'little bird,'" snapped Howells, "he'll do his warbling in an iron cage. I suppose you know you're confessing to a crime?"

"I tremble!" declared Julian cheerfully. "Have you anything more to impart? No? Not one thing? Alright. Now that you've told Papa the whole truth—even if Papa did know it already—Papa is going to reward you."

He smiled at the black scowl on the Inspector's face and proceeded, less facetiously, to tell him about the peculiar little man in the bowler hat and spectacles who had been hanging about Dorian House on the night of the murder.

"I don't suggest he played an active part in the killing," he added. "He didn't look as though he'd have the nerve to steal pennies from babies, far less commit a murder. But he's mixed up in it. Perhaps he's the writer of the anonymous letter."

The Inspector jotted down the details of the mysterious little man's description.

"I'll start a search for him at once," he said. "But you should have told me about him the other night. You'll find yourself in trouble one of these days, Mendoza."

"I'll risk it. There's another thing. Has it occurred to you that Singerman may have committed suicide?"

"Hardly. In that case the weapon would have been lying close to the body and there was no sign of a weapon in the flat."

"There's just a possibility," said Julian dreamily, "that the revolver was lying near the body when the dead man's brother and the liftboy discovered it."

Howells stared. "What the dickens are you driving at?"

"Simply that Hyman Singerman could have disposed of the gun after he sent the boy to the telephone."

"Why should he do that?"

Julian blew out a cloud of pungent smoke. "Don't take me too seriously. I'm simply theorising. All the best detectives do that. But it seems to me that if Singerman did commit suicide Brother Hymie might have a reason for wishing to hush it up. The effect publicity of that nature would have on the standing of the film company…an awkward clause in Jacob's insurance policy… I can imagine a dozen reasons."

"Then perhaps," said Howells, with heavy irony, "you can think of one reason why Singerman should kill himself?"

"That's easy. Miss Foster had just left and he did not know what action she might take. Possibly he pictured a trial for assault and the attendant publicity and disgrace and lost his nerve."

"He had played the same game with dozens of women without his nerve being seriously impaired," said Howells dryly.

"Ah! There's another possibility. His women must have cost money—plenty of money! And he was paying alimony to three ex-wives. I should look into his finances. Perhaps he wasn't the rich man he was supposed to have been."

"If I were you." grunted Howells, "I'd drop reporting and take up writing thrillers. You have that type of mind."

Nevertheless, as he departed, he made a mental note to investigate Julian's theory. After he had gone Julian put on a ragged dressing-gown, refilled his pipe, and sat by the fire staring into the leaping orange flames. So absorbed in his thoughts was he that he did not hear Mrs. MacDougal coming into the room. She looked at him with the secretive smile that women assume when they catch men daydreaming. Mrs. MacDougal was a romantic. Every woman is.

"She's a very sweet lassie," she murmured, as though she were thinking aloud.

Julian started. "Who is?" he asked, although he knew perfectly well whom she meant.

"The young ledy you brocht here yesterday."

"Was she?"

"She was," said Mrs. MacDougal. "But I dinna think sae muckle o' the young man. He had a richt dour face."

"Had he?"

"He had. They'll maybe be sweethearts?"

"What if they are?" growled Julian, striking a match.

"The lassie deserves better," replied Mrs. MacDougal, drawing the bedclothes back over the rail at the foot of the bed.

"A woman deserves the man she gets," said Julian roughly.

Mrs. MacDougal picked up the ravished breakfast tray.

"Conseederin' some men," she replied, "that's an unco' harsh judgment tae pass on women." There was a pause while she fumbled with the doorhandle, then:

"You'll be thinkin' o' getting' married yoursel', one o' these days?" she said.

"God forbid!" replied Julian hastily.

"Ah," she said, "then ye've been thinkin' o' it already?"

Julian Expounds a Theory

The burly commissionaire, resplendent in green and grey, with much gold braid and many gold buttons, looked down his long nose with a pitying smile.

"Sorry," he said loftily. "Mr. Singerman can't see anyone today."

"He hasn't been struck blind, has he?" asked Julian innocently.

"Not as I know of."

"Then he'll see me."

The commissionaire eyed him appraisingly from head to foot, taking in the dusty shoes, the baggy trousers, the worn overcoat, and the ancient, battered hat. He sniffed.

"I think not," he said. "Sir," he added, as an afterthought.

With an air of finality, he went into his den on the left of the impressive entrance hall and picked up the newspaper he had been reading when Julian interrupted him.

Julian crossed the black tiled floor to a door at the rear of the hall. The commissionaire appeared hastily, crumpling the paper in his hand.

"Hey! Wait a minute! You can't go through there!"

"Mr. Singerman's office is somewhere beyond that door, is it not?"

"What if it is?"

"I have informed you that I wish to see Mr. Singerman."

"Look here—" began the commissionaire truculently.

Julian's eyes grew hard. "I wish to see Mr. Singerman," he repeated.

The man took stock of him again and this time he looked at Julian's face and eyes instead of at his clothes.

"Orders are that he ain't to be disturbed on any account," he said mildly.

"I'm afraid you will have to forget about orders."

The commissionaire looked doubtful. It was not easy to be quite sure of his ground under the gaze of those hypnotic eyes.

"Wait a minute, sir," he said.

He disappeared into his tiny sanctum and Julian heard him speaking apologetically on the telephone. In a few minutes a cool, superior young lady sailed through the forbidden door into the reception hall. She approached Julian with a disdainful air, patting her back hair languidly.

"I understand that you wish to see Mr. Singerman?"

"I do."

"I'm afraid that is impossible," she replied with a supercilious smile. "If you care to state your business—"

"My business is with Mr. Singerman. Please inform him that Julian Mendoza is waiting to see him," he said, looking into her eyes. "Julian Mendoza," he repeated, with a certain emphasis.

He pronounced his name in the tone of one who is quite sure of his own importance. The girl was impressed. After all, only a person who was someone would dare to dress so slovenly; the nobodies usually wore white spats. She hesitated and was lost. "I'll see," she murmured, disappearing through the door by which she had come. Shortly she returned. "Mr. Singerman will see you," she said, with a fulsome smile. "This way, please."

She led him along a grey and green corridor, flanked with doors on which names were inscribed in gold lettering, and ushered him into a large room which might have been lifted bodily from an American film about a Napoleon of Business. Only a screen designer could have conceived such an office. And only a film magnate could have worked in it. The desk, elaborately carved, and littered with telephones, push-buttons and Dictaphones, covered an area as large as many modern rooms. Mr. Singerman had spent a lot of time sitting at that desk, looking like Napoleon, but now he was greatly changed from the self-important, genial little man he had been. He had become a pathetic, shrunken little figure, resting a round chin on cupped hands, and staring bleakly into space. His face was grey and haggard. His rotund body seemed to have shrivelled: his clothes looked as though they had been made for a much larger man.

The girl announced Julian and left the room, but Mr. Singerman did not look up. For a long time, he sat there lost in his thoughts, apparently oblivious to Julian's presence, then he raised vacant eyes and stated at him.

"Who the devil are you?" he asked in a dry, lifeless voice.

"I'm Mendoza."

"And who the devil is Mendoza?"

"We met the other night at Dorian House."

Singerman gazed at him for a long time, his head nodding slightly, seemingly of its own volition.

"I remember now. You are a detective—no, you pretended to be a detective."

"I am a reporter. It is necessary sometimes to pretend to be what one isn't in order to go where one wishes to go."

The film magnate considered that for some moments.

"Well, now you can get out of here as quickly as you like. I have nothing to say to you. I can't see anyone."

He dropped his head on his hands and withdrew into himself as a snail withdraws into its shell. Julian sat down and waited. Minutes passed before the other noticed him again.

"What, still here? I told you I have nothing to say to you."

"Mr. Singerman," said Julian quietly, "I am sincerely sorry to trouble you. I can see how greatly you are upset by the death of your brother."

"Upset!" Mr. Singerman snatched at the word and repeated

it bitterly. "Upset! My whole life is turned upside down. I am lost, alone. I cannot think. I cannot do anything. It is as though a part of myself had been wrenched away. Always we were partners, Jake and I, ever since we were children. We shared this office. He sat facing me across this desk. Everything we did we did together. For twenty-five years we have been building, building, always together—and now he is gone. Gone! How can I believe it? Often, I look up expecting to see him sitting across the desk." His voice sank to a whisper. "And I see him, I tell you! I see him. Not as he used to be, but as he was when I found him…dead… With an awful grin on his face and the coldness of hell in his staring eyes…"

He shivered and made a weary gesture. "But why do I tell you all this? What is it to you? Go, please. I wish to be alone."

Julian hitched himself forward. "Your brother meant a great deal to you," he said gently. "His death should not go unavenged. Won't you help me to find his murderer?"

Mr. Singerman raised his head slowly and stared into Julian's eyes. "Why should you think you can find him?"

Julian shrugged his shoulders. "I have succeeded in such matters before."

Mr. Singerman reflected for a few moments, then shook his head. "No, no, you must not interfere. The Police…"

"I'm afraid I must. It is my job to investigate these matters for my paper. I shall be handicapped if you refuse to help me, but I shall still do my best without your help."

"And you think you can succeed?"

"I do."

The film magnate drummed his fingers restlessly on the desk. "What do you wish me to do?" he asked.

"For one thing, I should like the run of the studios—not that I expect to find the murderer here, but because I wish to study the environment in which the greater part of your brother's life was lived—and, secondly, I should like to ask you a few questions."

"What can I tell you? I know nothing. Nothing."

"Can you suggest anyone who might have a motive for killing your brother?"

Mr. Singerman spread his fleshy palms expressively. "Is that not the question with which I have been torturing myself for hours on end? The answer is not easy to supply. Jake was a hard man. There were many who resented his superior brains. But I can think of no one who would kill him."

"He had incurred the enmity of more than one woman?"

"He was a fool over women," agreed Mr. Singerman, his puffy face darkening. "Yes. Some of them were his enemies. But they were the sort of enemies who can be disposed of with money, you understand. Jake was generous in those things, if not in business. And why should any of them wish to cut off the golden flow at its source?" He hesitated and studied Julian closely from beneath lowered eyelids. "I have thought—" he broke off abruptly. "But that is nonsense."

"What have you thought?"

Mr. Singerman leaned toward Julian confidentially. "If I tell you something, it will go no further Very well. You will laugh, but I will tell you. It is only a suspicion, you understand. A crazy one. I know it is mad. I tell myself so: but cannot get it out of my mind." He paused. "You have heard of Gustav Von Blon?"

"The film director?"

"Yes, the film director. What a man! Insane: crazy! And we were as insane as he, for we engaged him to make a picture for us. For a week a storm had been brewing between him and Jake. Mark you, they had quarrelled before. Almost every day since that madman came from Hollywood there has been words between them. But this was no minor argument. Only a few hours before he was killed Jake told me that he would throw Von Blon out of the studios if it cost us a hundred thousand pounds."

"I've heard of Von Blon," said Julian. "Rather extravagant, isn't he?"

"Extravagant?" Mr. Singerman spat out the word. "He splashes money about like a drunken sailor. My money. Jake's money. What do you think? When half the picture was made, he scrapped it, scrapped it after spending thousands of pounds on it, simply because it wasn't exactly what he wanted! Oi gewalt! It makes me go cold all over, to think of it! And Jake Well, you would have thought Jake was going to blow up any minute. If he had lived, he would have broken Von Blon's contract if it cost every penny we had in the world."

"Von Blon knew that?" asked Julian sharply.

"Jake told him so to his face, among other things. It would be easier to tell you the things he didn't call him than the things he did. And Von Blon simply sat there and smiled—where you are sitting, he sat."

"And you think that Von Blon—"

"Have I accused him?" protested Singerman, with a wide gesture. "But if you knew the man, you would realise that he is mad enough for anything. And this picture is his last chance as a director. He came over from Hollywood because none of the big companies on the other side would have anything to do with him. He is the finest director in the business, but mad as a March hare. Crazy about realism. He will spend a thousand pounds to get an effect which lasts only a few seconds. Films are his only interest; all he lives for. And if Jake had broken his contract, he was through."

Julian nodded thoughtfully. "And you think he would go to any lengths to save his career?"

Mr. Singerman pursed his lips and spread his hands again.

There was a silence. "There is one other thing which makes me think," he said at last. "Mr. Gustav Von Blon has a flat on the fifth floor of Dorian House."

The reporter was sunk in thought. "I'd like to meet the gentleman."

"That is easy. He is still marching about the studios as though he owned the place. And I am not going to interfere with him. I am too worried, too unstrung to start a fuss. Besides, I am not the fighter Jake was. I will let him finish the picture and pray it will be completed before I am forced into bankruptcy."

Drawing a pad of writing paper towards him, he scribbled a few words on it, tore off the top sheet, and handed it to Julian.

"This authorises you to go wherever you choose about the studios. It will be better if you run into Von Blon in that way than if I introduced you to him. You are a reporter. Interview him. He loves to be interviewed."

Julian thanked him and rose to go. He paused with his fingers on the door handle, then limped back and leaned across the wide desk.

"Mr. Singerman," he said, "are you aware that they are saying your brother committed suicide?"

The film magnate started. He leant back in his chair and looked up at Julian shrewdly. "Who says that?" he demanded.

Julian made a deprecatory gesture.

"Who can tell who starts these rumours?" he replied unblushingly. "It is spreading rapidly."

Mr. Singerman looked thoughtful. "It is a possibility...no, it is not. The police doctor says my brother died instantly. He would have had no time to dispose of the revolver—and none was found in his flat."

"Someone may have removed the gun," said Julian, eyeing him closely.

Mr. Singerman shook his head. "Impossible—unless you did it yourself. After I discovered Jake dead you were the only person to enter the flat until the police came."

"Even so, it is possible to shoot oneself, die instantaneously, and yet dispose of the weapon."

"How?" asked Singerman sharply.

Julian sucked on his empty pipe. "Quite a simple device would do it."

"A device? What do you mean—a device? Jake knew nothing about mechanical things."

A pause.

"It could be very simple," said Julian slowly. "A length of cord…some sort of weight. It's been done that way before."

"You are talking riddles," retorted Singerman irritably.

"The weight would be attached to the revolver by the cord and allowed to dangle out of the window. The window in the hall of your brother's flat was open when I arrived on the scene. I presume it was not you who opened it?"

"I did not go into the flat," replied Singerman hastily. "My God, no! A look was enough. It was open when I discovered the body—of course!"

"Ah! Then, when your brother pulled the trigger—this is merely a theory—the gun would be jerked out of his lifeless hand by the weight, dragged through the window, and drop eight floors to the ground."

"But in that case," frowned Singerman, "it would have been discovered almost immediately."

"Not necessarily," corrected Julian. "Below the hall window of your brother's flat is a small ornamental pond with a few fish in it. I noticed it yesterday, when I passed Dorian House. I don't know how deep it is: I looked into the water, but between mud and the large leaves of waterlilies I could not see the bottom.

If the revolver fell into that pond, it might not be found for weeks—possibly months. By that time the cord might be rotted away and there would be nothing to show how the gun came to be there."

"It sounds plausible," admitted Singerman thoughtfully.

"It won't be difficult to find out how much truth there is in my theory," said Julian. "I'll get in touch with Howells this evening and suggest dragging the pond."

Singerman nodded. "But I doubt whether you will find anything," he said. "Jake was not the man to commit suicide."

"I presume his financial position was sound?"

Singerman stared at him, with a curious expression on his heavy features. "Why do you ask?"

"There must always be a reason for suicide as well as a motive for murder."

The film magnate nodded again.

"That is so. As far as I know, Jake's affairs were in excellent shape. You will understand, of course, that I cannot speak with certainty until I have had time to investigate his private papers."

While he was speaking, Julian backed away softly and jerked open the door. Someone fell into the room and a sheaf of papers, dropping from his outstretched arms, slithered across the floor in wild confusion. The sallow-faced little man who had made this unconventional entrance sat up and blinked about him with a crestfallen air, then put a hand up to his nose as though he missed something which should be there.

"Your spectacles, I think?" murmured Julian, picking up a twisted gold frame and holding it out.

There was a ludicrous expression of dismay and apprehension on the face of the intruder which proclaimed that he had recognised Julian as certainly as Julian had recognised him.

For a moment he remained seated on the floor, staring up at Julian open-mouthed, looking as though he were about to cry; then he turned nervously to Mr. Singerman.

"I'm so sorry; so sorry," he whispered. "I—I was bringing in these papers—" indicating the litter of disordered pages which lay about him— "and I am afraid I leant rather heavily on the door. I assure you—"

"Pick them up," replied Singerman gruffly, "and get out."

"Yes, sir," said the little man eagerly. "Yes, sir."

Kneeling, he began to gather the papers hastily, his eyes averted, his trembling fingers making a seemingly interminable task of it, his thin, tearful voice muttering apologies to which the film magnate was not troubling to listen. When he had collected them into an untidy armful, he scurried to the door, with his head twisted at an angle.

"Your glasses," said Julian, still holding them out.

The little man cast a frightened glance over his shoulder; a glance which reminded Julian of a startled creature of the woods; and he put out a shaking hand and took the spectacles. A couple of papers fluttered to the floor. Julian picked them up and placed them on top of the others, smiling down sardonically into the watery blue eyes that flinched from meeting his gaze.

"Haven't we met before?" he asked.

"Oh, no…no…I'm sure we haven't."

"I'm quite sure we have."

The little man gulped convulsively and his Adam's-apple bobbed up and down. He cast another timorous glance at Hyman Singerman, murmured something desperately, and scuttled out of the room.

Julian looked at the film magnate and saw that he had again wrapped himself in the morbid shroud of his thought. Dwarfed by the huge desk at which he sat he was staring in front of him in the same hunched, forlorn attitude as when the reporter had first entered the room. Closing the door quietly behind him, Julian limped after the little man who was hurrying along the corridor as though his life depended on it.

Glancing back, the quarry saw that he was being pursued and quickened his pace almost to a run. He hastened into a lift and said something to the attendant, who drew the gates together. Julian lunged forward and thrust his stick between them. They swung open again and the attendant eyed Julian belligerently. Before he could express himself in the matter, the reporter flourished under his eyes the written pass he had obtained from Hyman Singerman and stepped into the mirror-walled cage. The attendant shrugged his shoulders and touched a lever.

"Which floor, Mr. Slee?" he asked, above the soft whine of the ascending lift.

The little man blinked tearfully at Julian.

"The—er—the fourth," he whispered.

"And you, sir?"

"The fourth, please," said Julian.

When the gates opened the little man bolted into the fourth-floor corridor and hastened along it with Julian swinging behind. The lift attendant, staring after them, pushed his cap forward and scratched the back of his head.

"Blimey!"

The little man started to run when he turned a bend in the corridor, but Julian thrust out his stick, hooked the handle through his arm, and drew him back. He pushed his frightened prisoner against the wall and placed a large hand on his chest.

"No, you don't, Little Man," he said softly. "You got away

from me once, but you won't twice. You and I are going to have a cosy little chat. Where can we talk undisturbed? Got an office on this floor by any chance?"

The little man shook his head. He was gazing into Julian's eyes with the petrified expression of a rabbit in the toils of a snake.

"Then why did you come up here?"

With a flicker of his tongue the little man moistened his lips, flabby, colourless lips, like fat grey worms.

"I—I wanted to get away from you," he squeaked.

"Well, you won't do that in a hurry."

"Are—are you a detective?"

"Never mind what I am."

The captive squirmed. "If you aren't you have no right to interfere with me," he whined. "Let me go."

"Not until we've had that chat. Well, can you suggest a quiet spot for it, or shall we hold our discussion here, in the corridor?"

"We—we can go to my office."

Julian released him. "Lead on," he said, "but watch your step. If you try to give me the slip. I'll wring your scraggy neck."

The other gaped in terror at the hairy, long-fingered hand which Julian curled menacingly under his nose and led the way downstairs to a tiny bare room on the ground floor. The reporter pushed him into the swivel-chair which stood in front of the desk—which, with a filing cabinet, comprised the sole furniture—and stood with his back to the door, eyeing him smilingly, with a soft, meaning smile, while he filled his pipe.

"First," he said, striking a match, "what's your name?"

"Slee," the little man gasped. "Simon Slee."

"And what proud position do you hold in this building?"

"I—I keep account of the various production expenses."

"And what, Mr. Slee, were you doing at Dorian House the other night—the night of the murder?"

Simon Slee gulped and ran a finger round his neck inside his collar band.

"I assure you I had nothing whatever to do with the murder. Oh, please, you must believe me. I didn't even know about it until the following morning."

"What were you doing at Dorian House?" Julian repeated coldly.

"I—I—it—it isn't easy to explain. I was—er—watching."

"Watching what?"

"Just—er—watching."

"Snooping, you mean? Spying on someone? On whom: Jacob Singerman?—or Gustav Von Blon?"

Slee gaped at him. "How did you know?" he stammered.

"Know what?"

"About—er—Mr. Singerman and Mr. Von Blon."

"Now we're getting along famously," said Julian. "So, something happened the other night between Singerman and Von Blon, eh? Tell me all about it."

An expression of cunning crept into Simon Slee's little eyes. "There's nothing to tell. Really there isn't. You've mistaken my meaning."

"Oh, no, I haven't." Julian leaned forward, clutched the lapels of the little man's jacket, and drew him half out of his chair. "You'll tell me what happened and tell me quickly, or I'll shake the miserable life out of you."

"I'll tell you," whimpered Slee. "I'll tell you."

"Alright." Julian let him drop back into the chair. "Out with it—and don't forget anything."

"I hardly know how to begin. For—er—reasons of my own I went to Dorian House the other night, as you know. I didn't wish to be seen going in, so I entered by a rear door and walked up the stairs. I hung about on the stairs between the seventh and eighth floor landings, expecting—er—a certain person to call on Mr. Singerman. He didn't come, but at a quarter to nine Mr. Von Blon came up the stairs and I had barely time to skip up and flatten myself against the rear of the lift shaft when he knocked at Mr. Singerman's door.

"Mr. Singerman answered the summons almost at once and his face fell when he recognised Mr. Von Blon. He told him he could not speak to him then as he expected a visitor, but Mr. Von Blon laughed and replied that all he had to say could be said in a few moments. He said that Mr. Singerman would be asking for trouble if he tried to break his contract. 'I intend to finish this picture,' he said, 'and I will go the limit to keep you from stopping me.' Those were his exact words. 'I'll go the limit,' he said. Mr. Singerman didn't seem a bit frightened. 'That suits me,' he retorted. 'I'm prepared to go the limit as well. We'll see who wins.' Mr. Von Blon swore. 'You know what this means to me,' he said. 'I warn you, I'm a dangerous man to trifle with.' Mr. Singerman said: 'So am I,' and slammed the door. Mr. Von Blon stood there for a moment with an ugly look on his face, then shook his fist at the closed door and went downstairs muttering to himself."

He hesitated and blinked at Julian, who drew on his pipe and returned the gaze steadily without speaking.

"Well—I can't tell you much more. I hung about and saw the girl—Miss Foster—admitted to the flat by Mr. Singerman about nine o'clock. I started to follow her when she came out… you know the rest."

"Why did you follow her?" asked Julian.

"Well…she…Well, she didn't seem to be Mr. Singerman's usual type. You—er—perhaps know his reputation with women… I was…interested. I—er—wanted to find out about her."

"For the purpose of blackmail?" suggested Julian.

Simon Slee looked shocked. "Oh, no!" he breathed.

"Oh, yes!" mocked Julian. "Blackmail's your little weakness, isn't it? Blackmail—and writing anonymous letters?"

The shot went home. Slee started and his sallow face turned almost green. He moistened his puffy lips, but he did not speak.

"You wrote an anonymous letter to Jacob Singerman a few days before his death, informing him that someone he trusted had robbed him of thousands and offering full information for two hundred pounds."

Slee shook his head and went on shaking it, like a pendulum, his popping eyes focused on Julian's face. "Oh, no, really, I didn't. I swear—"

"You're a stinking little liar," said Julian dispassionately. "Singerman agreed to your terms through an advertisement in the agony column of the Evening Globe. What happened after that? Did the deal go through? Or was he killed before you had a chance to sell the information." A thought struck him. "Of course—the 'certain person' you expected to see calling on Singerman the other night was the 'trusted' party himself!"

"I don't know what you're talking about."

"Yes, you do! Spit it out: who was the 'trusted' one?"

"I shan't tell you. I shan't! You can't make me. You can do what you like to me, but I shan't tell!"

"Supposing I 'phone Inspector Howells and have him come here at once?" suggested Julian grimly. "He'll have it out of you in about five minutes."

Trembling, Slee cringed back in the chair.

"He won't make me tell. Nothing will. You can threaten and bully me as much as you choose, but I shan't say another word."

Julian leaned back and nodded sapiently.

"I see. You won't tell because, now that Jacob Singerman is

no longer a prospective customer for your knowledge, you hope
to use it to blackmail the man who swindled him."

Slee was convulsed with violent emotion. Words poured in
a torrent from his quivering lips: "Well, why not? Why should
I give it away for nothing? All my life I've been giving myself,
every bit of me, the last ounce of nerve and energy, for nothing.
I've been a fool. Slaved for a pittance and watched other men
growing rich almost without effort. I've scraped and bowed, and
whined 'Yes, sir,' and 'No, sir,' to ignorant bullies who could
hardly write their own names, but yet rode in Rolls-Royce cars
and drank champagne and smoked cigars. I've eaten dirt…licked
their boots…crawled on my belly to them—and why?—simply
because they had money and I hadn't I And how did they get
it? Out of the sweated bodies of their employees, that's how.
By trampling on everyone else, by cheating and lying—by any
means, as long as they weren't found out. Why shouldn't I take
it from them as they've taken it from others? Look at me! I'm
fifty. I've had thirty-six years of slavery. It's made me a coward
that anyone can push about at his merest whim. You don't think
you'd dare bully me if I were rich, do you? You only dare to
do it because I'm only an underpaid bookkeeper, who doesn't
count. Thirty-six years of endless figures! Poor pay! Scraping and
pinching to exist. I haven't been able to save as much as a pound
a year for each of those bitter years. Blackmail, you say? Justice,
I call it! Why shouldn't I take what I can? Why shouldn't I?"

When he finished the words were coming in hoarse, sobbing
gasps. He fell back in his chair, shuddering, and closed his eyes.

"Blackmail's a dangerous game," said Julian quietly. "You
haven't the guts for it. I'll make you an offer. I'm a reporter on
the *Morning World*. I'll guarantee my paper will pay you two
hundred pounds for the name of the man who robbed Jacob
Singerman and the proofs in your possession."

"Two hundred pounds!" giggled Slee, shrilly, hysterically. "That was a week ago. A lot has happened since then… Such a lot! It isn't enough now. I want more. Much more. Thousands… Thousands!"

"Thousands!" repeated Julian. "I thought so; the swindler is also the man who killed Singerman!"

"I didn't say that!" panted Slee. "I didn't say that!"

"But you believe it. Well, watch yourself, Little Man."

"What do you mean?"

Julian struck another match and drew on his pipe until the tobacco glowed red.

"A man who has committed one murder isn't likely to stick at a second. You've got a ten-to-one chance of getting a bullet in your brain!"

It was the strangest pub Julian had ever seen. He had come through a padded door and almost run into it. Two walls were all it boasted: set at right angles to each other, one of them fronting on a strip of cobbled street which stopped short a few paces from a huge camera. In the doorway stood the landlord, in shirtsleeves, with a stained apron about his ample waist.

"You pop orf, d'you 'ear?" he exclaimed sharply.

The words were addressed not to Julian but to a faded little woman in a drab shawl and ragged skirt, on whose head bobbed a hat which sagged dismally in spite of its gay trimming of artificial roses. She flourished a jug at him.

"Sauce!" she retorted shrilly.

"Garn!" snarled the landlord, taking a step forward and raising his hand.

The woman swayed, lost her balance, and sprawled full length on the cobblestones. The landlord placed his hands on his hips, threw back his head, and burst into raucous laughter.

"That's better!" said a young man who was sitting in front of the camera. "Just run through it again and we'll call it a day."

Julian's eyes roved aloft to the ceiling of the long studio, a hundred and fifty feet above his head, divided by a system of trolley lines from which cameras, lights, and other equipment could be suspended and moved to and fro. They travelled to the galleries, on various levels, which lined the walls, and made out the pale blurs of faces and round outlines of giant lights, the latter not at the moment in use.

The exterior of the public-house occupied only a corner of the immense studio. Behind it he could see a three-walled set, built like a T, representing two adjoining rooms, and beyond the deck of a battleship, bristling with guns. The other scenes were deserted, but almost a score of studio workers were grouped about the front of the public-house set.

The dishevelled woman appeared in the doorway of the pub, clutching her jug in one hand and the gathered ends of her shawl in the other and shrieking insults over her shoulder. She took a sudden dive into the 'street,' propelled by the landlord's fat hand.

"You pop orf, d'you 'ear?"

A flourish of the jug…

"Sauce!" she shrilled…

"Garn!"

As she measured her length on the floor again, the young man rose. Tall and thin, with an untidy mop of sandy hair, he wore a canary-coloured pullover and grey flannels and held a sheaf of typescript in his hand.

"O.K.," he said. "That's as good as we can get it. The Chief wants to shoot that scene first thing in the, morning, so be on the set in your makeup bright and early."

He turned away and made for the padded door, but stopped short with a whistle of astonishment at sight of Julian.

"Mendoza, by all that's holy! What on earth are you doing here? Don't tell me you've sunk so low as to become a film critic?"

"Hello, Tommy. No, I'm still a humble reporter. And you? I heard you'd kissed Fleet Street goodbye, but I didn't know you'd stepped into the shoes of Cecil de Mille."

Tommy Halliday wrung his hand warmly. "I haven't. Far from it. Come downstairs to my room for a chat. I'm dashed glad to see you."

The ex-newspaperman's office was one of a row of diminutive rooms, barely larger than cubicles, each containing two chairs, a flat-topped desk, a telephone and a wastepaper basket, which housed the studio's swarm of minor executives. He tossed the typescript into a drawer, draped himself in a chair, resting on his spine with his feet on the desk and motioned Julian to the other chair.

"What's the lowest thing that crawls?" he asked, lighting a cigarette. "Whatever it is, that's what I've become. The trade name is 'assistant director'—but when one is under a certain pig-headed bully of a German, the trade name is only a polite euphemism for 'worm'."

"Meaning Von Blon?" suggested Julian.

"Meaning Von Blon," agreed Halliday bitterly. "If it wasn't that I've spent a year trying to break into the film world I'd bash in his ugly head with the first thing that came handy, and make anyone who was fool enough to want it a present of the worst blasted job a poor perishing heathen ever had."

"I gather," smiled Julian, "that you don't altogether like being Mr. Von Blon's assistant director?"

"That," almost spat Halliday, "is the impression I intended to convey. I haven't been able to call my soul my own above a whisper since I took the job. But let's talk of something else. I'm sick and tired of the—" In colourful, but unprintable, language he outlined his frank opinion of the great Von Blon.

"That's a pity," said Julian. "I want you to present me to him. I've a hankering to meet the gentleman."

"There's no accounting for tastes," replied the former reporter, with a shake of his head.

"But you'll have to curb your impatience for a while. Can't see him today. He's in conference with the principal members of the cast—and I'll give you twenty to one in old boots against the conference ending without a head or two being broken. You'll never guess the crazy Hun's latest idea. We're filming an 'eternal triangle' talkie and ever since we started Von has been going off into fits because the principals didn't put enough spirit into their parts to suit him. So, he got a brainwave—the maddest of the century—sacked the lot and engaged two actors and an actress whose private lives happened to coincide roughly with the main theme of the story. One of them took the other's wife away from him. The actress is the wife. Get it? Cute, isn't it? It won't be acting that the cameras will film. It will be a chunk of life in the raw."

"They'll never agree to it," said Julian.

The assistant director waved a hand at him. "You don't know Von Blon. He's the wiliest ape out of captivity. He signed them up individually without telling any of them who was to play the other parts. He's breaking the news to them in his office now. Golly! I'll bet there are sparks flying. But contracts are contracts. They'll play the parts, all right—although the heat they'll put into them may crack a few lenses!"

"What a lovable nature your boss must have," commented Julian dryly.

"As lovable as a rattlesnake," agreed Tommy Halliday.

He took a large oblong of pasteboard from a drawer and tossed it across the desk.

"That's the little darling," he said. "It often does me good, when I've been squirming under his tongue all day, to bring out his photograph and tell it exactly what I think of him."

Julian took the photograph and gazed with interest at the square face that scowled back at him. A cold face, humourless, callous, ruthless, hard, with sneering little eyes, pouched with flesh, in one of which gleamed a monocle; thin lips, compressed in a straight line; a short, pugnacious nose with wide nostrils; and an aggressive chin. So that was Von Blon!

A speculative look crept into Julian's eyes. Von Blon… No, he had never known a man of that name. And yet, he could have sworn that he had seen the face before: not in a photograph, but in the flesh. He searched his memory, which was a filing-cabinet of faces, and conviction grew stronger. He had seen the man before. He was sure of that. But where?

A cross... The memory was connected with a cross. He could almost see it, rough-hewn, ungainly, spreading uneven arms under a pitiless blue sky... A grilling sun beating down mercilessly on parched, barren soil and stifling heat steaming up out of it... A clamouring rabble of filthy, ragged men, like wild beasts, screaming all manner of foul obscenities, screaming themselves hoarse, snarling, threatening, spitting defiance...at the men in uniform who drove them back, smashing the butts of guns on naked, defenceless skulls, lashing starved, scarred bodies with whips. And another man lying still as a corpse at the foot of the cross...

"Don't happen to know him, by any chance, do you?" asked Tommy Halliday, curiously. "You look as though you might."

"Yes," replied Julian quietly. "I know him.

Von Blon Breaks the News

Russell Clayton stood by the window, his favourite profile turned to the other occupants of the room, his pose the austere, dignified one which had gone down so well with the audience when he played the strong silent lead in 'Other Men's Women.' The expression on his mobile face was out of the same play. Almost fifty, cosmetics and dye, cunningly applied, made him look fifteen years younger in most lights. He had left untouched a single silver lock above his right temple: it heightened his air of distinction. Corsetting and the devout attentions of a prince among tailors disguised the fact that his magnificent body, once as erect as that of a Guardsman, had run to seed. He had the dominant nose which is usually associated with successful barristers, but he had tried in vain to school his large soft mouth into an impressive firmness.

"It is quite out of the question," he said, in a deep vibrant voice (of which he was secretly proud). "I am astonished that you should suggest it. I presume you know my reasons. They were probably your own reasons for requesting me to take part in this…this distasteful affair."

"Then you refuse?"

"Definitely and irrevocably?"

Gustav Von Blon, his little black eyes inscrutable, his square, cropped head slanted a little, his thin lips ever so slightly smiling, turned his head and regarded the pale lovely woman who sat in a carved chair to the right of his desk. "And you, Madam? Do you also refuse?"

From beneath long eyelashes, Norma Lavery glanced at her husband who sprawled in a chair facing her, his head sunk on his chest and his hands tangled on his lap. Philip Dressler had spent over an hour in making himself presentable for the interview (he would not have been present if he had known whom he was to meet) but the pitiful shabbiness of his clothing was not hidden from her dissecting eyes. She felt an almost overwhelming pity for him. He looked ill. It was tragic to look upon the soiled remnant of his once remarkable beauty.

"I do," she said quietly. "The very suggestion is an insult."

The smile grew more scornful as the director turned to Philip. "Mr. Dressler?"

Philip raised his head slowly. He was very pale. "For a great director," he said bitingly, "you are a particularly choice specimen of the genus rat. It is all I can do to keep my hands from your filthy throat."

Von Blon pursed his lips and smiled with all but his eyes. "So."

There was an almost audible silence. He put a monocle in his right eye and his gaze travelled slowly from Philip to his wife and from Norma to the posturing mummer at the window—the man Philip Dressler hated more than anything or anyone in the world.

"So," he murmured again. "I think we will get on very well together. A certain animosity towards me on the part of my players is always a good thing, I find. It adds a certain fire and spirit to their interpretation of their parts. And, on occasion, it is good for some distaste to exist between the players themselves—in the present circumstances, for instance. Yes. I think we will get on very well together."

"If you think I'm going to act in your confounded film," retorted Philip, "you are damned well mistaken."

He became aware of Russell Clayton's contemptuous gaze on the worn patch in the sole of one of his shoes. Biting his lip, he drew in the foot.

"This is very odd," said Von Blon suavely. "I offer you excellent roles in the most ambitious talking picture ever conceived in a British studio, parts which might have been made to measure for you, and you scorn them. Truly, the artistic temperament is baffling. Baffling!"

Russell Clayton walked forward and leaned commandingly across the desk. "If you had the slightest spark of decency, you wouldn't have offered us such parts. You know perfectly well that it is impossible for either Miss Lavery or myself to appear with Mr. Dressler. Instead of appreciating the fact, you wish to trade upon it, for the delectation of the goggling morons who infest picture palaces. When I entered this room and found that we were all cast in the same film I thought at first it was a mere coincidence. I know better now. Well, you may dispose of your excellent part as you see fit, Mr. Von Blon. I certainly shan't play it."

With all the tremendous dignity that had ever been at his command, he turned to the actress. "We had better go, Norma."

Drawing her furs more closely about her rounded white throat, Norma Lavery rose. As she took Clayton's proffered arm, she caught her husband's eye and his satirical smile brought colour to her pale cheeks.

Von Blon allowed them to go as far as the door before he said: "One minute!"

The actor turned and favoured him with a haughty stare.

"Before you go," said the director calmly, "I wish you to understand that I shall require both of you in the studio at nine o'clock tomorrow morning. You also, Mr. Dressler."

Russell Clayton had a mocking laugh, cool, taunting, scornful, with which he had dared many a stage villain to do his evil worst. He uttered it now.

The director inserted a cigarette in a long ivory holder and lit it at a jade desk-lighter.

"I would rather not talk to you of law courts and contracts," he said smoothly. "With the exception of Mr. Dressler, you are financially capable of paying large damages for breach of contract without embarrassment. But I feel bound to remind you that a certain publicity would attend such an action. The unfortunate estrangement of Mr. Dressler and his charming wife and your own part in it, Mr. Clayton, is a tea-table topic among your friends, but not yet, mercifully, a subject for wider scandalmongering. Unhappily, in the event of an action at law, it would be certain to be disclosed as the reason you refuse to carry out your contracts. The newspapers would make the most of it. A savoury titbit, hein? It would not do any of you much good."

"You infernal swine!" exclaimed Philip, rising slowly, with his fists clenched.

Gustav Von Blon blew smoke in his face. "I shall expect you all at nine tomorrow," he said, still smiling…

*

Philip visited three public-houses on his way home to Angelus Row. As he passed the open door of Cicely's room late that afternoon, he saw her pouring tea at a low, round table, and a large man with an exceedingly red neck making toast at a glowing fire. Cicely waved the teapot at him in friendly fashion.

"Come in and meet my watchdog," she cried gaily, "and tell me all about your new part. You've been to the studios today, haven't you?"

He wavered in the doorway for a moment, then went on up the stairs without a word.

Cicely ran after him and caught his arm. "Philip! What is it? You look like a ghost. You haven't…haven't lost the part, have you?"

He uttered a mirthless laugh and she smelled the strong odour on his breath: that seemed to explain his queerness. "No, I haven't lost it. I couldn't lose it if I tried."

"Then that's all right. Come and have a cup of tea. It will do you good. I want you to meet Mr. Burke, my own special policeman. It seemed unfriendly to leave him out in the cold waiting to shadow me, so I asked him in to tea. We're becoming close friends. We go everywhere together."

Philip leaned forward until she thought he was going to topple downstairs on top of her.

"Listen, I've got a good joke to tell you. A swell joke"—again he uttered that chilling, mirthless laugh—"What do you think? My darling wife and Clayton and I are all in the same film! Norma's the faithless wife—that part will fit her like a glove—Clayton's the deceived husband—for a change—and I, I am the designing lover. I've got to lure her away from Clayton, just like Clayton lured her away from me. That's rich, isn't it? Funny as hell? Why the devil don't you laugh?"

Cicely felt no inclination to laugh. She hardly knew what to say or do.

"You should have heard Clayton when the stinking little Hun broke it to us! He was astounded, insulted, outraged, as only he can be. I said a few things myself. God knows why. I've sunk low enough this past year to do anything without turning a hair."

"You won't throw up the part?" Cicely urged. "No matter how much you hate it, it's a chance to get you on your feet again."

Philip shook his head.

"No, I shan't chuck it. I can't. The dirty little blackmailing swine of a director saw to that. But with Clayton and me in the same film, murder will be done before it's finished!"

Von Blon is Annoyed

"Pig! Clumsy idiot!" Mr. Gustave Von Blon pressed the glowing end of his long cigar against the neck of the man who was massaging his naked back. He did it deliberately, dispassionately, as one might crush a mosquito between thumb and fingers, replaced the cigar between his lips, adjusted his monocle, and dropped his eyes to the open book which was propped against a pillow in front of him. Adolf, the masseur, a burly German with the cropped head of a Prussian guard and the mashed features of an ex-prizefighter, drew in his breath with a hiss, but he bent his head subserviently and ran his thick fingers with an amazing gentleness down his master's spine.

"I am sorry," he mumbled, in the humble tone of one who has well merited a rebuke. "It was an accident."

"Pah! You do it on purpose, you schweinhund, you! Do you think I am made of iron, clumsy ox?"

But for the rhythmical ticking of the jade clock on the mantelpiece, the hands of which pointed to half-past eight, and the patting of Adolf's skilled palms, the room was as silent as though it had been situated in the Sahara Desert instead of in the heart of London. Dorian House was soundproof throughout—and Gustav Von Blon's servants were exceedingly well trained.

Without looking up from his book, the director stretched out a hand to a table which was placed within easy reach of the divan on which he lay face downwards and conveyed a tall glass mug of creamy black beer to his mouth. He half emptied it at a gulp, to the accompaniment of a loud smack of the lips, put the mug on the floor, groped for a liver sausage sandwich which he consumed in two bites; and chased that down with a pickled herring, which he carried to his mouth with his fingers.

He removed his cigar only to insert the food in his mouth and replaced it while he chewed noisily. Gustav Von Blon was not a pretty eater. 'Pretty' is an adjective which could not be applied to any aspect of him.

The bedroom door opened, so quietly that it might have been stirred by nothing more material than a breath of wind, and a soft-footed Japanese in white jacket and black trousers approached the divan softly and made a slight obeisance.

"Gentelman to see you, sir."

His master frowned up at him. Adolf's well-trained hands raised from the beefy thighs and paused in midair.

"Do I know him?"

"I no think so, sir. He is not that kind of gentleman. A noosepaper gentleman, name Men Do Za. I tell him I no think you will see him, sir, but he insist very strong."

"I cannot see him."

Von Blon turned back to his book with an air of finality. The Japanese left the room with a noiseless, fluid motion. He padded through the hall to the open door of the flat.

"Mistaire Von Blon he no can see you," he said blandly. "Sorry," and would have closed the door had not Julian's foot moved swiftly into the aperture.

"Tell him it is very important."

"Mistaire Von Blon no can see you," repeated the valet firmly.

His slanting black eyes dropped to the foot which was preventing him from closing the door and travelled slowly back to Julian's face with an unfathomable expression.

"Please to remove foot," he said softly.

Julian pressed his shoulder against the door and moved it and the valet a good yard. He followed his shoulder into the hall and looked speculatively at the row of doors behind one of which he was certain to find the man he had come to see. As he limped forward to try one of the handles the Japanese moved swiftly in front of him and barred the way.

"Mistaire Von Blon no can see you," he said again, an unmistakable menace in his soft voice.

Julian ignored the warning and found himself entangled with a lithe, muscular body which lost no time in getting a ju-jitsu hold upon his neck which should have hurled him headlong through the air. Instead, an astounded Japanese found himself somersaulting under the impetus of a counter movement which only an expert could have executed, and wound up on his knees with his right arm in a vice-like grip which relentlessly tightened.

"As a ju-jitsuist of no mean ability," murmured Julian imperturbably, "you will realise what must inevitably happen if I exert a little more pressure. Do I see Von Blon, or do I not?"

Perspiration broke out upon the saffron brow.

"I...theenk...you...see...him," the Japanese groaned painfully.

"Good," Julian released him and helped him to his feet. "Lead on."

Gustav Von Blon was not aware of their approach until Julian's shadow fell across his page. He turned his head angrily and sat up with an oath.

"Don't blame your valet," said Julian. "He did his best."

The director glared at him, then swung on his masseur, who was waiting in stolid silence for orders, his long arms dangling by his sides.

"Throw this man out!" he barked.

Adolf moved to obey, his eyes measuring Julian without animosity but with inflexible determination.

"Just a moment," said the reporter quietly. "Your servant is a clever little fellow, and this chap looks as though he could give an excellent account of himself. I dare say the pair of them together would make short work of chucking me downstairs. But before you set in motion a pitched battle which will certainly not enhance the tasteful appearance of this room, why not listen for two minutes to what I have to say? I promise it will interest you. You might get an idea for a film out of it—yes, I think it would make an excellent film."

As he spoke, he backed slowly, keeping pace with Adolf's unhurried approach.

"I can see the main scene vividly. A frenzied mob howling their hatred under a burning sky at a traitor they have nailed to a rudely-fashioned cross; tearing his swooning body with their nails; spitting into his drooping face… A powerful scene, don't you think, Mr…Braun?"

The director's heavy brutal features sagged into the staring grey face of an idiot, open-mouthed, goggling; then they were convulsed by a spasm of demoniacal fury. He sprang up and his hands, curved like talons, reached for Julian's throat. The reporter's calm gaze made him pause and with an animal snarl he turned on his watchful servants.

"Get out, both of you! Quick! Are you deaf?"

The beer mug, smashing against the doorpost, and slopping its contents down the wall, speeded their departure from the room. Von Blon's cigar was smouldering on the costly Persian carpet: with his naked foot he stamped it out and continued to stamp the crushed stump as though it were a venomous thing. He was trembling from head to foot with insane rage; he gave vent to it by blundering about the room, cursing and smashing things like a spoiled child in a tantrum. The clock, swept from the mantelpiece, accentuated his wrath by continuing to tick serenely on the floor in spite of its shattered glass. He snatched up a brass candlestick and pounded it furiously until the works flew out of the mangled case and rolled, tinkling, in all directions.

Gradually the madness spent itself. Panting, he dropped upon the divan, his chest heaving, his breath coming in shuddering gulps, and glared up at Julian, who had watched the frantic display in interested silence.

"It is a lie!" he screamed hoarsely.

Julian threw back his head and laughed. What an anti-climax to such an exhibition of blind rage!

"What is a lie? I have made no statement. And if I had, why become demented over a lie?"

"You—you—"

Von Blon struggled to control himself. "So," he panted. "You are a blackmailer, hein? You think you will get money out of me with your lies, eh?"

"No. I don't want your money. Your past means nothing to me. I merely implied my knowledge of it in order to force you to listen to me. There is no need to go off the deep end. I only want to ask you a few questions."

The director stated at him suspiciously. "Questions? What sort of questions?"

"What were your movements on the night of the murder of Jacob Singerman, for instance?"

"On the night of the murder," Von Blon repeated slowly. "Pah! You are lying. That is not what you wish to know. You are trying to trick me."

"I assure you I am not."

"What have I to do with this murder? I know nothing about it."

"You didn't see Mr. Singerman on the night he was shot?"

"Certainly not."

Julian straddled a chair, with his arms folded on the back rest, and gazed reprovingly at the nude director.

"Think again. You saw him at a quarter to nine."

"So, you have been spying on me!"

"This excess of temperament is beginning to pall," said Julian wearily. "It doesn't impress me a bit. Wrap something about that indecently fat tummy of yours and try to behave like a sane being."

An ugly look welled up in Von Blon's piggy little eyes, but he held himself in check, stung by the scorn in Julian's glance. He snatched up a towel and wrapped it about his middle.

"I am waiting for your questions," he said.

"You did see Singerman the other night?"

"Yes."

"At a quarter to nine?"

"Perhaps. I do not remember."

"Was there, by any chance, a later visit?"

"Do you think I had nothing better to do than pop up and down between his flat and mine?" exploded Von Blon.

"I should prefer you to answer 'yes' or 'no.'"

"No!" he bellowed.

"That's better. By the way, why did you walk up three flights when there was a, lift available?"

"That is not your business!"

"Was it because you did not wish to be seen calling on Singerman?" Julian pursued relentlessly.

"Mein Gott! Am I a suspicious character because I choose to walk upstairs?"

Julian produced his pipe. "Mind if I smoke?"

"I hope you smoke eternally in hell!" retorted Von Blon.

Taking that for permission, Julian lit his pipe. Through a blue haze he studied the other shrewdly.

"You told Singerman you would 'go the limit' to prevent him from breaking his contract with you," he observed. "What did you mean by that?"

"Pah! How can I remember the meaning of every word I speak?"

"I suppose the limit to one's efforts to prevent another man from doing anything would be to kill him," commented Julian.

"So! That is what you are trying to suggest, eh? That I—I, Gustav Von Blon—" remembering that Julian knew him under another name and as a less exalted personage, he broke off and finished lamely:

"Ach! It is absurd."

"Then in making the threat you were only bluffing?"

"I do not bluff!" roared Von Blon. "What I threaten I carry out."

"And within an hour or so of the threat being uttered, Singerman was shot."

"Listen," hissed the director, almost frothing at the mouth; "before I go mad, listen: I did not kill him, do you hear? I did not kill him. I...did...not...kill...him...!

"If you are quite sure of that," said Julian, rising, "I'll bid you good evening."

A torrent of Teutonic abuse followed him out to the hall, where he found the Japanese valet, whose bland visage expressed the philosophic reflection that life is but a bowl of cherries. A crisp pound note which Julian offered was politely but firmly refused.

"If you would show me how you broke my hold—" the Japanese murmured wistfully.

"Next time, I'll explain it to you step by step," promised Julian.

As he left the flat, he heard a hoarse bellow from the irate Von Blon. Julian smiled. The thwarted wrath of the director was about to be visited on some innocent head! He would not have smiled so placidly had he known who was to be the unfortunate victim...

Outside Dorian House he hovered about for a moment until the street was temporarily deserted, then stepped over a low railing and ran across the strip of lawn that skirted the building, to a patch of water, black as the night, framed in concrete, with dead brown leaves and the wide green leaves of waterlilies floating on its surface. He lit a pocket electric torch, dipped it into the pond, and let the beam travel slowly over the muddy bottom. A shoal of little silver fishes darted upward to the light like steel filings to a magnet and followed it on its sluggish exploration. In a little while Julian noticed a silvan gleam that was not a fish. Stripping off his jacket and overcoat and rolling up his shirtsleeve, he plunged his arm into the water and, after a few moments of fruitless groping, fished out a revolver to which a brick was attached by a length of stout cord…

Oddly enough, he said nothing about his find to Inspector Howells when he telephoned him at Scotland Yard a few minutes later. Julian always liked to keep something up his sleeve. He simply told him that he had discovered the writer of the anonymous letter.

"Your man's name is Simon Slee," he said. "You can find him during business hours at the Colossal Film Company's Studios at Turnham Green. He knows the murderer—or thinks he does. He admitted as much to me, but he won't talk."

"Oh, won't he?" said Howells, softly, ominously. "Oh, won't he…"

A Screen Test

The dark young man in the soiled raincoat and shabby grey felt hat who had been perambulating moodily up and down Angelus Row for a quarter of an hour, pausing to look up at a certain lighted window when he passed number twenty-three, halted in front of that undistinguished house, started to ascend the muddy steps to the door, halted on the third step, hesitated for a moment, muttered something to himself, and slowly descended to the pavement. The portly, bowler-hatted individual who had been watching him from the gloom of an adjacent doorway sauntered across the street with a cigarette in his hand.

"Got a match?" he asked.

The other looked round with a start, then silently fumbled for a box of matches and handed it to him. A yellow flame flickered in the darkness between the cupped hands and the man in the bowler hat scrutinised his vis-a-vis closely while he drew on his cigarette. He saw a lean, frowning face, with sullen dark eyes and a tiny moustache above sensitive lips.

"Live here?" he said affably.

"What if I do?"

"You're Mr. Archer, aren't you?"

"I am," growled Kenneth, "though I haven't the slightest idea who you are, or how you know my name."

"You were walking up and down last night as well," said the portly individual pleasantly. "For the best part of an hour, it must have been. Hanged if I could make head or tail of what you were up to—at first. Seemed odd for a man to be pacing the pavement outside the house in which he lived."

"I don't see that it has anything to do with you," retorted Kenneth bluntly.

"It hasn't. But if we all minded our own business this world would be a dull place for most of us."

"Who the devil are you, in any case?"

"It isn't my policy to disclose my identity to all and sundry, but since you ask so polite and friendly, I'm Brown—Detective Brown. Detailed to keep an eye o' nights on the young lady whose window seems to interest you so much."

"Oh," said Kenneth.

"And a particularly nice young lady, too," mused Detective Brown. "Burke—he's keeping an eye on her during the day—seems to think the world of her."

"Confound his impertinence!" snapped Kenneth. "As though it weren't enough for her to be followed wherever she goes—"

"Friend of yours?" asked Detective Brown equably.

"In a way," admitted Kenneth guardedly.

The Scotland Yard man eyed the glowing end of his cigarette with exaggerated interest. He remarked that there was no accounting for tastes. Now he, for instance, would not dream of patrolling outside a lady's window on a chilly evening if he knew her well enough to be inside having a cosy chat.

"I had my spell of walking up and down below a window," he said, reminiscently. "But that was before I found someone to introduce me to the young lady concerned. After that I was inside seven nights out of seven, consolidating my position, so to speak."

"She's Mrs. Brown now," he added.

Kenneth said that was all very well. But supposing the present Mrs. Brown, early in their courtship, had told him that she never wanted to see him again: what then?

"Bless you, she did," chuckled Brown. "A score of times. But I always turned up the following evening, full of repentance, and promised never to do it again."

"But if you hadn't done anything," protested Kenneth. "If the fault were all on her side?"

"Then I apologised twice as much, and she always relented and forgave me very kindly."

They fell into step and walked to the corner and back. Kenneth said that women were the deuce. Detective Brown agreed that they had their little ways, but opined that a good 'un had qualities which compensated for her contrariness. They were all right if you knew how to handle them.

"I don't," groaned Kenneth.

"To let you into a secret, neither do I. But I'll tell you my system: always do the opposite of what you feel like doing. If you feel like shaking the life out of her, kiss her. It may annoy her a bit at first, if she's hankering for a good row, but women are competitive creatures. They can't bear to be outdone. Pretty soon she'll be doing her best to beat you at reasonableness."

They had halted outside number twenty-three. Detective Brown glanced at the front door and then, with a smile, at Kenneth. The young man laughed.

"I'll try it," he said. "Good night."

"Good night, sir."

Kenneth ran up the steps and let himself into the house. He knocked at Cicely's door, determined to surprise her by his mollifying attitude, but the manner of his reception was not encouraging. She frowned.

"You don't seem very pleased to see me," said Kenneth humbly.

"I'm not."

"Oh," he said.

He hesitated. "May I come in?"

Cicely walked from the door to the hearth with a gesture which implied that it mattered very little to her whether he did or not. Kenneth entered. They looked, at each other in silence.

"You've been browbeating Philip," she said, severely, at last.

"Oh, no," replied Kenneth hastily. "I merely asked him what you were doing in his room the other morning."

"And threatened him with a black eye when he couldn't remember anything about it!" "Well…"

"You needn't deny it. Mrs. Mould told me. She was listening."

"I don't intend to deny it," Kenneth was stung to retort.

"If you must discuss me," said Cicely aloofly, "I'd rather you didn't do it in the hearing of a charwoman."

"Cicely, please don't let's quarrel. I admit I don't see eye to eye with you in the matter. I've been brought up to think it odd that a girl should spend an hour at dawn in a man's room with very little on…but you seem to think such conduct entirely reasonable, so I'm prepared to say no more about it."

"Oh, you are, are you?" retorted Cicely in a tone very far from that which he had expected. "It is very kind of you, I'm sure, to be so condescending, but, as it so happens, I don't care two pins what you say or think, Mr. Archer."

"Cicely," he said patiently, "let's be reasonable."

"I like that!" she exclaimed. "You've been reasonable all along, I suppose? You didn't fly off the handle and rant and storm and refuse to give me a chance to explain—"

"Why, I've been begging you to explain all along!" Kenneth protested.

"Exactly," she said, shifting her ground. "A man who lo— trusted me, would have seen no need for explanations. He would have believed in me implicitly no matter how much appearances were against me."

When you feel like shaking the life out of her, kiss her… Kenneth tried it and was slapped for his pains. Hadn't he insulted her enough already? Who was he to treat her like a child, to be scolded and reproved one minute and complacently kissed the next?

Kenneth swore.

"If you are going to use that kind of language," said Cicely frigidly, "you had better go."

"I shall!" stormed Kenneth. "And I shan't come back!"

"Good!" she rejoined.

He had no sooner closed the door behind him than he opened it again. "I was going to tell you about my job—but I don't suppose you're interested."

Cicely checked the enthusiastic exclamation which rose to her lips. He had not yet been sufficiently punished for daring to doubt her. "You've found a job?"

"A temporary one, at the Colossal Film Company's Studios. They want me to crash a car for a talkie they're making. I expect so insignificant a trifle has escaped your memory, but I showed you the ad. They're paying me fifty pounds—and all hospital expenses."

"Hospital expenses!" she repeated swiftly.

"Yes," he said, with a bitter laugh. "Hospital expenses!"

Kenneth slammed the door again and went upstairs. He paused on the landing above and waited for her to call him back. After a fruitless wait of some minutes' duration, he went morosely to his own room.

It was all Cicely could do to refrain from calling him back, but she had made up her mind that he needed a lesson in self-control. There was another reason why she smothered the impulse. She was not at all sure that her feelings for him were as they had been. A lot had happened lately. She had met Julian. It was ridiculous, of course, for her thoughts to dwell on the huge, barbaric reporter, but for all that she could not get him out of her mind…

The gas flickered and almost went out. By the light of the crumbling fire, she fruitlessly searched her bag for a shilling to put in the meter. While she was debating whether to run out for change or go early to bed, she heard the low hum of a powerful engine and, looking out of the window, saw a Rolls-Royce limousine gliding to a halt at the kerb below. A man in a fur coat stepped out and she saw the red glow of a cigar and the white gleam of a shirt front as he started to ascend the front steps. The doorbell shrilled…

A few moments later, the door opened and a dishevelled head peered into the room.

"Oh dear, she ain't in," muttered Mrs. Mould.

Cicely turned quickly from the window. "I'm here," she said eagerly. "What is it?"

"There's a gen'leman downstairs, miss, what wants to see you most particular. A foreign-looking gen'leman, in a posh fur coat…smokin' a cigar, an' all…"

"Yes, yes, I saw him from the window," exclaimed Cicely impatiently. "Who is he? What is his name?"

"Vong Blong, or somethin' of the sort," whined Mrs. Mould. "I was too flustered to rightly catch it."

"Von Blon!" Cicely clasped her hands ecstatically. "Von Blon! Oh, Mrs. Mould, are you sure?"

"That's the name he told me—I can't say no fairer than that."

Cicely thrust a ten-shilling note into her hand and pushed her to the door.

"Get me some change for the meter," she gasped frantically. "Hurry! The gas is going and I can't see him in the dark."

A thickset figure came up the stairs with a heavy, deliberate tread.

"You need go to no trouble," declared a guttural voice. "What I have to say will not take long."

"You are Mr. Von Blon?" stammered Cicely nervously.

The director loomed in the doorway, his outline blocking

out the faint light from the landing. There was something disturbing, vaguely threatening, about his shadowed bulk. He ignored the question.

"You are Miss Foster—Miss Cicely Foster?" he demanded harshly.

"Yes. I'm terribly sorry to receive you like this. The light will be all right in a moment, if you don't mind waiting."

Cicely motioned to Mrs. Mould to go for change, but the director did not stir from the door.

"The light does not matter. I have no wish to see you, Miss Foster." There was a sneer in the cold voice. "I have had a letter from your mother. A very stupid letter. She says you have told her you are working for me. She asks me to be kind to you. Pah! What does she think I am?—a nursemaid to her lying brat?"

The German was seething with rage. He had been forced to bottle up much of his wrath during the interview with Julian and the letter had arrived while he was casting about him for a victim on whom to vent it. His valet, who had read every line of the newspaper reports of the Singerman case, had furnished him with Cicely's address.

He stormed at her, abused and reviled her. How dare she concoct her lying stories about him? Did she not know that to be directed by the great Gustav Von Blon was an honour for which the most famous actors and actresses fought? What was she but a miserable chorus girl? Pah! A wretched, degraded liar! He knew her type. Doubtless she had some vile scheme in mind. Hoped to blackmail him, perhaps. Women like her were always playing their scurvy games on great men. No doubt her mother was in the plot! But let her be warned! He was not a fool, to be tricked by such as she! He would show her up for what she was. He would kick her into the gutter, where she belonged...

Cicely felt as though her naked body were being lashed

with whips. The words stung. They seemed to burn themselves on her brain. Dazed, she stood and listened, unable to utter a word in her defence.

Spitting out a last stream of foul abuse, Von Blon turned on his heel and clattered down the stairs. Cicely shivered and fell limply on her bed.

"Coo!" whispered Mrs. Mould, who was trembling with excitement, "that was a bit 'ot!"

Suddenly Cicely thought of her mother and sat up with a cry. Von Blon might answer her letter: she could almost see the bitter, insulting words he would write. The man was a brutal beast, capable of any cruelty; her mother was so frail, so sensitive, it would kill her… Panic stricken, she tore the door open, ran downstairs and into the street. The director was getting into his car. She darted forward and caught his arm.

"Mr. Von Blon, please listen to me for a moment," she gasped. "I—I'm sorry, terribly sorry, for what I did. I must have been mad. You see… I couldn't tell my mother I was out of a job… she would have worried so…so…well, I made up a story about being employed in the films…and—somehow—your name came into my mind. Please, I beg you—don't—"

Her heart sank. The heavy-jowled face which frowned down at her was frigid, callous; the murky yellow light from the street lamp overhead threw it up in harsh relief. As soon expect mercy from a man-eating tiger as from a man with a face like that!

Von Blon adjusted his monocle and stared at her. Roughly, he drew her under the light, placed a hand beneath her chin, and tilted her face upward. For a while he gazed at her in silence, then he made a little sound with his tongue and teeth.

"So!" he said.

"I can't tell you how sorry I am—" she began again.

"Shut up! I am thinking."

The appraising eyes seemed to strip the garments from her lithe youthful body.

"You want to be a film actress, eh?"

"Yes," she stammered.

"Well, perhaps I can do something with you." He motioned to the luxurious car. "Get in."

Cicely hesitated.

"You are afraid, eh?"

She shook her head. "No, only…well, I haven't a hat…I'm wearing an old pair of house slippers…"

"What do I care about your hat and your slippers? Get in!"

He grasped her arms and bundled her into the rear of the car, got in beside her, and picked up the speaking-tube. "The studio, Otto," he said curtly.

As the limousine glided away, purring like a sleek cat, Detective Brown ran from the shadows and hung on to the luggage grid behind. In Shaftesbury Avenue he dropped off and, hailing a taxi, ordered the driver to keep the Rolls in sight.

Cicely dropped back on the deep, yielding cushions, dazed and bewildered, but with a warm glow of excitement stirring in her veins. Von Blon ignored her. He put his feet up and lay back with a cigar in his mouth. During the smooth run through streets crowded with traffic and thronged with pedestrians he spoke not a word. When the car drew up outside the ten-storied concrete studio building at Turnham Green which, even at that hour—ten o'clock—was ablaze with light, he got out and marched in, leaving her to follow. The commissionaire on duty in the reception hall saluted the director and eyed curiously the girl who trailed at his heels.

Von Blon led her through a long corridor and into a large, sumptuous office. He perched on his desk, lifted the receiver of one of the row of telephones and jiggled the hook impatiently.

"Hello…Put me through to Mr. Klein…Klein…? This is Gustav Von Blon. I want you to be on that drawing-room set on stage four ready to make a test within five minutes… Nothing is impossible. Be there." He recalled the operator. "I want to speak to the chief sound engineer…Is that you, Cummings? Gustav Von Blon speaking. I want you to have the drawing-room set on stage four ready to make a test within five minutes…Well, you will have to forget about home for an hour or two." Again, he jerked the hook up and down. "Get me Miss Edmunds…Miss Edmunds…? Von Blon. Is there anyone in the studio tonight who calls himself an actor? …Neville? …Yes, he'll do. Send him up to stage four to help with a test."

Replacing the receiver, he lit a fresh cigar. A faint smile twisted his thin lips. Nothing pleased him more than to know that Klein, the camera man, and Cummings, the sound engineer, were both cursing him, although neither dared to disobey when he cracked the whip. It would have been more convenient for everyone if the test were postponed until the morning; but it was a rule with Von Blon never to study the convenience of others.

"Come," he said.

Cicely obediently followed him out of the office and into a lift.

"Fifth floor," said Von Blon.

An electrician, working in one of the galleries which surrounded the sound stage, was whistling gaily when they entered, but he dried up abruptly at sight of the German director. He winked at one of his mates and made a gesture as though to drop a heavy pair of pliers on the cropped head below. Klein was sullenly focusing his giant camera on two adjoining walls, set at right angles to each other, and decorated and furnished as a modern drawing-room. The sound engineer glowered at Von Blon's back through the glass window of his booth. A battery of lights were being manoeuvred into position above the set.

A young man in makeup sauntered in. "Want me, Mr. Von Blon?"

"Yes, Mr. Neville. Miss Foster is going to have, a test and I want you to help." Von Blon dropped heavily into a choir. "I shall give you a test which is a favourite of mine, Miss Foster. You are a happy wife, with one child, who is waiting for her husband to come home from work. There is a knock at the door, and you run to it gaily. A man stands on the threshold: one of your husband's friends. He takes off his hat and fumbles with it. You sense that something is wrong. 'Joe!' you cry, 'What is it? You look so queer…It isn't…Harry?' The man cannot answer. You stare at him in horror. 'Not…not dead?' you whisper. He is silent, but you realise at once that you have guessed the truth. For a while you stand quite still. Your body sags. You are stunned. All the joy is drained out of your face. Suddenly you remember your child. We will imagine that the armchair in the corner is the cradle in which he is lying. You cry: 'My baby!' run across the room, and drop on your knees beside it. You throw your arms about the child and let your head droop until it is resting on the arm of the chair. You sob…And that is all.

"Do you understand what you have to do?" he asked sharply.

Cicely nodded silently.

"Good. And you, Mr. Neville?"

"Yes," replied the young man.

"Very well. Miss Foster, you will stand over there. Before the knock you will be busy with something—doing something to that table, perhaps. That is right. Are you ready?"

He turned his head.

"Ready when you are, Mr. Von Blon," called a voice.

"Good. Lights!"

The set was bathed in radiance.

"Sound! Camera!"

And then Cicely found herself paralysed with fear. She could not think. She could not move. She clung tenaciously to the thought that she was a young wife waiting for a husband who would never come home. Whatever else deserted her, that must not. She was a young wife waiting for her husband to come home. In her mind she repeated it over and over again until it beat like waves on her brain. Everything was drained out of her, but that. Her arms and legs were moving, but not at her conscious direction. She heard her own voice speaking and thought vaguely how strange it sounded. It was as though her soul had left her body; as though she were a marionette, dangling on wires; a doll with a voice…

"Joe! What is it? You look so queer! It isn't…Harry?"

But of course, it was. His eyes told her that.

"Not…not dead?"

Yes, Harry was dead. The husband she loved, dead. She knew it. She could read it in the averted face of the man who was standing in the doorway. Harry! Dead! No…No…it couldn't be true. It couldn't! That would be too cruel. They had been so happy together. So happy. It couldn't be over, just like that! But it was. All over. Everything that mattered. No—not everything. There was one thing left to her, one thing. Her child.

She stumbled across the room and dropped to her knees with a wordless cry…

"Cut!" said Von Blon sharply.

Cicely did not move. She was still kneeling beside the armchair, sobbing as though her heart would break. The young actor walked across the set and touched her arm.

"That's all, Miss Foster," he said.

She started and looked up, tears trickling down her cheeks. He eyed her curiously.

"You're a funny kid. Do you always throw yourself into your

part like that?"

"My part…" She passed a trembling hand over her moist forehead, then glanced at him swiftly. "Did I make a mess of everything?"

"You were marvellous!"

Von Blon called her to him.

"Report to me in the morning," he commanded.

"Then…then I was all right?"

"Pah! How do I know? It looked all right, yes: but how did it look to the camera? That is the question. The answer may be: 'Rotten!' It often is. I will know in the morning. See me then."

Apretty girl was no rarity in the life of the commissionaire at the Turnham Green Studios of the Colossal Film Company. Dozens of pretty girls tried their wiles on him every day; he often said to his wife that it was a fair treat to return to the domestic hearth and see a homely face for a change. He smiled pityingly at Cicely at nine o'clock the following morning, when she asked to see Mr. Von Blon.

"He won't be in for a good hour yet, miss," he replied, with a glance at the clock.

"I suppose it will be all right for me to wait?"

"Bless your heart, yes," he said cheerfully, nodding to the open door of the waiting-room. "They all wait; some of 'em all day, every day… It's a wonder they don't bring their beds."

Apparently, he did not recognise in her an embryonic film star. (As a matter of fact, it would have made no difference if he had. Greta Garbo herself would have tried in vain to pass him unless he had orders to admit her.)

The walls of the green-and-gold waiting-room were decorated with coloured photographs of such ornaments of the talking screen as were then under contract to the Colossal Film Company and lined with scores of armless chairs, unoccupied save for a hungry-looking young man with a receding chin, long, unkempt hair, pince-nez, and a bulging brief case, who was slumped down in one of them, looking as though he had been sitting there all night—as he may have been. Cicely perched on the edge of a chair, ready to spring up quickly when her call came.

An hour passed and the room began to fill up, mainly with women of every type and condition, young, old, short, tall, fat, lean, pretty and distinctly plain, who eyed each other with the jealous antagonism of ravenous wolves assembled about a carcase. A dowdy, elder-y woman with a lined, patient face and wrinkled yellow hands which betrayed long association with the wash-tub sat next to a scented, fur-swathed, henna-haired exquisite who nursed a Pekingese, and whose other neighbour was a hatchet-faced middle-aged woman with a pink, golden-haired, blue-eyed, long-legged little girl in tow. When someone who looked important passed through the hall beyond the open door one or other of them would dash out and buttonhole him, but after a conversation in eager whispers on one part and eloquently negative shrugs on the other, the hopeful one invariably returned to her seat with a defiant air.

At half-past ten Cicely went out and bearded the commissionaire. "Hasn't Mr. Von Blon arrived yet?"

"He's busy," he responded, without looking up from his paper.

"Have you told him I'm here?"

"Listen, miss, there are eighty people in the waiting-room who want to see Mr. Von Blon and he don't want to see any of 'em. Now, if you was him and you was busy and the perishin' idiot who was employed to keep 'em out kept 'phoning through to tell you that they were here, what would you do? I'll tell you. You'd take the poor bleeder by the scruff of the neck and throw him into the street, that's what!"

"But I have an appointment!"

"That's what they all say."

"Then you won't tell him?"

"Not on your life, miss."

He turned away with an air of finality. Cicely went back to the waiting-room, trying to look as though she had been asking the time, but the rows of cynical faces were not deceived. Someone had taken the opportunity afforded by her absence to appropriate her chair and she was forced to stand with the growing knot of latecomers by the window.

"Waiting to see the Great Gustav?" drawled a girl with a tiny hat clinging to the back of her head, and a foot-long cigarette holder in her moist red mouth.

"Yes."

"I've been trying to see him for three weeks."

"Oh, but I've had a test," replied Cicely, with her chin up.

"So have I—but it hasn't got me very far."

Cicely looked out of the window. The dreams which had blissfully filled the night were melting into crushing despondency. Had her test been a hopeless failure and was this the German director's brutal method of letting her know it? Her lip trembled and she bit into it until her teeth drew blood, determined to keep her end up in front of the others.

Time dragged on. Eleven o'clock. Twelve. The atmosphere became foul with cigarette smoke and mingled perfumes. At last, she could bear the hopeless waiting no longer. With her head held high, she walked out of the room. The commissionaire said: "Good day, miss," as she passed through the wide doors into the street. Her eyes were smarting with tears.

She had gone no more than a dozen paces when someone shouted: "Oi!" Turning, she saw the commissionaire beckoning to her.

"Is your name Foster, miss?"

She nodded.

"Then you're wanted, miss. I've just had a message."

In her eyes, tears; in her heart, a bounding joy. She followed him into the hall and he summoned a diminutive page.

"Take this lady to Mr. Halliday."

The boy led her along one of the long corridors which riddled the building like a rabbit warren and ushered her into a small, bare room in which sat a long-limbed, thin young man with a shock of sandy hair, wearing a canary-coloured pullover and soiled grey flannels, who took his feet from the desk as she entered.

"Miss Foster? My name's Halliday; I'm Mr. Von Blon's assistant. Won't you sit down? A cigarette?" He held a match for her, then lit his own cigarette. "I've just seen your test screened, Miss Foster. Congratulations. It was excellent."

"I'm so glad. What did Mr. Von Blon think of it?"

"He hasn't seen it. As a matter of fact, he had forgotten all about it—we've had a busy morning—until I asked him half an hour ago which of the three young ladies whom we've had under consideration, was to play a small part in a scene we're doing this afternoon. He told me to look at the result of your test and take you on for the part if you were alright. Well, if you want it, it's yours. It isn't much of a part, frankly, but it may lead to something better. Even a 'bit' under Mr. Von Blon's direction usually does."

"Oh, I'll take it, no matter how small it is."

"Then that's settled. We'll want you today—at once, in fact. Rather short notice, but that's the way the Chief works. Lord knows how he gets the results he does. He never decides anything until the last minute. Lucky for you, as it happens—if I'd had my way, we'd have given the part to one of the three other girls days ago."

He pressed a button and in a few moments a page entered the room.

"Take Miss Foster to the wardrobe mistress," said Halliday.

He scribbled something on a slip of paper and handed it to the lad.

"See you later, Miss Foster."

A long corridor; a lift; another corridor and into a large room, hung with long rows of dresses, noisy with the steady whir and clicking of sewing machines. A stout, friendly-looking, middle-aged woman took the slip of paper, ran an expert eye over Cicely's trim figure, and reached down a two-piece tweed suit.

"This ought to fill the bill. Let's see how it fits you, Duckie."

It appeared to fit admirably, but the wardrobe mistress frowned. She gave it to a sewing machine operator for minor alterations. In ten minutes, Cicely stood before a long mirror and admired herself in the heather-mixture suit, a smart blue hat with a jaunty feather, stockings to match the suit, and brown brogue shoes. A bell rang. The wardrobe mistress spoke a few words on the telephone and turned to Cicely.

"You're wanted, Duckie. I'll send a boy to show you the way."

In the ground floor corridor, Cicely ran into Julian, who was slouching along with his pipe in his mouth. He stared.

"What on earth are you doing here?"

"I've just been given a part in Mr. Von Blon's film," she told him ecstatically.

Julian frowned.

"You don't look very pleased," she said, a little crestfallen.

"I'm not. I'm not enamoured of the gentleman."

"Well, I am," she retorted.

She laughed at his startled look.

"—as a director!" she added.

Tommy Halliday's tousled head appeared in the doorway of his office.

"You're going for a run in the country, Miss Foster," he said briskly. "You'll find three cars waiting in front. You'd better go in the rear one."

With a smile of farewell to Julian, Cicely hurried away. The assistant director drew on a shapeless felt hat and glanced keenly at the reporter.

"Friend of yours?"

"Yes."

"A pippin, isn't she?"

"Tommy," said Julian, "be a good chap and keep an eye on her for me."

Halliday winked. "I'd half an idea of keeping an eye on her for myself." He closed the door of his office. "Can't stop to chat. We're shooting a scene in the country this afternoon and we've got to be forty miles from here by one o'clock. See you later."

Julian glanced after him thoughtfully. Turning away, he collided with someone who was scuttling breathlessly along the corridor. It was Simon Slee. His eyes were glistening behind his thick-lensed spectacles.

"Hello," said Julian. "What's all the hurry?" Slee blinked up at him.

"I've got to speak to Mr. Singerman at once."

"What's up?" asked Julian, keeping a grip on the little man's arm.

"It's Mr. Von Blon—"

"What's he done?"

"He…he's filming a scene in the country this afternoon—"

"That's what he's paid for, isn't it?"

"Yes, but he's planning to wreck a very expensive car. A brand-new car. Mr. Singerman will be furious when he hears of it."

Julian released him and he hurried off as fast as his short legs would carry him, in the eager haste of all bearers of ill-tidings. The reporter rubbed his chin reflectively. It looked as though there was going to be a clash between Hyman Singerman and Gustav Von Blon. It would be worth seeing. He turned on his heel and limped out to the front of the building where three cars were drawn up to the kerb.

The German director was climbing into the leading car, a Rolls-Royce limousine. A dark-moustached young man whom

Julian seemed to recognise was at the wheel of the second, a Hispano-Suiza; in the rear of which sat Philip Dressler and another man. Cicely was sitting in the rear seat of the third car and Tommy Halliday was about to get in beside her.

"Mind if I go along?" asked Julian. "I'd like to see the great man in action."

The assistant director hesitated. "Oh, alright. Jump in."

The cortege moved off.

"We're going to a spot about two miles from Hambly, a village in Kent," he remarked, settling in his seat until he was resting on his spine. "There's a stretch of road there that might have been made for our purpose."

"That's Kenneth Archer driving the car in front, isn't it?" asked Julian.

"Yes. Know him?"

"Slightly."

"Wish I had his nerve," said Halliday, "although I wouldn't have his job for a thousand quid. He's doubling for one of the principals in a car smash we're going to shoot this afternoon. Too dangerous a job for the actor concerned. He might be laid up for months."

Cicely drew in her breath sharply.

"Archer's an idiot to risk his life for a paltry fifty quid, but one can't help admiring his nerve. Takes a lot of it, you know, to drive a car into a brick wall at sixty miles an hour."

Julian heard Cicely's gasp, but the assistant director did not notice it.

"The Chief picked him out of a score of applicants for the job," he continued blithely, "because he didn't seem to care a hang whether he was killed or not. That's the kind of stunt driver Von likes."

The reporter hacked his ankle and Halliday swore. Julian

nodded furtively at Cicely. After a glance at her white fate, the assistant director subsided into silence.

In little over an hour the cars turned in one by one to the drive of a low, rambling house standing slightly back from the main road. A squad of electricians and other technical workers had taken possession of the grounds early that morning; cables curled like snakes across the lawn; a gigantic film camera was trained on the front of the house; and behind it a temporary sound booth had been erected. The Hispano-Suiza was parked on the drive with its nose pointing to the road and the other cars drove over the lawn and halted behind the camera.

A few minutes after they arrived, the assistant director paraded Cicely, Philip, and the actor for whom Kenneth was later to double before Gustav Von Blon for orders. The great man sat on the running-board of his limousine with a sheaf of papers in his hand and a long cigar between his thin lips.

"Mr. Hammond runs out of the house," he snapped, rolling the cigar to the corner of his mouth with a twist of his lips, "and is about to jump into the Hispano-Suiza when Miss Foster, who knows that the steering-gear has been tampered with, hurries after him and tries to stop him. He will not listen. Thrusting her aside, he jumps in and drives away, accelerating rapidly. Miss Foster runs a few paces down the drive, shouting; 'Stop You'll be killed!' and Mr. Dressler, who has been standing behind the shrubbery skirting the drive, springs out, grapples with her, and, in spite of her frenzied struggles, drags her back into the house." He fixed them with a steeling glance. "Do you all understand what you have to do?"

Hammond said: "Yes," and the others nodded.

"Good. We will run through that sequence at once."

They rehearsed the scene twice, then went over it two more times for the benefit of the camera. Von Blon signified that he was satisfied and the Hispano-Suiza was brought back up the drive. The camera was removed to a platform which had been erected on the embankment at the side of the road a few hundred yards away, within twenty yards of a low wall which curved with a turn in the road.

Von Blon called Kenneth to him and gave him his instructions. "You understand fully what is expected of you?"

Kenneth's jaw hardened. "Yes, sir."

"Very good."

Kenneth had one foot on the running board when Cicely ran forward and caught his sleeve.

"Kenneth, please don't go through with this," she pleaded.

"I've got to," he said grimly. "I couldn't back out now even if I wanted to."

"But you may be killed!"

"Better be killed than confess myself a coward."

"Kenneth, for my sake…"

He looked down at her with a scowl on his pale, lean face. "What does it matter to you, in any case?"

Cicely felt an almost overwhelming impulse to throw her arms about him and refuse to let him go. If she did that, he would listen to her, she knew. But she hesitated—and the opportunity was gone.

"Mr. Archer, are you ready?" barked Von Blon.

"Yes, sir," replied Kenneth steadily.

With an odd, twisted smile at Cicely he climbed into the driving seat.

"Kenneth!" she cried, but the quickening engine drowned her voice. She stood staring down the drive long after the car was out of sight. At a touch on her arm, she turned with a start and found herself alone with Julian. The others had decamped to the platform overlooking the spot where the smash was to occur.

"You'd better stay here," said Julian gently.

She shook her head. "No. Whatever happens, I want to be near."

A Rolls-Royce glided up the drive and halted beside them. Hyman Singerman sprang out, followed by Simon Slee.

"Where is Von Blon?" panted Singerman.

Julian pointed and the fat little film magnate waddled quickly down the drive, with Slee at his heels. Julian and Cicely followed in silence. Wheezing painfully, Singerman climbed the embankment to where the director was standing.

"What is this I hear?" he demanded, his face purple with anger. "You are planning to smash a two-thousand-pound car… Is that true?"

"I cannot discuss it with you now," replied Von Blon calmly. "I am busy."

"I demand an answer!" bellowed Singerman hoarsely. "Is it true?"

"Perfectly true," said the director, watching the road through a pair of field glasses.

"My God! You are mad…mad! Two thousand pounds for a few feet of film! Do you think I am made of money? You must stop this at once, do you hear? At once!"

Almost a mile of the deserted road was visible from the platform. Von Blon exhaled a puff of fragrant smoke with evident satisfaction and pointed to a tiny speck in the distance.

"That is your two-thousand-pound car," he said imperturbably, "travelling, if Archer is obeying my orders, at seventy miles an hour. Nothing will stop it except"—he pointed to the white wall at the bend of the road—"except that wall!"

"But it must be stopped, I tell you! God of Abraham! Two thousand pounds!"

"A film is not made for nothing."

"And are you making this one for nothing? Over fifty thousand pounds you have spent on it already, and what can you show for it?"

The director shrugged his shoulders, his eyes following the approach of the speeding car.

"Stop him, I tell you!" screamed Singerman in his ear.

"My orders are that he is to crash against that wall, and I have arranged no signal to countermand them," retorted Von Blon coolly. "If you can think of a way to do it, stop him yourself."

But Singerman could think of no way to stop the car. He could only stand and stare, in dazed horror, at his two thousand pounds hastening to destruction.

*

The white road, winding between hedged fields, like a ribbon threaded through green cloth, unravelled beneath the spinning wheels. Kenneth clung to the steering-wheel, his dark eyes staring in front of him. His right foot held the accelerator pedal down as far as it would go. Icy fingers were holding his heart in a chilling grasp, but he was going through with this, through to the end, whatever the end might be. The car rocked, swayed, bucked, but held the road by a seeming miracle, the tyres screaming on the rough surface, the engine whining with ever-increasing volume.

Nearer…nearer to the white wall and whatever fate awaited him. He thought of Cicely and his courage wavered, but he set his teeth and held a steady course. A few seconds and his fifty pounds would be earned—although he might not live to spend it.

Suddenly something which looked like a bundle of rags fell into the path of the hurtling car. Kenneth swung the wheel, but felt a mudguard hitting something solid with a jarring bump.

The wall leaped to meet him. Now... He closed his eyes. His last conscious thought was to wonder if it would hurt...

*

Philip Dressler was the first to reach the twisted form which squirmed like a sliced worm on the roadway beneath the platform. It was the funny little man who had come with Hyman Singerman. His clothes were torn and dusty. A thin red trickle came from the corner of his colourless lips. He was vainly struggling to rise. Philip slid an arm about his shoulders and raised his head.

"Kent..." babbled Simon Slee drunkenly. "Kent... Did it that way... Tell po—"

He dropped back unconscious. The others crowded round. Philip was elbowed back by Halliday, who opened the injured man's shirt and felt his heart.

Standing in the background, Philip felt eyes burning into the back of his head. He turned sharply, but no one appeared to be looking at him.

Julian Mendoza yawned and rubbed his eyes. He was tired. Dog tired. The table on which his elbows were propped was littered with scribbled sheets of paper and the ashtray overflowed with spent matches and tobacco ash. A coffeepot and a soiled cup were crowded perilously near the edge of the table.

Coffee—a murderous black brew, kept simmering on the fire—and the inevitable pipe had been his companion through the still night hours while he vainly tried to fit together the jumbled pieces of the jigsaw puzzle which was the Singerman case, and now, in the middle of the morning, unshaven, dishevelled, clad in his ancient dressing-gown, he was still at it—and no nearer to the solution. He never would approach the solution, he realised wearily, until he was able to accept and explain an apparent impossibility.

There was a knock at the door and Mrs. MacDougal came in with a disapproving frown on her prim face.

"Inspector Howells tae see ye," she snapped.

Julian swept the papers into a drawer. "I'll see him at once."

The good woman showed Inspector Howells up and uttered an emphatic 'humph!' as she left the room. There had been a row when she found at breakfast time that Julian's bed had not been slept in, and it was still bubbling within her.

The Inspector had a folded newspaper in his hand. He flattened it on the table in front of Julian and jabbed a finger at an item on the front page.

"I want to know all about that," he said.

Julian glanced at it.

REAL LIFE TRAGEDY IN FILM EPISODE
SPEEDING CAR HITS ONLOOKER

During the filming of a talkie which Mr. Gustav Von Blon is making for the Colossal Film Company, Mr. Simon Slee, an employee of the Company, was seriously injured. An incident in the film is the crashing of a car at high speed. Mr. Slee was standing with a group of other spectators on the embankment at the side of the country road on which the smash was to occur, and as the car roared towards the wall with which it was to collide, he fell forward directly into its path and was run over. He was removed to hospital and has not yet regained consciousness. It is feared that he will not recover.

The accident was caused by Mr. Gustav Von Blon stumbling against the unfortunate man and causing him to lose his balance. Mr. Von Blon, who was greatly distressed by the tragic happening, stated that he was not sure whether he had himself been pushed from behind, or whether he had been carried away by the excitement of the moment and leaned forward further than he had intended to.

The driver of the car was taken to hospital, suffering from a broken leg.

Julian looked up. "That's a fairly complete account of what happened. I wrote it myself."

Inspector Howells dropped into a chair. "You told me on the 'phone the other night that Slee knew the identity of the murderer—or thought he did. Isn't it significant that this should happen to him?"

"It is. I warned the poor little beggar myself. He was asking for it."

"Then you think the man who killed Singerman engineered this 'accident'?"

"I'm sure of it."

"I sent a man to the studios yesterday to pick up Slee," grunted Howells. "If he had got there five minutes earlier … before Slee left with Hyman Singerman I'd have had the name of the murderer out of him and this wouldn't have happened."

"Don't be too sure of that," replied Julian. "Slee is a stubborn little cuss. I don't believe any amount of questioning would have made him divulge his secret."

"I've just come from the hospital. He hasn't regained consciousness. The doctors say he may die in a state of coma."

"Taking his secret with him to the grave," added Julian.

"I suppose you've discovered nothing that indicates the identity of the murderer?"

The reporter rested his chin on his hands and stared out of the window. "I know who he is," he replied deliberately.

Howells started to his feet. "You do? Who is he?"

"I'd rather not say. I can't prove it."

"That's nonsense," retorted the Inspector angrily. "Who is he? Von Blon?"

"I could make out a better case against Von Blon than against anyone else," replied Julian evasively. "Look here, Howells, this is a delicate matter. I want to work it out my own way. Give me time to do that and I'll hand you the case in a bag. Move too precipitately, and you'll muck it up."

"It is your duty to tell me what you know without delay," snapped the Inspector.

"Duty or no duty," said Julian doggedly, "I'm going to keep it under my hat for forty-eight hours. After that, whether I've proved my case or not, I'll tell you all I know—and suspect."

The Inspector argued, threatened, cajoled, but Julian

remained obdurate, and in the end he was forced to agree to allow the reporter the time he required. But beyond that, he said grimly, he would not go. He would have the facts out of him if he had to charge him as an accessory after the fact.

"As it is," he grumbled, "it will be the deuce of a job explaining the position to the Deputy Commissioner."

"Don't explain," responded Julian blithely. "Put him off with the usual bunk; the police are unremittingly on the trail; an arrest is hourly expected…"

"You've given up the suicide theory?" asked Howells, ignoring the other's flippancy. "I never thought much of it myself."

"It was an excellent theory," mused Julian. "But utterly wrong."

"I looked into Singerman's financial position, as you suggested. You were right; he wasn't the rich man he was supposed to be. He had been dabbling in the stock market and lost heavily."

"Now that," murmured Julian, "is very interesting."

After the detective had gone Julian tumbled into bed and slept soundly until late in the afternoon, when he rose, shaved, had a cold bath, and dressed. He walked along to Piccadilly and took a bus to Turnham Green. The pass Hyman Singerman had given him gained him unquestioned admittance to the studios. He ran into Cicely as he limped along a corridor.

"Hello," he said. "Where are you going?"

"Mr. Von Blon is rehearsing a scene on sound stage number four," she replied. "I'm not in it, but I'm going up to watch."

"I'll go with you. I was just wondering why I came. Now I know. It was to look at you."

Cicely made a mock curtsy. "'Thank you, kind sir, she said'…"

"Have you heard how young Archer is faring?" he asked, as he followed her into the lift.

"I enquired at the hospital this morning. His leg was set last night and he is doing nicely."

"Wouldn't they let you see him?"

She frowned. "I didn't ask."

"Oh." Julian glanced sideways at her. "Still a chilliness between you two, eh?"

"Oh, I'm not pig enough to carry on our quarrel now that he's hurt," said Cicely slowly. "I'm only too ready to drop it and be friends again. Only…well, I know if I go to see him now I shan't be able to refuse him anything he asks…and…I'm not quite sure… Oh, it isn't easy to explain."

"I understand," said Julian quietly—and Cicely had an uncomfortable feeling that he did.

He asked no more and she volunteered nothing. Outside sound stage number four there was an electric sign with the following warning in large green letters:

REHEARSAL IN PROGRESS

ENTER QUIETLY

They went in on tiptoe.

Grotesque shadows crowded in on a splash of amber light which was thrown by a shaded lamp on an armchair in which a man was sitting with an open book on his lap. Blue smoke curled from the stump of a cigar which had been permitted to burn away to ash on a silver tray at his elbow.

The man was tall; his long legs, protruding from the chair, showed that, and his age must have been about fifty, judging by the deep lines of his face and the silver that streaked his hair at the temples.

His eyes, dark with anger, kept straying from the book to the clock on the mantelpiece which remorselessly ticked away the seconds. Tick…tick…tick…tick… The sound of it filled the room and the man's long, slender fingers tapped restlessly on the arm of the chair, keeping time to the ceaseless rhythm. He was waiting…waiting…

Over another chair a heavy travelling coat was draped and on it lay a brown felt hat. On the floor beside the chair lay a kitbag, plastered with labels.

The clock chimed three times.

At a faint sound the man reached up swiftly and turned out the light above his head. He sat quite still in the darkness. Moments passed, then a silvery, high-pitched laugh floated on the air and a pencil-line of light showed as the door opened softly. There followed the swish of a silk dress and the murmur of a deep, baritone voice. Another laugh. "Frank, you are a fool!"

Then the room was flooded with light.

By the door stood a beautiful woman in evening dress, her wrap slipping from her shoulders, revealing the firm, rounded outline of her breasts; her fingers still pressing the light switch and her free arm about the neck of a young man who was kiss-ing her ardently, hungrily, as though he would never let her go.

"A touching little picture," was the dry comment of the man in chair.

With a startled cry the woman tore herself free and stared at the grim face across the room. "Arnold! My God! I thought…"

"That I was a hundred miles away? You would have been perfectly right, my dear, but for the unfortunate death of the client I went to see, which made it possible for me to come straight home. Sorry to have disappointed you—and Mr. Gregory!"

The young man swung round. "You can drop that sneering tone, Haddon. I'm damned glad you did come back. I'm glad you saw. Now we can have the matter out, as I've told Inez we should have done long ago."

The woman shrank back, with terror in her eyes. "Frank, please!"

Her 'husband' uttered a laugh that was horrible with hatred. "He doesn't understand me as you do, Inez. He wants to have the matter out—very well, he shall have his way. Come in, Mr. Gregory."

"Frank"—the woman's voice was hoarse with hysteria— "for the love of God, go!"

"No, dear, I intend to stay. We'll let him have his say—we owe him as much, I suppose. Afterwards I'll take you away."

He drew her shrinking, reluctant form into the room. Her 'husband' rose, letting the book fall unnoticed to the floor, went to the door, locked it, and pocketed the key. A little cry burst from the woman's lips at that, but the young man put a reassuring arm about her shoulders.

"Let's dispense with the melodrama, Haddon," he said curtly. "This isn't the thirteenth century. Inez and I love each other. You've seen enough to know that. I'm glad. It saves a lot of explanations. You must have realised that her marriage to you was a mistake. It could never have succeeded; the disparity in your ages was too great. Now that you know the truth, I'm going to ask you to—"

"To do the 'decent thing'!" The 'husband' spat out the words. "To set her free—for you."

The 'lover' stood his ground. "To set her free from a bond which is hateful to her."

There was a pregnant silence while they stared into each other's eyes. Stark hatred flamed in that tense glare. The atmosphere was charged with the potency of their mutual loathing. They appeared to have forgotten the woman who cowered silently in the background. Hate filled their minds to the exclusion of all else.

"You poor fool!" hissed the 'husband' suddenly. "As though I should surrender that which is mine. Inez should have told you; what I have I hold. And you—you—"

"You sound like Jove," sneered the 'lover', "—about to hurl a thunderbolt!"

"Frank! Don't talk like that!" gasped the woman. "You don't know him as I do—he'll stop at nothing!"

"It's all right, Inez; he's only blustering. Don't be frightened. I'm going to take you away." The 'lover' turned confidently to the other man. "You hear? I'm going to take her away, whether you like it or not!"

The 'husband' stood silently looking at them and his head began to shake slowly from side to side. His lips were twisted in a grin that bared his teeth. "No," he said, still shaking his head, "you're not."

His hand dropped swiftly to the table and pulled out a drawer. It came up holding a revolver. Almost in the same movement, he fired.

The 'lover' uttered a hoarse cry and into his eyes leaped an expression of ludicrous amazement. His hands clawed the air as he pitched forward on his face. Tick…tick…tick…the seconds slipped away as steadily as though nothing had happened.

Then, ignoring the shrinking woman, the 'husband' walked forward and rolled the other man on his back. Already a dark stain was spreading on the white shirt front.

"Dead…" he said, in a tone of awful malignity.

*

"Lousy!" shouted a guttural voice. "Lousy! Du Leiber Gott! What do you call yourselves? Actors?—or stuffed dummies?"

A faint murmur of conversation rose from the onlookers, who had been silent while the scene was in progress. Philip Dressler rose and dusted his trousers. Russell Clayton shrugged his shoulders and placed the revolver on the table.

"What is the matter, Mr. Von Blon?" asked Norma Lavery. "I thought the scene was going very well."

Gustav Von Blon strode forward with the military swing that was famous wherever films were made. His beady little eyes flashed venomously; his jaw jutted belligerently; even the cropped hairs on his square skull seemed to bristle with anger.

"And why should the scene not go well when I, Gustav Von Blon, have rehearsed you in it for hours? The scene will do—up to a point. But where you are shot"—he shook a quivering finger under Philip Dressler's nose—"there it is hopeless. Lousy!"—he rolled the word on his tongue as though savouring the taste of it—"Mein Gott! I could make a wax doll act the part better than you! I could take a pickled herring and make it look more like a dead man! Over and over, I have said that when the shot is fired you must fall to the floor dead. Dead!—I tell you! Dead!—do you hear me? Dead. As though a bullet had gouged the life from your body. Not as though you were lying down for a little rest!"

"I'm doing my best," retorted Philip.

"Your best!" raved the director. "Your best! What is that to me? Will an audience say: 'He does not look very dead, but, poor fellow, he is doing his best'? No! The audience will have paid to see the picture because it was directed by Gustav Von Blon and it will expect you to look dead, because when Gustav Von Blon makes a picture, every situation is real, vital, convincing!"

He waved his stubby hands. "For today, this is enough. I am flesh and blood, like any other man. I cannot go on for ever pouring my soul into lumps of clay who call themselves actors. Tomorrow we will try again—and tomorrow, my friend, you will die like a dead man, or you will go back to the gutter, where you belong."

Turning to Tommy Halliday, he barked: "Have everything ready tomorrow morning at ten o'clock."

"Yes, Mr. Von Blon."

The director's Japanese valet, his face impassive as that of a bronze idol, held up a long, military cloak and, drawing it about his shoulders, Von Blon clicked his heels in the approved Prussian manner and marched from the sound stage.

Philip glared after him and muttered something under his breath.

"Say a few words for me while you are about it," grunted the assistant director. "You got it just now, but I get it all the time. Believe me, this picture's taking years off my life!"

Russell Clayton lifted Norma Lavery's wrap, which had slipped from her shoulders to the floor, and held it for her with a gallant air.

The bitter eyes of Philip Dressler followed his wife and the other actor as they left the stage. Suddenly he turned. He had seemed to feel again the burning gaze he had felt the previous afternoon when he bent over the crumpled body of Simon Slee… Was someone glaring at him from the shadowy bulk of the plaster 'battleship' that towered in another part of the studio? The feeling was so strong that he went to look. He fancied he heard retreating footsteps as he approached. No one was there…

"What's the matter Philip?" asked Cicely. "Anyone would think you had seen a ghost?"

"I fancied I felt one," the actor replied, turning to the girl and Julian, who had crossed the stage to where he stood. "It's rather odd. Once or twice lately I've had an uncomfortable feeling that I was being watched by malevolent eyes." He laughed. "Silly of me, isn't it?"

Cicely introduced the reporter.

"Pleased to meet you," said Philip, shaking hands. "Care for a cocktail? I've the makings in my room."

He caught Cicely's disapproving glance and assumed a meek expression.

"Just one," he pleaded, in the tone of a child begging for sweets. "I need it, after what I've been through."

Cicely smiled. Philip had the natural charm of a schoolboy, when he cared to exert it.

"By the way, Mr. Dressler," said Julian, as they walked toward the actor's dressing-room, "did Slee say anything to you when you ran to him after the accident yesterday? I've been meaning to ask you, but I haven't had an opportunity."

"The little chap who was hurt? He tried to speak, but I didn't catch more than a few disjointed words."

"Can you remember them?"

Philip wrinkled his forehead. "I daresay I could, if I concentrated; but, if you'll excuse me, I'd rather not try at the moment. The scene we were rehearsing was a terrific strain and my brain is wrung dry. Some other time."

His dressing-room was little larger than a good-sized cupboard. They were forced to crowd together and make themselves as small as possible in order to close the door. A table, littered with the paraphernalia of theatrical makeup, the surface of which was a mirror, stood against one wall, below another mirror, ringed with small electric light bulbs. A bentwood chair and a wicker armchair were the only other furnishings, except for a curtained recess in which Philip's clothes hung on hangers. Philip put a hand under the curtains, groped about the floor of the recess, and produced a bottle of gin, one of vermouth, and a silver cocktail shaker.

"Martinis or nothing," he said, pouring gin into the shaker. "'Fraid this room doesn't lend itself to this sort of thing. There isn't room to shake from side to side: it has to be an up and down motion: and only nightclub addicts, used to dancing for hours on one square inch of floor, are much good at that."

Cicely was honoured with the only glass. Julian and Philip drank the cocktails out of a chipped cup and the top of a flask respectively, and found them good. Drawing the bent-wood chair up to the mirror-topped table, Philip smeared cold cream on his face, rubbed it in with his fingers, and wiped off the greasepaint with a stained towel.

He put a cigarette between his lips and struck a. match. At that moment the clear tones of a feminine voice floated in through the open transom above the door. The match flamed in mid-air, while Philip listened with his head on one side.

"I'm not very keen, Russell. I have a headache."

"Oh, but you promised," replied a man's deep voice. "Besides, it will do you good; take you out of yourself. Giovanni has a new band, and the food's good. We needn't stay more than an hour or so, if you don't feel up to the mark."

"I'll think it over…"

"Good. I'll call for you about nine."

Footsteps passed down the corridor. The flame scorched

Philip's thumb and he dropped the charred stick with an oath. He ground the unlit cigarette to dust between his fingers and sat staring at his own haggard reflection in the glass on the wall.

"They would have to stop outside my door to make their assignation," he muttered.

He reached for the gin bottle and splashed a generous measure into the flask top, tossed it off, and was tilting the bottle to pour another when Cicely's hand pushed it up. "Drinking doesn't help," she said.

Philip shot her a twisted glance. A lock of lank dark hair fell over his pale brow and made him look more than ever like a dissipated boy.

"Oh yes, it does," he retorted bitterly. "When I'm drunk, I don't care. Drink is the only thing that has kept me from killing the swine with my bare hands."

His tortured eyes seemed to stare through and beyond her. "If you knew the purgatory I'm going through playing in this infernal picture…seeing her…holding her in my arms…kissing her… My God! Kissing her…"

"Giovanni's" he murmured.

He turned to Julian with a dry, mirthless laugh. "You're a reporter, aren't you? If you want a good story, be at Giovanni's tonight!"

*

Shortly after nine that evening Philip came out of his room, clad in a dinner jacket which had been in pawn until a few hours before, and started to descend the creaking stairs. Cicely was standing at the door of her room. Although Philip's gait was perfectly steady, his glassy eyes and waxen face informed her that he had already consumed enough strong drink to floor three average men. He brushed past her without appearing to notice that she was there.

"Philip!"

He glanced over his shoulder, his face ghastly in the flickering light of the gas jet which illuminated the stairs. "Come here," she said.

Shaking his head, he continued down the stairs. Cicely ran after him and caught his arm.

"You're being an awful idiot, you know."

Philip shrugged his shoulders. "Always have been."

"If you make a scene at Giovanni's, Norma will never forgive you. There'll be no further hope of a reconciliation."

"I wouldn't give that"—he snapped his fingers —"for my chances as it is. She doesn't care two pins for me."

"What are you going to do?"

"I don't know. Depends on how drunk I get."

Cicely remembered what he had muttered at three o'clock on the chilly morning when she helped him to his room. 'Someday I'll kill the swine…' You could never tell when Philip was talking seriously and when he was not. Had he meant it? She did not know, but she was afraid. He was capable of almost anything in his present black mood.

"If you must go," she said. "I'm going with you."

"Like blazes you are. This won't be any party for a lady."

"Norma's a lady, isn't she?"

"Norma's a block of ice. Tonight, I'm going to find out whether she has feelings to hurt. I doubt it."

With that he was gone. Cicely snatched up a wrap and ran after him. She caught up with him at the corner of the street.

"If you think I'm going to be a little gentleman because you're with me, you're jolly well mistaken," said Philip sullenly.

Giovanni's was in a quiet street off Leicester Square. An unpretentious entrance, guarded by a burly man in gold-braided uniform, gave admittance to a long room dotted with little round tables, gleaming with snowy linen and bright silver, and lighted with shaded lamps which illuminated the tabletops and left the spaces between discreetly shadowed. The lights shone on rounded white shoulders; dim shapes flitted to and fro in the gloom between. The ripple of gay laughter, the tinkle of silver, was half-drowned by the clamour of the jazz band. The blaring cackle of a trumpet…delirious moan of a saxophone on a three-day jag…frenzied wail of a tortured violin, like mad music tormented from the intestines of a living cat…demented snarl of a muted cornet…staccato stutter of a distraught banjo…deep bass mutter of a hag-ridden sousaphone…maniacal clash and clang of cymbals…a moon-struck clarinet shrilling high above the rest…

Giovanni, olive-skinned and smiling, his back arched like a question mark, politely regretted that there was no vacant table. (He knew every current scrap of gossip which was worth knowing and had no desire to entertain Mr. Dressler, his wife, and the gentleman who was rumoured to be the lady's lover, on the same evening.) Philip was not listening. His eyes roved over the room until they found his wife and Russell Clayton at a table across the dance floor. He made a beeline for an unoccupied neighbouring table, leaving Cicely and Giovanni no course but to follow. Giovanni regretted that the table was engaged. Philip sat down. With an eloquent Latin shrug, Giovanni drew out a chair for Cicely and motioned to a waiter. Norma Lavery looked up and caught her husband's eye. Philip smiled mockingly. She flushed and said something to her companion. Clayton looked round, and to his cold, sneering glance Philip returned another sardonic smile. The older man leaned across his table and said a few words to the woman and they rose and descended unhurriedly to the dance floor. On the other side of the room, they halted and, after a consultation with Giovanni, followed him to another table, screened with palms from the rest of the room. A waiter came and removed the actress's bag and wrap.

"They'd love to cut and run, but pride won't let 'em," muttered Philip darkly.

He drank brandy, his mood growing more bitter with every passing minute, his smouldering eyes staring at the screening palms.

"Let's dance," suggested Cicely.

"I didn't come to dance."

"Then let's go. This isn't particularly amusing. No, I don't want anything to drink. Philip, be sensible and come away."

Philip laughed, a harsh sound which made her shiver.

Know what I am?" he demanded, slopping the amber liquid on the immaculate cloth. "I'm a spineless worm. Ask Clayton—he'll tell you that. A man would—"

"A man would have the decency to leave," retorted Cicely.

He sat silently brooding for a few minutes, then he rose unsteadily to his feet. "It's all right," he assured her, with a wave of his hand. "I'm only going to telephone. Got a call to make."

Anxiously, Cicely watched his wavering progression to the end of the room. A pillar hid him from sight, but a little later he appeared at the table behind the palms. She saw Russell Clayton's head and shoulders as he stood up quickly. Panic-stricken, Cicely hurried across the dance floor. Two waiters and Giovanni converged on the spot. Their black-clad backs blocked her view of what was going on. She heard a crash. Pushing between them, she saw Norma Lavery standing by the table like a figure of stone and Clayton sprawling on the floor with a hand to one eye. The waiters pounced on Philip. At a signal from Giovanni, the band played even louder than before…

"One moment," said a cool voice.

It was Julian, his tall, rakish figure in striking contrast to its surroundings. Giovanni frowned.

"You needn't worry about publicity," said Julian, "if those gentlemen take their hands off Mr. Dressler without delay."

Giovanni hissed something and the waiters withdrew. Russell Clayton staggered to his feet and lurched at Philip.

"Sit down," snapped Julian. There was a glitter in his eyes which compelled obedience. He turned to Cicely.

"There's a door behind you; supposing you and Miss Lavery make use of it?"

Cicely helped the older woman into her wrap and hurried her through the emergency door into a lane behind. Clayton made a move to follow, but Julian hooked his stick through his arm and drew him back.

"We three are going to have a drink together," he remarked quietly. "After that you're free for the evening."

"Look here, if you think—"

"Sit down," said Julian, "unless you want another black eye. Champagne, Giovanni."

Minutes passed. Clayton fumed and glanced constantly at his watch.

"Alright," said Julian, draining his glass, "you can go. I advise you to put some beef-steak on that eye without delay. It's a beauty."

With an angry retort the middle-aged actor departed. Julian tapped Philip's shoulder. "Let's go," he said.

Philip was slumped across the table with his head on his hands. He raised tragic eyes. "I must have been mad. What an utter swine I've made of myself."

"It's a man's privilege to act the fool," said Julian, "but you abuse the privilege."

*

"I suppose you think I'm as hard as nails?" asked Norma Lavery. She addressed Cicely, who was sitting by the fire in the drawing-room of her flat. "Well, you don't know what I've been through with Philip. He can be charming; when he's sober, he's the dearest person in the world; but how often is he sober? And when he's drunk—well, you saw him tonight!"

She paced the room restlessly, clasping and unclasping her long, graceful hands. "For years I tried to break him of drinking. My God! How I tried! If I hadn't slaved eternally to keep him sober, he'd never have become the star he was until a year or two ago. The moment I relaxed my grip on him he slipped down the ladder faster than I had dragged him up it. You can't imagine what our life together was. Once, at the beginning, when we were poor and unknown, I pawned my wedding ring to get money to pay the rent. I didn't mind that. We were in love and it was rather a joke. But that afternoon, when I came in from a round of the agents and found the rent collector on the stairs, the money was gone. Philip had taken it. I made up some story for the collector, swallowed his insults and threats, and sat down to wait for Philip to come home. He came in at six, uproariously drunk, with his arms full of parcels—champagne, chocolates, fruit, a Spanish comb, Heaven-knows-what—chuckling with glee over a winner that had come home at twenty to one. What was the use of saying anything? That was…Philip. Scolding him for risking our last penny would have been as uselessly brutal as slapping a week-old child. He had tickets for a show; rushed me into my pitifully shabby 'glad rags' and took me to Frascati's for dinner. Between the acts he went out for a drink—just one, he promised faithfully—and didn't come back. It was four in the morning when he rolled home, minus his hat and collar, with an armful of flowers. He had searched the West End until he found a florist who lived over his shop, dragged him out of bed and bought me roses with his last pound. Rent? The pawned ring? They had slipped his memory…

"I forgave him and went on forgiving him through a succession of similar episodes. Between outbursts he was manageable, but as we rose in the world the outbursts became more and more frequent. Success went to his head. One night he came to the theatre blind drunk. We were appearing together; it wasn't safe to trust him out of my sight. I locked him in his room, gave out that he was 'indisposed' and the play commenced with his understudy in his part. During the second act he broke out and came on to the stage. There was a terrible scene. The curtain was rung down and the management sacked him. I left him. I couldn't stand it any longer. After that, no one would give him a chance. A year later he turned up at my flat in the middle of the night, unshaven, filthy, verminous, pitifully thin, and half-dead. I took him in and nursed him through an attack of pneumonia; for weeks he hovered between life and death. When he was convalescent, he swore that he was going to turn over a new leaf. I believed him—and persuaded a manager to believe him."

She gestured wearily. "But—well, he was…Philip. The same thing happened again. This time, I left him for good."

"And yet," said Cicely softly, "you still love him."

Norma Lavery lit a cigarette, but crushed it out after a few puffs. There was a haunted expression in her lovely dark eyes. "Yes," she said bitterly, "I do. I'll never be fool enough to take him back—but I'll never stop loving him. It wrings my heart to see him looking so pale and ill."

Cicely took from her bag the letter she had appropriated from the hoard Philip kept behind a picture in his room.

"I want you to read this," she said quietly.

"...Like Mad Dogs..."

At ten minutes to ten the following morning the studio in which the current sequences of 'Illicit Loves' were being made seethed with activity like an anthill or a boiling pot. Bustle. Clamour. Confusion. Men in overalls hurried to and fro, testing mechanisms and adjusting cables; the cameramen were putting reels of film in their giant cameras; the sound engineer and his assistant were tinkering with the recording apparatus; a gloomy property man, with a list of 'effects' in his hand was drifting about the set, muttering to himself that some people loved to make the jobs of others harder: "...never content to leave things so's a man can lay 'is 'and on 'em...allus muckin' abaht wiv wot don't concern 'em..."; and Tommy Halliday, the assistant director, was issuing orders right and left, while his eyes roved over the two-walled room, making sure that everything was as it must be when Gustav Von Blon came on the scene.

Aloof from it all, his empty pipe between his teeth, Julian Mendoza was an interested spectator. "Much ado about nothing," he muttered softly.

"I think it's wonderful," breathed Cicely, at his side. "Only think—out of all this entertainment for millions will grow."

"I'm thinking," said Julian. "Clammy hand holding clammy hand in the dark... chocolates being sucked into fat red mouths...middle-aged women learning to be discontented with the lukewarm attentions of their husbands. There's Singerman—looks ill, doesn't he?"

Cicely turned and her eyes softened as they rested on the worn, haggard face of Hyman Singerman, who was standing, looking a little as though he had lost himself, in the background.

"Pathetic," she agreed.

Norma Lavery was standing at the table in the middle of the set, toying absently with something that gleamed between her fingers. The assistant director snatched it from her and thrust it into the table drawer. "You know better than to play with the props," he growled. "That's the way things get mislaid."

"Oh, shut up, Tommy," she retorted wearily. "Good heavens, can't anyone in this crazy studio utter a civil word?"

"Sorry, Norma," he grinned, "but if anything's missing when it's wanted the Chief will have my blood."

He raised his head to the ranked arc lights above and bellowed an order.

Russell Clayton came into the studio, made-up more thickly than usual, to hide the traces of the previous night's conflict with Philip Dressler. He crossed to Norma's side and said something in a low tone. With a muttered word she turned away to find her husband frowning morosely at her from the door.

At precisely ten o'clock a sudden hush came over the set as Gustav Von Blon approached, followed by his Japanese valet and a pale, bespectacled male secretary, who carried a stuffed portfolio. In impressive silence, the director permitted the valet to relieve him of his military cloak, while his eyes, hard and disdainful, travelled over the set.

The Japanese placed a Turkish cigarette in an ivory holder fully eighteen inches long and handed it to his master. There was a placard a few feet away stating: 'No Smoking' in letters half a foot high, but what did rules matter to Gustav Von Blon? A frantic rustling, and half a dozen hands held out flaming matches. Ignoring them, the director lit his cigarette from the enamelled lighter which appeared, as though by sleight-of-hand, in the valet's yellow fingers.

"What a showman!" whispered Cicely.

Julian nodded silently.

At that moment the director's cold gaze lighted on the reporter, who smiled sardonically. Von Blon's bloated features grew livid with vitriolic fury; Julian chuckled. They were both thinking of the same thing: a convict crucified in the broiling sun by his own comrades… Almost at once, the director's face froze again into an imperious grey mask. He turned away and looked appraisingly at each of the small cast in turn.

"You were not wearing that ring yesterday"—he pointed to Norma Lavery's left hand—"take it off! Halliday!"—he scowled at the assistant director—"why the devil do you not attend to these things before I appear? Must I do your work as well as my own?"

Philip Dressler looked oddly at his wife. Biting her lip, the actress removed the ring and hastily put it in her bag, which was lying on a chair beneath the cameras.

The director marched across the set and moved a lamp a fraction of an inch. "The first part of the scene will do as it is," he said brusquely, turning on his heel, "but I intend to alter the climax of the scene. Simply to shoot the lover: that is too flat, too dull. It lacks grip, sting. No, I have a better idea."

His piggy little eyes flickered from Dressler to his wife and from his wife to Clayton.

"As Mr. Clayton seizes the revolver, Mr. Dressler will grapple with him. They will fight—Oh, furiously they will fight! Back and forward, to and fro; a desperate, frenzied struggle, with death the reward of the loser."

His eyes narrowed and his thin lips parted in the ghost of a grin. "And I shall give no orders as to who shall win. That we will see. It depends "—another sly, evil grin—"upon you, Mr. Dressler—and you, Mr. Clayton. We will see which is the better man. This is to be a real fight, not a sham! Each of you will strive to the utmost to win. And he who wins, who captures the revolver, will fire at the other. The other will fall dead. He will fall, not like a sack of potatoes, but like one who is dead. You understand, both of you? I want a thrill here that will lift audiences from their seats!"

A sound, half sigh, half mutter, rose about the set like the breathless swelling of the atmosphere that comes before the breaking of a typhoon. Someone uttered a laugh, shrill and hysterical.

Julian felt Cicely's hand grasping his arm tightly. "Good God!" she muttered. "The devil wants to set these two deadly enemies at each other's throats like mad dogs!"

"He's mad," said Julian. "With the magnificent, ruthless insanity of the Borgias."

"But, Mr. Von Blon, you can't do that!" protested a tall lanky man (Julian later discovered that he was the author of the scenario) who was standing behind the cameras. "The script—"

"What do I care for your script?" hissed Von Blon. "When the script interferes with my conception of a picture, I tear up the script! Tear it up; do you hear? I, Gustav Von Blon, am not to be tied down to rules like a verdammt clerk!"

"But if the lover were to win it would ruin the whole story! The plot—the climax—"

"I will devise another climax!" retorted Von Bion. "And the plot"—he snapped his fingers —"if the plot does not fit, I will alter it!"

"But—"

"Mein Gott! Do you still argue? It is I who am making this picture, do you hear? I will decide what is to be done, and you, my friend, will mind your own business!"

"Look here, damn you!" said Philip Dressler suddenly, "we're not going through with this!"

"Silence!" thundered the director.

Russell Clayton walked up to him belligerently. "This is one time you are not going to have your own way, Mr. Von Blon," he said icily. "I'm an actor, not a bruiser. I refuse to take part in the scene as you have outlined it."

"You are engaged to do what I tell you," snapped Von Blon, every word like the lash of a whip, "and you will do it!"

Hyman Singerman came forward, his face ashen, his hands trembling. His lips twitched so that for a moment he could not speak.

"Are you crazy?" he demanded hoarsely at last. "Do you think you can ride over everyone else like so much mud? I tell you—you—cannot. You will not sweep aside the story like this. You will not do this mad thing. I forbid you!"

Von Blon glared. "So! You forbid me, hein? Read my contract, Mr. Director-of-the-Company, and you will find out how we stand. You will see that although you can harass me with your eternal whining about pennies, you cannot interfere with my making of the picture!"

His manner was terrific. The hypnotic force of his personality, insolent, tremendous, seemed to charge the atmosphere like electricity. In the dead silence that followed, the dropping of a pin would have been audible. No one spoke. No one stirred. He walked to his chair and sat down.

"Lights!" he shouted.

The set was bathed in brilliance.

With a gruff command and several deft motions of his hand, Von Blon marshalled the two men and the woman into position for the scene which was to follow. The actors looked at each other uncertainly, but neither of them spoke. They appeared to be stunned.

"Camera!" he barked.

Death in the Studio

The unbreakable rule of film studios while a scene for a talking picture is in the making is silence. On this occasion there was no need for the warning light that glowed above the set. The script girl's jaws halted on an unmasticated caramel. The sprinkling of spectators felt no urge to sneeze or shuffle their feet. Even the electricians and the other studio workers, usually blasé and bored during the shooting of a scene, were watching the lighted set with tense interest.

Here was drama! Life in the raw; not a greasepaint and spotlight simulation of it.

The men who faced each other in the two-walled room were genuinely burning with hatred. They played their parts as though they were living them and as the climax of the scene approached the tension was terrific. The white-faced woman, who cowered behind the younger man, was living the intense horror which was painted on her distorted features. Her lips moved as though she were trying to say something, but no articulate sound came.

Clayton's dash to the drawer was an explosion. The revolver came up in his hand like a streak of light. And, like a spring released, Philip Dressler leaped for the older man, shot one fist to his jaw, and snapped the fingers of the other hand over the wrist which held the gleaming weapon as a steel trap might dose on a squirming animal.

The table went over with a thud as they staggered back together, struggling desperately, viciously, for the advantage. The bottled-up enmity of months at last found an outlet. All that was primitive, brutal, ugly, welled up in them.

A splintering crash of shattered glass…

The grunts which follow the dull impact of fist upon flesh…

A sudden flow of blood from Clayton's nose…

A red smear across his cheek as Philip's fist smashed again into his face…

The hoarse wheezing of the younger man as his adversary's thumb found his windpipe…

A vicious kick…a knee upthrust into the pit of the stomach…

Suddenly, it was over.

Clayton staggered back, with both hands clutched to his abdomen. Philip swayed drunkenly on his feet with the revolver dangling from his fingers. He shook his head to clear it and passed a shaking hand over his moist forehead. His breath was coming in shuddering gasps.

He looked dully at the weapon and, like a child remembering a lesson, raised it slowly…

At that moment the woman uttered a wild frantic scream and threw herself forward. "No! No! Don't shoot!"

A stab of orange flame; an echoing report; the acrid odour of burned powder…

The paralysed silence of the moment was broken by the script girl's piercing shriek, which heralded an attack of hysteria.

The older man threw up his arms with a strangled cry and toppled to the floor.

Norma's whole body seemed to cave in and she fell in a dead faint.

Moments passed before Philip dragged himself forward and rolled Clayton on his back. "Dead," he said tonelessly.

Then his eyes widened and he dropped on his knees beside the sprawling form. He put out a trembling hand to touch the crimsoning breast, but drew it back with a sharp cry.

"My God! He's dead!" He stared wildly at the pale blurs of faces and huge outlines of cameras that comprised the third wall. "He's dead, I tell you! Don't you understand! Dead! Really dead!"

*

The paralysed silence of the moment was broken by the script girl's piercing shriek, which heralded an attack of hysteria. Gustav Von Blon, who had been watching the scene with strange, gloating eyes, promptly turned and slapped her face. She swallowed her caramel and was heard no more.

"Cut!" he cried, and the camera stopped.

Pandemonium reigned. Above it the tearful voice of Hyman Singerman was heard, urging others to a control of themselves which he could not himself maintain. Julian limped across the set and knelt beside the motionless form. He took the limp wrist between steady fingers, while the others waited in hushed expectancy for his verdict.

"Yes," he nodded gravely. "He's dead."

A murmur ran through the group of white-faced onlookers like wind through a field of corn. They drew nearer to each other.

"Someone had better telephone the police," he added. "And all those who were here when the shot was fired had better stay where they are until they arrive. Mr. Singerman, I advise you to—"

But Hyman Singerman was in no condition to do anything. He had collapsed, quivering, into a chair, and was staring in front of him with dull, twitching eyes.

Julian took command. He posted guards to keep away intruders and sent the screenwriter at a run to the nearest telephone.

"Pull yourself together," he said sternly to Philip, who was trembling with nerves and horror. "Your wife is coming round. See if you can keep her quiet."

Philip knelt beside Norma and placed an arm tenderly about her shoulders. As she sat up slowly, he murmured something in a soothing tone.

Von Blon walked on to the set, his grey face lit up with excitement. "What a scene!" he exclaimed gutturally. "Du Lieber Gott! It will make the picture!"

Hyman Singerman raised his head slowly and stared venomously, furiously, at the director.

"That's what you think, eh?" he gasped hoarsely. "Then let me tell you it will finish the picture. The censor will never allow it to be shown. And you, you gonof, you robber, you cutthroat, have thrown away thousands of pounds of my good money on it! Thousands of pounds! My God! I could kill you! But make no mistake, mister, this is your finish as well. You will never direct another picture!"

"But—" for once the great director was without words.

"You would send them like dogs at each other's throats! You would change the story to show how clever you are! You were too big, too important to listen to anyone. And now, all you can think of when a man is lying dead is a scene in a picture which will never be shown!"

"I don't understand," muttered Von Blon. "The revolver was loaded only with blanks."

"That's right, sir," chimed in the property man, in a shaking voice. "I loaded it meself fust thing this mornin'."

"Sure you didn't make a mistake in the boxes?" asked Julian.

"That's impossible, sir," replied the man quickly, trembling for his job. "We ain't got nothin' but blanks in the property room."

"Then someone must have changed them."

"And who?" panted Hyman Singerman, rising unsteadily. "Who but a madman would have done such a thing? Ah! But there is a madman in the studio! A man who has neither sympathy nor compassion for his fellows! A man to whom human beings are merely puppets. A man so crazy that he will smash a brand-new car for a few feet of film! A man who sets bitter enemies at each other's throats like snarling animals! A madman who will stop at nothing to provide a thrill for the camera!"

He pointed a wavering finger at Von Blon.

"Yesterday you thundered at Dressler because he did not 'die' convincingly enough to please you. You declared that before you were finished with him he would die like a dead man!

Dead, you said. You repeated the word over and over, as though it fascinated you. Dead! Dead! Dead! And now you have a dead man lying at your feet, you murderer!"

"This is too much!" screamed Von Blon. "You dare to suggest that I—I, Gustav Von Blon—"

"Yes, you! You knew that if the picture failed your career would be ended. You could see it failing at a crucial point. And it is known wherever films are made that you do not care what you do, or who suffers, so long as your pictures turn out as you wish them. You are crazy! Mad!"

The director suddenly grew calm. He smiled, and his expression was not pleasant to look upon.

"This is absurd. You do not realize what you are saying. Who would believe such a story? Gustav Von Blon, the greatest director in the world, killing a man because he could not act? The police will laugh at you as I—I—"

And then he grew pale, for his eyes rested on the grave, shrewd face of Julian Mendoza, and he realised that half a dozen words from the reporter would prepare the police to believe anything of him.

Within fifteen minutes Inspector Howells arrived, with two other men at his heels, and Julian briefly related what had happened. Frowning, the Inspector examined the body and the revolver with which the fatal shot had been fired. The cartridge chamber of the revolver contained the empty case of what had been a live cartridge, two unfired live cartridges, and three unfired blanks. Snapping it shut, Howells balanced it on his hand.

"I'll have a lot to say to you in a few minutes," he told Julian ominously. "Meanwhile, I'll find out what the others know about this."

Everyone in the sound stage was marshalled under his critical inspection. He held up the revolver.

"Who was responsible for loading this?"

The property man came forward nervously.

"I, sir."

"You loaded it this morning?"

"Yes, sir—but only with blanks—I swear it! If I should be struck down dead on this spot—"

"That will do for the present, my man," said Howells sharply.

He eyed the fidgeting crowd sternly.

"How many of you have handled the gun since it was loaded?"

There was a pause. Everyone waited for someone else to speak to. Then Tommy Halliday waved his arms expressively.

"Any one of us may have done," he replied. "The revolver lay in the table drawer; it is Mr. Von Blon's rule that props must never be removed from a set until the scene is finally completed. Almost anyone in the studio could have found an opportunity to change the cartridges. It would only take a moment."

A sudden light flickered in his eyes.

"Good Lord—"

"Well?" asked Howells keenly.

"Oh, nothing. An idea occurred to me, but it is quite absurd."

"Supposing you let me be the judge of that?"

The assistant director shuffled his feet uncomfortably.

"Well…I happened to see Miss Lavery handling the revolver about ten minutes or so before the scene was shot, but, of course, that doesn't mean anything—"

At the mention of her name, the actress came forward slowly, leaning on her husband's arm. Beneath her slight makeup she was very pale.

"You are Miss Lavery?" asked the Inspector.

She nodded, her eyes straying in morbid fascination to the still form which lay a few yards behind him.

"Is this true?"

"Yes, I was toying absently with the revolver," she admitted, "but I didn't interfere with the cartridges. I didn't even realize that it was in my hand until Tommy—Mr. Halliday—scolded me for touching it."

Suddenly, all eyes were turned on Von Blon, who had uttered a Teutonic oath.

"You cried: 'No! No! Don't shoot!'" he said accusingly. "At the moment when Dressler was about to fire you cried out. Why? The words were not in the script. You uttered them spontaneously. It was as though you knew the shot would kill!"

There was a breathless silence. Everyone who had watched the scene was remembering the actress's frantic cry. Norma swayed and would have fallen but for the support of her husband's arm.

"I see it all now!" declared the director, striding up and down as he always did when the creative urge was upon him. "According to the script, Clayton was to shoot your husband.

You loved Clayton and wanted to rid yourself of your husband, so you changed the blanks for live cartridges. And then I changed the action of the scene. I made them fight for the revolver. And when you saw your husband about to shoot the man you loved and knew that the shot would kill, you lost your head and cried out."

"No! It isn't true!"

"Then why," he thundered, "why did you cry 'Don't shoot?'"

"The scene was so vivid," she stammered. "I—I was carried away. For a moment I imagined that it was really happening—not just a bit of acting for a picture—naturally I cried out…"

"As any woman would have done," said Philip fiercely. "By God! You'll have me to reckon with, Von Blon, if you try to put the blame for this on her!"

Actor and director glared at each other for a tense moment, then Von Blon turned away with a shrug of his shoulders. Norma passed a trembling hand over her forehead.

"If I might sit down—" she murmured.

"Certainly," said Howells.

He drew a chair forward and picked up the embroidered handbag which lay upon it.

"Is this yours?" he asked.

"Yes, it's mine." The actress's voice trembled lightly. "Please give it to me."

The Inspector held it out and she reached for it with a sigh of relief, but he shook his head and drew it back.

"It seems to me you're a little too eager to have it. Perhaps I'd better take a look inside first."

"Please give it to me," she pleaded. "There's nothing in it which has any connexion with all this…"

Ignoring the anxious entreaty in her voice (or perhaps because of it) Howells opened the bag.

"Hello!" he exclaimed, putting in his hand. "What's this?"

He held out his find in his open palm. 'This' was a box of cartridges from which three were missing!

Philip Dressler gasped. His wife's hand flew to her throat.

"Perhaps you'll be good enough to explain, Miss Lavery?" said Howells quietly.

"I—I can't," she faltered. "I haven't the slightest idea how they came to be there. I didn't put them in my bag—I swear I didn't."

"But you didn't want me to examine the bag."

"Yes, I know…that was silly…but it wasn't because of the cartridges, truly it wasn't. Oh, please believe me! I didn't know they were there. I objected to you looking in my bag because—because there is a letter in it which I didn't want anyone to see." Frantically, she turned to her husband. "Philip, a letter to you. I wrote it last night, but I didn't send it—I couldn't— Instead I wore my ring today."

"The ring I gave you when we became engaged," said Philip.

"Yes. I hoped you'd see it and make some sign."

The Inspector rubbed his chin reflectively; then he beckoned to one of his assistants, who came forward quickly.

"Take Miss Lavery over there"—he pointed—"let her sit down, and stay with her for the present."

"Then you're going to arrest me?" cried the actress, white to lips.

"At the moment, madam, I can't answer that question. I haven't yet decided what I am going to do. If you'll go with the officer—"

Philip accompanied the plainclothes man and his wife, and Inspector Howells made no objection. Julian waited until the Inspector was engaged with one of the others, then he went across the stage and drew Philip aside.

"I want you to try and remember exactly what Slee said to you after he was injured yesterday."

Philip wrinkled his forehead.

"The exact words," said Julian. "It's most important."

"He said: 'Kent'—yes, that was it—the word 'Kent' twice, and then he said: 'did it that way…tell po—' and fell back in my arms before he had completed the last word. 'Tell po—' Good Lord! Could he have meant: 'tell police'?"

"That's exactly what he did mean," said Julian grimly.

He turned back to Norma Lavery.

"Your husband is in grave danger," he told her earnestly. "If you value his life, on no account let him out of your sight for the coming twenty-four hours."

Feeling a savage grip on his arm, Julian wheeled to find Von Blon glaring up at him.

"Do you intend to tell this Inspector Howells what you know about me?" whispered the German director.

"I haven't decided," retorted Julian, shaking him off.

Quite casually, Julian drifted to the other side of the stage, toward a door that no one was watching. When Howells looked for him a little later the reporter was nowhere to be found. That afternoon the Inspector was called to the telephone to speak to someone who would not give his name. It was Julian.

"Where the dickens have you got to?" demanded Howells angrily. "I want to see you at once."

"Can't be done," responded Julian calmly. "See you later—possibly not until morning—be at the studios bright and early. Meantime, if you don't want another mysterious fatality to solve, you'd better detail two of your heftiest policemen to keep guard over Philip Dressler and Hyman Singerman."

Julian Loses a Tooth

Although Mr. Hyman Singerman had been sitting in front of his drawing-room fire for over an hour with an evening paper in his podgy hands, he had not read a single word. He was holding the paper partly as a screen from the eyes of his wife, which had a trick of seeing more than was actually in the flesh before them—of seeing the innermost thoughts of her husband, as well as his material presence—and partly from habit. Every evening of his married life he had settled down after dinner to a study of the day's news, and the habit of twenty years was difficult to break, although tonight the lines of type blurred before his eyes. His brain was in a bewildered tangle which made concentration impossible.

"Becky," he said, in a soft, caressing voice, "play something for Papa."

A pretty, dark-eyed, olive-skinned little girl of about ten put down the doll she had been lecturing gravely on the perils of overeating and climbed on to the piano-stool, her rounded legs dangling a foot from the floor. "What shall I play, Papa?"

Mr. Singerman hummed something in a husky, unmelodious voice which brought a bubbling, silvery laugh to his daughter's red lips.

"That's 'The Spring Song,' Papa."

"Play it, Becky."

The child's small hands travelled inexpertly over the keys, with many a slip and false note, but Mr. Singerman, beating time with a thick finger, and smilingly nodding his head, found no fault with her execution. As she played, the paper slid from his hands and he lay back with a sigh and watched his little daughter with an expression of pride and love on his, sad round face.

The wireless uttered a sudden squawk; a youth whose oily black hair lay flat upon his sleek head was fiddling with the controls.

"Myron!" exclaimed Mrs. Singerman sternly, "you know Papa hates the wireless when he is resting after dinner."

"Nu, Leah," said Mr. Singerman gently, "let the boy amuse himself. If he stays in at night to please me, we should let him do something to please himself."

Leah crossed the room, perched her plump, shapely body on the arm of her husband's chair, and put an arm round his shoulders. A change had come over him lately, she reflected. He had not always been so tolerant of his son, who was at a difficult age. He was missing his brother, she knew; since the awful night when he had found Jacob's dead body in the hall of his flat, he had been a different man. One night in bed he had wept and told her that he felt utterly lost without him.

"Leah," said Hyman, almost in a whisper, "I've got something to tell you. Something of which I am ashamed. The diamond necklace I gave you for our tenth anniversary… I sold it and replaced it with paste."

"I know," she replied, stroking his pink bald head. "Wasn't I brought up in the trade? They don't make paste that could fool me."

"You know—and you are not angry?"

"Why should I be angry? Everything I have; I got from you, Hyman."

A tear trickled down Singerman's fat cheeks. "And everything I've got that's worth having I got from you, Leah."

The door opened and a trim maid announced that Mr. Mendoza wished to speak to Mr. Singerman. The film magnate frowned.

"If you don't want to see him," said his observant wife, "Sarah can tell him you are out."

"No, I had better see him. He is the reporter I told you about. But…if you would take the children away… He will probably talk about Jacob's—er—death and the less they hear about that the better."

"Don't let him bother you long, Hyman," she said, rising and patting his arm. "You are tired. Come, Becky…Myron… your Papa wants to talk business with a gentleman."

There was a hunger in Singerman's eyes as he watched his family leaving the room. With a sigh, he rose to meet Julian.

"Sit down, Mr. Mendoza," he said, with forced warmth. "A cigar? Sarah, bring a decanter of port—or would you prefer a brandy-and-soda, Mr. Mendoza?"

Julian had frustrated the maid's attempts to relieve him of his hat. "If you don't mind, I shan't have either," he replied. "I can't stop for more than a minute. Forgive the intrusion. I merely dropped in to ask you about a man named Kent who was formerly in your employ."

Singerman stared at him, with a curious expression on his sagging features. "Kent…" he repeated, in a dry tone. "Kent… But he is dead."

"I know that. One of your technical staff told me so this afternoon. What I meant to ask is whether you know the whereabouts of the plans on which he was working at the time of his death."

For a full minute no sound broke the silence but the ticking of the ormulu dock on the mantelpiece.

"No," replied Singerman. "No. I am sorry. I am afraid I don't. Probably they have been destroyed. Although he was attached to the technical staff, he did most of his work alone in a small laboratory of his own and never breathed a word of his ideas until they were completed. I believe he used to take his plans home at night for greater secrecy."

Julian thanked him and turned to go. "Oh, by the way,"

he said, "don't be alarmed if you notice a man lurking about outside tonight. So many strange things have happened lately to people connected with the Colossal Film Company that Inspector Howells has sent one of his men to see that nothing happens to you."

"That is very thoughtful of the Inspector," said Singerman dryly.

"Oh, I thought of it," replied Julian.

His host escorted him to the door. On the doorstep, Julian thought of something else. "I didn't know Sam Finklebaum was a relative of yours," he remarked.

"Do you know him?" asked Singerman, his face darkening at mention of the brother-in-law who had so frequently sponged on him.

"Slightly. I ran into him at the Crescent Turkish Baths this evening and he mentioned that you are his brother-in-law. Well, I mustn't detain you at the door or you'll catch a chill. Good night."

The reporter wended his way home through the Park. The night air was crisp and invigorating and he swung along briskly in spite of his crippled leg, his stick beating a rhythmic tattoo, to the slithering accompaniment of his dragging right foot, his pipe glowing red in the darkness.

At the corner of the quiet street in which he lived a man stopped him and asked to be directed to a certain number. Julian stretched out his hand to point to a house across the way and it was seized in a powerful grip. At the same time a lithe dark form darted from the shadows, with one hand raised in which something gleamed. Julian lashed out with his stick and the shining object described a glittering arc through the air and tinkled into the gutter. A fist, sheathed in brass knuckles, smashed into his face and drove him, reeling, against the iron railings which skirted the pavement. He felt a hard substance in his mouth and a warm flow...

The assailants closed on him menacingly. Shaking his head to muster his failing senses, Julian staggered to an upright position and drove the point of his stick, like a sword, with all the power of his muscular body, into the belly of the foremost. The man collapsed with an agonised groan, but the other leapt on Julian's back like a tiger and the reporter felt his head bending forward under a relentless pressure. Sweat stood out on his forehead as he struggled desperately to break the hold which in another moment must snap his neck like a twig. The pain was excruciating. There was a roaring in his ears. His frantic hands found their objective, and he put every ounce of nerve and sinew into the only manoeuvre that could save him. With a scream, the clawing burden flew from his shoulders and fell, with a sickening thud, into the area below.

Julian spat out a tooth and leaned helplessly against the railings. He was trembling and his breath was coming in shuddering gasps. He wavered forward and picked up the curved knife which lay in the gutter. The other man was writhing on the pavement with both hands clasped to his abdomen. Julian grasped him by the hair, dragged back his head, and looked into the pain-wracked face of Adolf, Von Blon's masseur.

"When you feel well enough to rise," said Julian grimly, "you'll find the Japanese valet in the area—with a broken neck, I hope."

Adolf squirmed and his eyes widened as the knife in Julian's hand came close to his face. With a hoarse laugh, the reporter dropped it on the pavement. "Tell your master to use it on his throat," he said, "—or he'll wish he had when next I meet him!"

He reeled away, clutching the railings for support.

Mrs. MacDougal was at the telephone in the hall when he opened the front door. She stared at him with a horrified gasp and covered the mouthpiece with her hand.

"Guidsakes, man! Whit have ye been daein' wi' y'r face?"

"Polishing brass," replied Julian with a painful grin.

"Inspector Howells has been ringing up for ye all evening. It's him on the wire now."

"Tell him you don't expect me tonight."

She gave the message, hung up the receiver abruptly, and, hurrying after her lodger, who was unsteadily mounting the stairs, caught the tail of his coat and drew him back.

"The lassie's upstairs," she whispered.

"What lassie?"

"Ye ken fine who I mean. Miss Foster."

Her eyes searched his face. "She's a bundle of nerves, poor girl," she said. "And nae wonder, after all she's been through lately. If ye've a spark o' manhood in you, ye'll tak' her in your arms and kiss her fears awa'."

"You're a silly old woman," retorted Julian sharply.

His room was in darkness, save for the dancing firelight, which shone on Cicely's exquisite profile and red-gold hair. As he entered, she sprang up, with a cry of relief, from the stool on which she had been sitting.

"Julian! I had to come… I've been so frightened!"

His hand dropped from the light switch. The sight of his bruised face would afford her no comfort.

"Sit down again, please," he murmured. "You were looking lovely just then."

Julian was all in. Only his indomitable will kept him from collapsing at her feet. She sat down and somehow, he managed to drag himself across the room and drop into a chair beside her without betraying his weakness.

"It was outrageously unconventional of me to come," she said. "But I couldn't bear it, alone in my room. I kept thinking of all the dreadful things which have happened lately; the murder of

Mr. Singerman…that poor little man being run over…Kenneth's broken leg…the ghastly affair in the studio this afternoon. Oh, I thought I'd go mad!"

"You've been in the midst of it all," said Julian quietly. "Poor kid!"

He stroked her hair. It seemed, somehow, perfectly natural that he should.

"I went to the hospital early this evening and saw Kenneth," she remarked, staring into the fire. "I—I only stayed for a few minutes. I—"

There was a pregnant silence. "You are still not quite sure whether you love him?"

She glanced up swiftly. "How did you know?"

"I've seen a lot of life," Julian replied, in an odd, strained tone.

Another silence… Cicely shivered. Silence conjured up the horrors of the past few days. "Talk to me, Julian. I don't want to think."

"What shall I talk about?"

"Tell me about some of the places you've been to. The pleasant places."

Julian leant back, his eyes closed, his unlit pipe dangling limply from his fingers, his voice coming in a low, dreamy whisper, as soothing as soft music. He spoke of islands dreaming in a golden sea, of birds wheeling and dipping above wind-filled sails, of cloudless azure skies where the sun shone always, and people with eternal laughter in their hearts. Swimmers, breasting the waves with glossy brown arms, rising upon planks, and, still as statues, beautiful as gods, riding to shore on a white-headed comber, a mile long, with the thunderous speed of an express train. Naked brown children playing in the ruffled fringe of the sea; naked, high-breasted maidens bathing in placid, translucent pools which gathered their cool, clear water from the lacy spray of tumultuous falls.

A breathtaking beauty which almost hurt the senses, painted by nature with the most vivid colours of her palette, jade green, emerald, turquoise blue, sapphire, tangerine, gold, red and shining white. Magic nights, deathly still, with no faintest breeze to stir the foliage; the thunder of the sea; music and deep, rich laughter about the leaping flames of a fire on the beach that tossed gay plumage to the smiling, starflecked heavens…

His voice died away, lingering like the last notes of a sweet song.

Cicely's eyes were wet with tears. "Islands dreaming in a golden sea…" she repeated tremulously. "Oh, Julian, what endless happiness to live there!"

"All my life I've searched for such a spot," said Julian. "And never found it."

"If we could only find it together!"

Hungrily, he gathered her into his arms and pressed his lips upon her smooth white throat. Trembling, he thrust her from him almost roughly.

"Come," he said, when his shaking voice would let him. "I'm going to take you home."

At the corner of the street, he hailed a prowling taxi and helped her into it. He started to climb in beside her, but changed his mind. He gave the driver her address.

"Good night," he said.

"Julian!"

But he turned away and the darkness swallowed him up.

For hours he wandered through silent streets, waging a battle within himself for the happiness of the girl he loved. Dawn was breaking when, weary and haggard, he let himself in to the slumbering house in which he lived.

The Murderer

It would appear an impossibility to look more like a policeman in mufti than in the regulation blue uniform, but it was achieved by the sad-eyed man who lounged in the entrance hall of the Colossal Film Company's studios on the morning after the murder on sound stage number four. If he had stood at a busy corner directing traffic, in his bowler hat, serge suit and heavy-welted number ten boots he would have commanded the unquestioning obedience of even the least amenable motorist. No one could possibly have mistaken him for anything but a policeman in 'plain clothes'. He cocked an eye at Julian when the reporter passed through the plate glass doors into the building a little after ten o'clock.

"The Inspector wants to see you," he remarked. "He's been kicking up blue blazes. Sent a man to fetch you half an hour ago."

Julian looked worn and tired. His chin, blue with stubble, was sunk in the upturned collar of his shabby coat. "Where is he?" he asked wearily.

"In Mr. Singerman's private office. Been popping out every five minutes to see whether you'd arrived."

"Is Von Blon in?"

"Yes—by special request of the Inspector. He tried to leave the country by 'plane at midnight, but one of our chaps was trailing him and turned him back."

The reporter limped along the ground floor corridor and entered the German film director's private room without knocking. Von Blon, who was seated at his desk, turned his head sharply; the angry rebuke died on his lips as he recognised the intruder. Julian locked the door and, his face livid, Von Blon tugged open a drawer and snatched up a blunt-nosed automatic. "Get out!" he hissed.

Julian pocketed the key and advanced steadily across the room, his eyes, glittering redly, holding the other's apprehensive gaze. The director slid out of his chair and backed slowly away, levelling the pistol at Julian's breast. "Get…out…of…my…office." The window halted his retreat.

"Do not come any nearer," he snarled. "I warn you—I will shoot!"

Julian approached implacably and Von Blon's finger tightened on the trigger. In the split second before the roaring report, Julian swung up his crippled leg and his boot thudded violently into the pit of the other's stomach. The bullet went wide and scored a long groove in the plastered wall. Von Blon crumpled up and the pistol dropped from his fingers to the floor with a clatter. With one hand Julian gripped his bunched lapels and held his limp, sagging form upright.

"I intended to batter your ugly face to a pulp, blacken your eyes, knock a few teeth down your miserable throat," he said, without heat. "You are a filthy dog and thoroughly deserve a beating. But you weren't man enough to face even a cripple with your bare fists, so if at this moment you feel that the lower half of your body is missing—and still aching like hell—you've only yourself to thank. I was raised in a hard school. I can be as dirty a fighter as anyone. Now, take a tip from me: in a few hours you'll be free to leave the country: beat it, and hide yourself, for tomorrow morning my paper will tell the world that the great Gustav Von Blon is none other than Erich Braun, a fugitive from a French penal colony, a mockery of a man, without heart or guts, who curried favour with the officials by betraying his own comrades—and was crucified by them during the wildest outbreak in the history of the colony!"

He released his hold and Von Blon slid with a groan to the floor and lay there, twisting and clawing at his stomach in exquisite agony. No one who has not experienced such a ferocious kick in the abdomen as the one Julian had administered can realise the diabolical torture which was consuming him.

Julian unlocked the door and went out, closing it behind him. There were one or two people in the corridor, but the unconcerned way in which they went about their business proved that the insulated walls of the building were everything that was claimed for them. Obviously neither the shot nor the scuffle had been audible outside the room.

"So, you've condescended to arrive at last!" exclaimed Inspector Howells scathingly as the reporter hobbled into Hyman Singerman's private office.

Without replying, Julian crossed the room to the massive desk behind which sat Singerman in the spineless, ungainly attitude of a rag doll. Their eyes met and in Singerman's there was a pitiful plea. He was ashy pale and his hands were trembling. His mouth opened, but no sound came.

"I didn't expect to see you here this morning," said Julian.

Singerman did not answer. He watched Julian's face with the stricken eyes of a suffering animal.

"I warned you last night as plainly as I could," said Julian bitterly.

A sigh fluttered through the twitching grey lips of the film magnate. It seemed to come from the depths of his being. "I know," he whispered brokenly. "I…tried to end it…but…I hadn't the…courage…"

"It would have been easier for everyone if you had. I should have been able to forget what I know, for the sake of the innocent ones who must now suffer."

"I couldn't do it. I tried…but I couldn't. I clung to the hope that you didn't really know."

"Know? Of course, I knew. You gave yourself away. I laid a

trap for you when I suggested a means whereby your brother might have committed suicide and disposed of the weapon and you fell into it head over heels. I had already searched the ornamental pond beneath his window and found it empty. When I discovered the gun in it that night, I knew who had put it there. But it was only last night that I discovered how you had contrived the actual murder. Before that I hadn't a shred of proof."

Inspector Howells stared from one to the other in sheer bewilderment.

"What on earth does this mean?" he stammered.

"It means," said Julian, "that Mr. Singerman is the man you are here to arrest."

"Mr. Singerman!" exploded Howells. "But…but it's impossible! He was at a Turkish bath in Coventry Street at the time his brother was shot. His alibi is supported by half a dozen reliable witnesses."

"They are telling the truth," said Julian. "He was at the bath at the time of the murder—nevertheless, he committed it. To cover it up he attempted to kill Slee; and was indirectly responsible for the death of Russell Clayton."

The Inspector took a step forward. "Is this true?" he demanded of the drooping figure which sat motionless behind the desk. "Wait! It is my duty to warn you that—"

Hyman Singerman sighed and a heavy load seemed to slip from his shoulders. "It is perfectly true. I am glad you know. I am glad it is all over. Now, perhaps, I will find peace. I will tell you everything. Everything…"

And then, in a low, dry whisper, in halting, broken sentences, he told the most dreadful story to which Howells had ever listened…

When it was over, the Scotland Yard man took a deep breath,

His palms were moist. He was hardly able to credit the evidence of his own ears.

He was too dazed to strike down the automatic pistol which appeared—by magic, it seemed in Singerman's hand. There was an echoing report and Singerman swayed slowly forward. A dark red pool began to form on the massive walnut desk at which he had spent so many hours looking like Napoleon.

It was afterwards discovered that the pistol was one which belonged to Gustav Von Blon, but it was never explained how it came into Singerman's possession. Julian might have explained. But he never did.

Goodbye!

J ulian turned the corner from the clamour of Fleet Street into the narrow lane in which the antiquated, smoke-blackened building which housed the editorial and printing departments of the *Morning World* was situated. The lane was congested with vehicles: carts laden with huge rolls of paper; box-tricycles, manoeuvred recklessly by nonchalant youths who cheerfully exchanged profanities with those they narrowly missed running into; delivery vans parked at the despatch platform, or mounting the broken pavements in their drivers' voluble efforts to find a way out of the maze. Boys everywhere: dodging under the heads of horses, skipping in front of moving vehicles, barging into everyone who got in their way—and boys loafing along with their snub noses stuck in lurid weeklies and urgent messages in their pockets.

He limped up the rickety wooden stairs, past the cubbyhole of the portly doorkeeper, who gave him a solemn wink, and into the long, bare reporters' room. The floor trembled beneath his feet with the thundering of the giant presses in the basement as they swallowed miles of paper and rivers of ink and spewed them out in the shape of hundreds of thousands of copies of the World's afternoon publication, the Evening Herald. The atmosphere was heavy with the pungent odour of printing-ink.

Two long desks, each made to accommodate five men, stood against two of the pencil-scrawled walls of the reporters' room. Two more stood back-to-back in the middle of the room. A row of telephone booths against the third wall, half a dozen battered typewriters on a table beneath the grimy windows, a score of unsteady bentwood chairs, a dozen wicker wastepaper baskets, a few tattered books of reference, and a calendar showing a month-old date completed the furnishings.

The floor was strewn with crumpled newspapers, torn sheets of copy-paper, spent matches and cigarette ends. The wastepaper baskets were almost empty. When a reporter wanted to dispose of something he never thought of placing it in the basket beside his chair: he aimed it at a basket across the room, or, more often, tossed it on the floor. Every now and then a match thrown down alight would set fire to the litter on the floor and one of the men would calmly put his foot on the blaze—or beat it out with someone else's hat.

As Julian entered, three reporters were scribbling busily at the two centre desks, a fourth was apparently having hysterics in a telephone booth, and a fifth was sitting on the table beneath the windows, poking an idle finger at the shaky keys of a typewriter, and addressing a flow of remarks to his industrious colleagues to which none of them paid the slightest attention.

"Hello," he exclaimed. "How's the Sleuth of Fleet Street?"

Without replying, Julian dropped into a chair, lit his pipe, grabbed a wad of copy-paper, and began to pound for dear life on the keys of one of the typewriters.

This is what he wrote:

After confessing to a series of astounding crimes, including one of the most amazing murders of recent years, Mr. Hyman Singerman, managing director of the Colossal Film Company, shot himself dead in his office this morning before the Scotland Yard official and the *Morning World* reporter, to whom the statement was made, could move a finger to prevent him.

He made the staggering admission that although he was in a cubicle at a Turkish bath at the time when his brother, Jacob Singerman, was fatally shot in his luxurious flat in Dorian House, Mayfair, five days ago, he was actually responsible for the crime. It was contrived by an ingenious apparatus invented by Rodney Kent, a young employee of the film company, who died some months ago. This device, an arrangement of springs, coils and hinges, which was designed to fire a revolver on the opening of a door, was taken to Hyman Singerman by Kent shortly after he created it, with the suggestion that it might be used in a mystery film. Shortly afterwards, before he had mentioned his invention to anyone else, Kent caught a chill, contracted pneumonia, and died, leaving his secret in the possession of his employer. For months the appliance lay forgotten in a drawer of the film magnate's desk.

At that time, according to his confession, Hyman Singerman was heavily involved in disastrous financial speculations and in a vain attempt to regain his losses he used his brother's name in a number of similarly unfortunate dealings on the Stock Exchange, forging his signature for that purpose. Trusted implicitly by his brother, he was able to draw large sums from the firm's banking account, against fictitious entries. This was discovered by Simon Slee, an employee of the company, who, desirous of turning the information to his own benefit, sent an anonymous letter to Mr. Jacob Singerman, hinting at the facts and offering full details for a payment of two hundred pounds. Mr. Jacob Singerman accepted the offer and, on the afternoon on which he was killed, Slee sold him the information. Furious, he charged his brother with defrauding him and, in a violent scene, obtained an admission that the allegations were true. An appointment was made for Mr. Hyman Singerman to go to his brother's Mayfair flat that night at ten o'clock to make a clean breast of his defalcations.

In his confession this morning, Mr. Hyman Singerman stated that in spite of the strong bond of affection between them he had no hope of mercy from his brother, who was ruthless in his dealings with those who betrayed his trust and would almost certainly prosecute him for forgery and fraud. In his desperate efforts to think of a plan to prevent that, the idea of killing his brother came into his frenzied brain. At first, he rejected it, but as the afternoon wore on he came to accept his brother's death as his only way out, and to wonder whether it could be achieved without risk to himself. It was then that he remembered the appliance in his desk drawer and decided to use it for his awful purpose.

There were three telephones in his brother's flat and one of these, which was not listed in the telephone directory, was reserved solely for use in communication between the brothers in order that there might always be a clear line for discussion of such urgent matters as might arise outside of business hours. A sedan chair, converted into a telephone booth, housed this instrument. Late that afternoon, Hyman Singerman admitted himself to the flat with a key in his possession and fixed the apparatus inside the sedan chair at a level with his brother's head, adjusted so that the revolver would be discharged when the door was pulled open. He knew that his brother would have no reason to use that particular telephone during the evening since they were meeting at ten o'clock and since he had not given him any address at which he might be reached before that hour, merely stating that he would be occupied somewhere in town.

From his brother's flat he went to a Turkish bath where he passed the time until the hour of the appointment. At ten o'clock he instructed a pageboy at the bath to telephone the number of the fatal instrument. There was, of course, no answer. His brother, opening the door of the sedan chair to answer the telephone, had instantly fallen dead with a bullet in his brain. There was no need for Hyman Singerman to fear that the report might have been heard and the alarm given, because Dorian House is soundproof throughout. Dressing at leisure, he took a taxi to Dorian House, and, in company with the liftboy, made the 'discovery' he had expected to make. Sending the boy to telephone to the police, he went into the flat, hastily dismantled the apparatus and hid the separate parts in his pockets.

It must here be mentioned that it was only by chance that his carefully planned alibi was not rendered useless. When making the appointment with his brother for ten o'clock that evening, Jacob Singerman had apparently forgotten an earlier engagement he had made with a certain young actress whose name has been widely mentioned in connection with the murder. She kept the appointment, but left shortly before ten o'clock. Had she remained in the flat a minute or two longer she would have heard the shot fired—possibly witnessed it—and given the alarm. The appliance would have been discovered and Mr. Hyman Singerman's alibi tendered valueless. He, of course, had no doubt that his brother would be alone at ten o'clock, considering the vital importance to both of them of the subject they were to discuss; otherwise, he would not have dared to attempt the murder by the means he did.

His unshaken alibi saved him from suspicion and, although he stated that from the moment he laid eyes on his brother's lifeless body he was never free from the pangs of horror and remorse, he felt himself safe from the consequences of his crime until Simon Slee, who had been spying on him, hinted at knowledge of the means whereby the crime had been committed and demanded five thousand pounds as the price of his silence. Unable to pay, Hyman Singerman begged for time to raise the money and began to cast about him for a means of disposing of the would-be blackmailer. The opportunity arose during the filming of a scene in a talking picture which was being taken on a country road, when Singerman and Slee were standing with others on a platform above the road, watching the approach of a speeding car which was to be crashed against a wall a few yards from where they stood. Under cover of the general excitement Singerman pushed into the director of the film, thrusting him against Slee, with the result that the unfortunate man was thrown from the platform into the roadway, run over, and seriously injured. It is still doubtful whether he will recover.

To his consternation, Singerman saw his victim muttering something to Mr. Philip Dressler, the actor, who had run to his aid, and although the injured man fell back unconscious almost at once, he feared that his guilty secret had been communicated to the actor. He expected every moment to be denounced, and, when the accusation did not come, his distraught brain jumped to the erroneous conclusion that Dressier, too, had blackmailing intentions. Unable to reason coherently, he felt only that here was a new menace to his safety which must speedily be removed. 'I was mad,' he confessed, 'but I was so terribly afraid...' Again, his chance came during the filming of a scene in the same talking picture, taken, this time, in the studios at Turnham Green. He had watched the scene in rehearsal and knew that in it a revolver, loaded with blank cartridges, was fired at the man he feared. Before the actual 'shooting' of the scene he managed to substitute live cartridges for some of the blanks and, fearing that he might be searched, hid the box of cartridges in a handbag belonging to an actress engaged in the film. An unexpected change in the action of the scene caused Russell Clayton, the well-known actor, to receive the deadly discharge intended for Dressler. (A full account of the tragic happening appeared in yesterday's edition of the *Morning World*.)

Julian took his hands from the keys and read what he had written. Yes, the bare bones of the narrative were there: the sub-editorial staff would skilfully pad it out to four times the present length. He took the last page of the story from the typewriter, inserted a fresh sheet, and tapped out the following paragraph:

> It was announced to a *Morning World* representative today that Mr. Philip Dressler and Miss Norma Lavery, the renowned stage players, who are, of course, man and wife, will leave within the coming week for a cruise to the West Indies.

As he assembled the pages of copy, a lad with a round, cheeky-looking face popped a ruffled head into the room.

"Lady to see you, Mr. Mendoza," he called.

Julian turned with a frown. "Did she give a name?"

"Foster, she said her name was." The boy winked. "A proper peach, if you ask me. She's in the waiting-room."

For a while the reporter was sunk in thought. "Tell her—" he began. "No—you needn't trouble—I'll see her myself." He tossed the typewritten pages to the lad. "Here, take these to Mr. McQuisten."

Cicely was standing by the dusty window of the waiting-room. Her face lit up when he came in. "I hoped to find you here," she said.

The reporter scowled at her and sat on the edge of a table littered with newspapers. "You shouldn't have come," he said gruffly. "I meant to write and bid you goodbye."

"Goodbye!" she repeated, her face falling. "Julian! What are you talking about?"

He stabbed his stick viciously at the toe of his shoe. "I'm going away. I can't stand London any longer."

"Oh," she said quietly. There was a silence.

"Where are you going?" she asked.

"I don't know. Thousands of miles away. China…Mexico… It doesn't much matter."

"You're going because of me?" she said, in a still, small voice.

Only his eyes answered her. She turned away with a gulp and stared out of the window.

"Do you know," she said, with a shaky laugh, "I've been an awful fool. I had an idea you loved me. Funny, isn't it?"

"Not a bit. I do."

She turned round with a glad cry and her eyes lit up.

"I love you," said Julian, "so much that I'd cut myself in little bits rather than cause you pain. That's why I'm going away."

"But that's rubbish," she retorted, coming closer. "Julian, you'll hurt me terribly if you go away. I love you, too."

Julian shook his head. "No," he said huskily, "you only imagine that you love me. You think so because I'm different from the other men you've met. You see colour, glamour in me that isn't in them. You don't recoil from my slovenly appearance and uncouth manners because you think them romantic, picaresque, like a rakish cloak, a plumed hat set at an angle, and a swaggering oath. You haven't thought what time would do to your conception of me. The scales would drop from your eyes, you know. You would see me as I really am. Every time you looked at me you would wonder what you ever saw in so outlandish a boor—and you would look at me, seeing me as I really am, a hundred times a day. You think not, my dear; you imagine that the glamour would last, but I've seen a lot of life and I know. I know myself and I know you. Perhaps you think I would change: learn to wear correct clothes decently, smoke cigarettes, and comb my hair… I never would. It isn't in me to be other than I am. I am thirty-seven and I have squandered the best years of my life. Yours is still before you. There is nothing for us to say to each other, except—Goodbye!"

He forced a fleeting smile. "I'm going to let you into a secret. You love Kenneth Archer. You're not sure of it yourself, but it's true. He loves you. He'll make you a first-rate husband when time has corrected his one important failing—youth. You'll be happy with him. You're both young enough to make what you will of each other."

He took one of her slim white hands in his own hairy brown hand, bent his head, and kissed it. And then he was gone, leaving her slowly to comprehend the undeniable truth of the things he had said. Julian had done a lot of thinking in the still hours of the night.

*

The news editor of the *Morning World*, a lanky, raw-boned Northerner, looked up from the pages of typescript which he was reading with unholy glee and smiled at Julian as the reporter entered his untidy private room.

"Man! I'm going to splash this all over the front page. It's the story of the century!"

"Glad to hear it," said Julian, "for it's the last I'll ever write. I'm going abroad. Thought I'd better let you know."

"Going abroad? In the name of heaven, why? And where to?"

"The first doesn't concern you," replied Julian rudely. "As for the second, any place where things happen. I've heard there's a revolution brewing in one of the South American republics. If there isn't, I'll start one."

The news editor started to remonstrate with him, but before he was properly launched the telephone bell rang. He said:

"Hold on a minute!" to Julian and lifted the receiver irritably. "Hello…? Yes, this is McQuisten… What's that you say…? Dead, is he…? Think it's murder, do they…? Repeat the address and I'll write it down… 44, Haggard Street…? 'H' for Hannah; 'A' for apple; 'G' for—" He broke off and stared at Julian, who was swinging the door open.

"Hey! What's your hurry?"

But Julian did not answer. He was hastening to 44, Haggard Street as fast as one sound leg and a crippled one would let him.

THE END

THE SUNDIAL DRUG MYSTERY

Buffeted by the wind, lashed and swept by rain, the little car staggered and lurched along the country lane, its tyres slapping and sucking in the muddy cartruts, its wheels skidding at times perilously near the ditch which flanked the narrow roadway. The driver, a tired-looking, shabbily dressed man of thirty-five, clung desperately to the steering-wheel, his eyes vainly trying to pierce the curtain of velvet darkness shot with scudding rain which loomed always a few yards in front of the car.

Two women were crushed into the seat behind him. One, a year or so younger than the man, was inclined to rotundity and her ample figure made it a tight fit. The other was a girl of twenty or thereabouts, tall and slim. They were both utterly miserable. One of the straps which held the hood in place had parted, making a large gap above the windscreen through which the rain poured in on them. A myriad of little holes in the canvas above their heads dripped water down their necks. The side-curtains were in an advanced stage of dilapidation; through the broken celluloid the gusty wind blew a shower of drops in their faces.

"Trust you to land us in a mess like this, Joe Carey," said the elder of the two women bitterly. "We were only eight miles from Norwich when you took this confounded short cut. We've done about ten already and there's no sign of this miserable lane coming to an end."

"We come onto the main road about a mile farther on," retorted the man, without turning his eyes from the little patch of road made visible by his failing headlamps. "And don't exaggerate, Rose. We've only done six miles by the speedometer."

"The speedometer!" she jeered. "The speedometer's like the rest of the car!"

"Whose idea was it to buy the blasted thing?" parried Carey indignantly. "You were so gloomily sure we'd save a fortune in railway fares if we had a car."

"A car—not a rolling mousetrap! You were an easy mark, Joe Carey, paying twenty pounds of our hard-earned cash for this portable pudding-basin. Twenty pounds!"

"What did you expect for twenty pounds? A Hispano?"

Rose moved her plump shoulders impatiently.

"How Bloomberg will laugh when we turn up at Norwich looking like drowned rats!" she said. "We'll never hear the last of it."

Her husband nodded gloomily. Bloomberg was certain to laugh. Nothing amused him more than the troubles of other people. Ike Bloomberg was the manager of the third-rate theatrical company with which Joe and Rose Carey and Diana Venner were touring the provinces in that stirring romance, 'All for Love'. In addition to being something of a humourist, the manager was considerably more of a miser. He paid his 'All Star Cast' little better than starvation wages. As an economy, the Careys and Diana had clubbed together a portion of their slender savings and bought the two-seater which had been expected to pay for itself in a short time through the consequent saving in railway fares. It seemed now that they had expended twenty pounds of their good money to no better purpose than to provide Ike Bloomberg with a new joke!

The day was Saturday and the hour was almost midnight. They had left Bury St. Edmunds in the car directly after the second performance of the play was over and were on their way to Norwich, where the company was opening on the following

Monday night. Rain and wind had kept them company all the way, and to make matters worse, the two women were beginning to suspect that the driver hadn't the faintest idea where they were!

As though resenting the insulting descriptions which had been applied to it, the car coughed and spluttered, then rolled to a standstill with a last despairing wheeze of its asthmatic springs. Carey pressed the self-starter and was rewarded with a single grating groan—then silence! With a muttered curse he clambered wearily over his drenched companions to reach the only door, and stepped out into the fury of the night.

His knowledge of the mechanics of a car was limited to knowing where to put petrol, oil and water, and how to change a wheel. He opened the bonnet on both sides and stared gloomily at the rusty engine; made a tentative jab at the carburettor; examined the magneto unenthusiastically, and coated his hands with oil without result. He swung the starting-handle with vigour born of despair, but desisted after a dozen vain—and back-breaking—crankings. Walking round the derelict two-seater, splashing through mud up to the ankles, he relieved his feelings with a flow of colourful profanity.

"Joe Carey!" stormed Rose. "Will you stop that language before Diana?"

The girl roused herself apathetically and brushed a wisp of damp, golden hair from her forehead. "Oh, I endorse every word," she said wearily. "He's said exactly what was in my mind, only I couldn't find words to express it!"

Carey poked his head through a hole in the side-curtains. "She's given up the ghost," he said gloomily.

"The dealer told you she was good for twenty thousand miles!" stormed Rose.

"He meant if we pushed her, I suppose."

"Don't be a clown!"

Standing in the rain, with the brim of his sodden felt hat drooping about his ears and his shabby overcoat soaked through, Joe Carey contrived the ghost of a grin. "Well, there's no need to worry about that shortcut for the present, at least. Here's where we stop!"

Carey did not hear the question. He had gone a few paces away and was peering into the darkness. In a few minutes he splashed back to the car.

"There's a pair of ornamental iron gates a few yards along the road," he observed.

"You don't say so!" exclaimed his wife bitterly, shaking her head to dislodge a raindrop from the end of her nose. "Pity it isn't daylight—you could get a snap of them for your album!"

Diana Venner roused herself again. "Joe means," she translated, "that where there are ornamental gates there must be a house."

"Then why can't he say so? Are there any lights showing?"

"No."

"Let's go and throw ourselves on the mercy of the people who own the house," suggested Diana. "They can't very well refuse us shelter on a night like this."

Joe opened the dickey seat and removed two of the three suitcases it contained. Diana climbed out and hefted the remaining suitcase. With a sound halfway between a sigh and a groan, Rose Carey stepped into the mud, shuddering as it engulfed her shoes and she felt its clammy embrace on her ankles.

They squelched and splashed along the lane and through the gates which were conveniently open; up a gravel driveway, Rose complaining bitterly at every step. In front of them loomed the dark shape of a low, rambling house. They huddled together in the shelter of the wide portico while Joe rang the bell. It echoed through the house.

"That's a blessing," said Rose. "The kitchen door must be open or we wouldn't hear the bell. Even if everyone's in bed they're bound to hear it as well. Give it another yank, Joe. I'm too cold to remember my manners."

Joe rang again—and again—but there was no sound of life within the dark house. "That's torn it," he said. "The place is empty."

"Just our luck!" mourned Rose. "We'll have to camp here all night and we'll all be dead of pneumonia within a week!"

"We can't do that!" protested Diana. "Isn't there any way we could get in?"

They looked at each other, then out at the night, which was gaining in fury.

"D'you suppose we could—break in?" whispered Diana.

"If I were a man," said Rose bitterly, "I know what I'd do."

With a shrug of his shoulders Joe disappeared. A few moments later they heard a tinkle of broken glass, then footsteps sounded inside the house. The hall lights went on suddenly and Joe opened the front door with a grin on his tired face.

"Broke in the scullery window and climbed in," he explained. "Enter, fellow housebreakers!"

They crept in on tiptoe, feeling that the occasion, called for furtive stealth. They had put themselves within reach of the law!

The front door opened to a large panelled hall. Rose stopped suddenly and sniffed the air.

"There's a smell of floor polish," she said. "Someone's been in this house today!"

Diana had opened a door on the left. "Ooh!" she cried. "A fire!"

They crowded in and found themselves in a large, pleasant room, with a huge fireplace in which the embers of a fire were glowing. Joe opened the coal scuttle and stoked the fire lavishly. "In for a penny, in for a pound," he said.

"I don't like this," declared Rose. "If there are people in the house, they're bound to have heard us. Why don't they come?"

"Because there isn't anybody," replied Joe, warming his hands at the blaze.

"Then why the fire? And anyone can see that this room's been tidied and dusted today."

She shook her head. "I don't like it."

"Look!" said Diana suddenly, pointing to the mantlepiece.

A square white envelope was propped against a brass candlestick which stood to the left of the mantlepiece. Diana walked over and examined the inscription on the envelope.

"Mr. Malcolm Channing," she read aloud.

"Channing," murmured Rose. "Channing…I've read that name in the papers recently."

"Sounds familiar," agreed Joe.

Rose shrugged her shoulders. "Oh, well, I expect there are hundreds of Channings." She shivered. "Holy smoke, I'm cold! I'm going to change into dry clothes."

"Good idea," commented Joe. "You girls make yourselves comfortable. I'll change in another room."

He left them alone together. Rose discreetly drew the curtains across the French windows and they began to strip off their soaked garments. When she had shed her overcoat and close-fitting little hat, Diana Venner was revealed as a ravingly beautiful girl. Rose, looking critically at her exquisite figure and perfectly moulded features, wondered, for the first time, why no London producer had thus far realised Diana's potentialities. They must be blind, she decided, if they couldn't see what a delicious eyeful she made.

They were clad scantily in filmy underwear when Rose suddenly caught Diana's arm.

"Listen," she said tensely. "Do you hear anything?"

Diana cocked her neat little head on one side and listened intently.

"Not a thing," she said at last.

"Neither do I—now," replied Rose solemnly. "But I could swear I heard a footstep on the gravel outside a moment ago."

"You're imagining things," smiled Diana affectionately.

"Maybe," was Rose's cryptic reply.

She shivered.

"I don't like this," she said again.

CHAPTER 2

There was a discreet knock on the door and they heard Joe's voice calling: "Are you decent, girls?"

"Just a minute," replied Diana hastily. She quickly stripped off her wet stockings and replaced them with dry ones from her suitcase; she stepped into a blue serge skirt and drew a closefitting pullover over her head. By this time Rose was also respectably clad.

"Alright, Joe. You can come in now," she cried.

Joe entered the room carrying a tray laden with an interesting assortment of cold food, a pot of coffee, cups and saucers, plates knives and forks, a bottle of whisky—and one glass. A length of stout cord was coiled over one arm. He had changed into baggy flannel trousers and a shabby tweed jacket.

"I've been exploring, girls," he said cheerfully. "And I only wish I'd known ten years ago that an explorer's life could be such fun. I'd never have become an actor."

He placed the tray on a long table in the centre of the room.

"Make yourself useful, Rose," he said, tossing the length of cord to his wife. "Tie that cord along the mantlepiece and we can hang our clothes to dry on it."

Diana was investigating the tray.

"Mm! Chicken!" she exclaimed. "Salmon sandwiches! Pickles! Assorted biscuits! It's a feast! Joe, you deserve a medal!"

Joe picked up the bottle of whisky and patted it affectionately. With tender care he poured a generous amount into the glass and diluted it slightly—very slightly—with soda-water.

"When we return to civilization," he said, holding the glass to the light and gazing into its amber depths with immense satisfaction, "and reporters ask me how I contrived to survive the hardships and perils of the wilds of Norfolk, my answer will not be 'chicken' or 'salmon sandwiches', or 'pickles', nor yet 'assorted biscuits'. They must have known I was coming," he added reflectively, raising his elbow and tilting his head backward. "This is my favourite blend."

There was a musical gurgle, then a sigh of contentment from Joe. He smacked his lips appreciatively. Rose looked up from the fireplace where she was draping their wet clothes.

"The mess we're in won't be improved by your becoming blotto," she said severely.

"No," said Joe gloomily. "I suppose not."

When they were seated about the fireplace, eating the appetising food, and drinking the life-giving hot coffee, Joe remembered another discovery which he had made. He produced it; a week-old copy of a London morning paper.

"Listen to this," he said "I'll skip the headlines and get into the story. It's going to interest you."

"The mysterious disappearance of Sir Mortimer Channing from his country house, The Grove, Norfolk, three days ago is still unexplained, and the police frankly confess that they are completely baffled by the affair. There is a total absence of clues to the means of the disappearance, or the reason for it. It is rumoured, however, that the view held in official circles is that Sir Mortimer has absented himself voluntarily for reasons of his own. Why he should wilfully disappear without explanation to his solicitors or his servants is not readily understandable, but in the absence of any indications of a violent abduction, the theory is not feasible.

"It will be remembered that in the evening on which he was first reported missing, Sir Mortimer informed his butler that he was going for a walk. He set out down the driveway of his house, hatless, clad in brown tweed lounge suit and carrying a stout ash-plant. Alarmed by his master's lengthy absence, John Hobbs, the butler, communicated with the police, who shortly arrived to investigate. They found traces of Sir Mortimer's footprints on the gravel of the drive and on the narrow lane directly in front of the gates of the house, but there the trail ceased. There were distinct tyre-marks on the muddy road and it was surmised that Sir Mortimer must have been picked up at the gates of his house by a motorcar. If this is so, it lends colour to the theory that the baronet disappeared of his own volition, for Sir Mortimer was a powerful man and, armed with a stout stick, it would have been no easy matter to abduct him against his will without at least leaving obvious traces of a struggle. There was no evidence of anything of the sort.

"It is expected that Mr. Malcolm Channing, Sir Mortimer's cousin, will take charge of the missing baronet's affairs on his return from a lengthy sojourn abroad, which is expected shortly."

The actor finished reading and cast a shrewd, whimsical glance at his wife and Diana, who were both looking more than a little alarmed.

"Now we understand why our host is so remiss as to leave us to shift for ourselves," he said with a grin. "He is unavoidably detained elsewhere."

"Don't be a clown, Joe," retorted Rose. "I don't like this. I felt in my bones that there was something wrong the moment I put foot in this house. I had a feeling—"

"Yeh, you're funny that way," agreed Joe. But why worry? Even if the 'goblins' have got the good Sir Mortimer, that doesn't mean that they're going to get us. Besides we'll sheer off first thing in the morning. 'When the rosy fingers of the dawn first tinge the morning sky'—" he broke off abruptly as he saw Diana preparing to launch a cushion at his head. "If we can't get the old 'bus to start, we'll walk."

"I don't like this," reiterated Rose for the fourth or fifth time.

"Aw, change the record," was her husband's ungracious retort.

"People have been put in prison for a lot less than we've done tonight," Rose pointed out.

"We won't wait to be put in prison," interjected Diana with a laugh. "In the morning we'll leave money for the window Joe broke and the food we've consumed, and make our—our getaway—isn't that the correct expression?"

She had thoroughly enjoyed her meal and was feeling relaxed by the warmth of the fire and the comfort of the padded armchair in which she sat. Fumbling in a pocket of her skirt she produced jade cigarette case and extended it toward her companions. They both refused. Rose because she was in a restless mood; Joe because he preferred his pipe. He tossed his matchbox to Diana, who caught it dexterously.

She struck a match and was about to light her cigarette at its flame when it flickered and went out. With an exclamation of annoyance, she turned her head to investigate the source of the draught.

Her eyes suddenly widened with alarm and she sprang to her feet. "Look!" she gasped, pointing to the French windows.

One of the windows was slightly ajar and a large hand was holding it to prevent it from swinging open wider. At the girl's exclamation the hand disappeared and the window swung into the room admitting a gust of wind and rain. There was a crash of shattered glass as one of its panels broke. They had brief glimpse of a burly figure disappearing into the night. Running footsteps sounded on the gravel path outside.

Joe ran to the window and looked out, but the darkness was impenetrable at a few yards distance. He shut and locked the window and walked back to the fire with a serious expression on his face.

"Lord knows how long he's been listening," he said. "At least he's bound to know that we've no right to be here. He must have heard that much."

"Do you suppose he'll tell the police?"

Joe shook his head. "Not he. If he'd had legitimate business here, he'd have come in and ordered us out. You can bet he wasn't up to any good himself, or he wouldn't have been skulking in the garden after midnight on a night like this."

"Why don't you go after him and find out who he is?" demanded Rose.

"And play hide-and-seek with him in the rain? And get a crack on the head for my trouble if I caught him?"

He glanced from Rose to Diana. "I had intended to go upstairs and select a couple of bedrooms for us to sleep in comfort," he added. "But we'll wash out that plan. We'll all camp in here for the night."

"Then you think there is danger?" asked Diana, looking anxiously at his face.

There was a brief pause before he answered. "I think that if 'official circles' knew about that johnny they wouldn't be so sure that Sir Mortimer disappeared of his own free will," he declared grimly.

"Joe," Rose gulped hastily. "Joe, we've got to get out of here! I don't like this."

"Forget it, darling," Joe's voice was weary. "How can we leave now in the wind and rain with the car crocked up? We'll get out early in the morning."

Rose looked about her fearfully as though she expected to see a lurking figure in every corner. She shivered. "If you leave me for a moment until daylight, Joe Carey, I'll scream!" she declared.

"I'll hold your hand all night," promised Joe hastily. "When you start screaming, you'd give a wooden image a headache!"

They settled down beside the fire again, but huddled together closer than before. They shared a feeling of something dark, sinister, foreboding, that seemed to hang over the house. The conversation dwindled. When one spoke, the others started at the sound. They had reached an unhealthy—but natural—state of fear. And yet there was no definite menace of which to be afraid.

Suddenly a bell shrilled a peremptory summons which echoed through the house. They rose to their feet simultaneously and stood looking at each other uncertainly. Rose Carey grasped her husband's arm in a grip that hurt. She was trembling from head to foot.

"It's the front door bell," said Joe mechanically.

"Don't answer it, Joe! Don't answer it! Let it ring!"

He patted her shoulder reassuringly. "Now, now, darling! What are you afraid of?"

"I don't know, Joe. I don't know," her lower lip quivered. "All I know is, I'm scared to death, and I don't want you answering that bell."

Once more the imperative summons shrilled through the house.

"Let it ring, Joe," whispered Rose again.

Diana took the older woman's arm and pressed it gently.

"Brace up, Rose," she said. "We're letting our nerves run away with us. We're imagining bogies where none exist."

"That's right, darling," agreed Joe. "Take a pull at yourself, old girl. You've usually got sufficient nerve for six."

With an effort, Rose forced a smile and relinquished her grip on her husband's arm.

"If you don't want Joe going into danger," added Diana, "we'll go with him and look after him."

Like three ghosts they slipped noiselessly into the hall and turned on the hall lights. Rose in the middle with one hand on

Joe's arm and the other on Diana's, they tiptoed to the front door and listened. They could hear nothing—and the ringing had ceased.

"There's nobody there," breathed Rose, with a sigh of relief.

"Better make sure," said Joe manfully.

He threw open the door and peeped out. The others looked over his shoulder with wide eyes. Then they laughed with relief.

"There's nobody there!" repeated Rose.

Joe stooped and picked up something from the floor of the porch. A piece of white paper with a few lines of pencilled writing scrawled upon it. He shut the front door and held the paper up to the light.

"This place is unhealthy for Nosy Parkers," he read aloud. "If you don't want trouble, get out at once. You've got half an hour to clear. After that, look out for fireworks."

The storm outside seemed to increase in fury. A gale if wind raged about the house, rattling the windows and screaming down the chimneys. Beneath the high-pitched wail of the wind, they could hear the rain pattering on the window-panes.

"Joe!" cried Rose. "Let's leave this awful place at once! I'm frightened, I tell you. I'm frightened!"

Joe shook his head. "We'll take a chance on the fireworks, Rose. We're not going out into that. I don't think…"

He never finished the sentence, for just then another bell began to ring. Three pairs of startled eyes turned automatically to a telephone which was standing on a table at the rear of the hall.

CHAPTER 3

There was a long pause while they stood stock still, grouped uncertainly beside the front door with their eyes on the telephone receiver which seemed, somehow, to suggest a new menace. Low, shrill and insistent, the bell clamoured to be answered.

"Well," said Joe, "a telephone can't hurt us."

"No-n-n-no," agreed Rose hesitantly.

"Of course not," said Diana. "Joe, will you answer it—or shall I?"

"I suppose—I suppose we must answer it?" asked Rose fearfully.

"Why not, darling?" responded Joe cheerfully. "We can't let it ring all night. Brace up, old girl. There's nothing to be scared of in a telephone."

He walked briskly across the hall and picked up the receiver. Rose flew after him as though she were afraid to let him go beyond reach of her arm.

"Hello…" There was a pause, then Joe covered the mouthpiece with his hand and turned to the two women.

"It's a man," he whispered. "He wants to know if I'm Hobbs."

"Who's Hobbs?" asked Rose anxiously.

"The butler," Joe replied.

"Tell him yes," counselled Diana.

Joe turned back to the telephone.

"Yes, this is Hobbs. What's that? Oh, Mr. Bland, Sir Mortimer's solicitor? Yes. Yes. I see. Very well, sir. I beg your pardon? I didn't catch that last remark, sir."

He jiggled the hook impatiently.

"Are you there, Mr. Bland? Operator…operator…"

He replaced the receiver on the hook and turned away with a shrug of his shoulders.

"The wire's gone dead," he said.

"What did he say?" demanded Rose at his elbow.

"Let's go back into the warm room and I'll tell you all about it."

They returned to the big, cheerful living-room and Rose and Diana dropped gratefully into their comfortable armchairs. Joe helped himself to a stiff glass of whisky before following suit. His face, as he poured the drink behind their backs was sober and grave.

"We've got to think fast, girls," he said, dropping into the third chair beside the fire with his half-empty glass in his hand. "That was Sir Mortimer's solicitor, 'phoning from his house at Norwich. Sir Mortimer's cousin, Mr. Malcolm Channing, has turned up unexpectedly and is coming here. You know what that means—at the best he'll probably turn us out into the rain. At the worst, he might call the police and make things hot for us. We've made ourselves pretty free of the house, you know. Not to mention the broken window in the scullery."

"But we can explain—" began Diana.

"It is only ten days since the mysterious disappearance of his cousin," Joe pointed out grimly. "When he finds three strangers in the house, he may not be in the mood to listen to explanations."

They bit on that and found it not at all to their liking. To be turned out in the rain would be almost as bad as to be turned over to the police.

"Whatever happens," added Joe, "we won't leave this house of our own accord. And it'll take more than one man to turn us out. We're safe here—from the storm, at least."

Rose shivered as she remembered the man—or men—who might even now be lurking in the garden. On consideration she found that she did not care to face the unknown dangers outside the house. At least there was no lack of lights inside.

"I suggest that we open that letter," put in Diana, pointing to the envelope on the mantlepiece.

"Think so?" Joe glanced sharply at her.

"Certainly. I admit that opening a man's private letter is a bit thick, but now that we're in this mess up to the neck we might as well go the whole hog. It's pretty certain that the letter was written by the person who was in the house today and it may give us information that will help us."

Joe glanced at Rose. "What do you say, darling?"

"Diana's right."

"We're all agreed, then. But we mustn't do it clumsily. We must be able to seal it again as though it hadn't been tampered with. Rose, you remember when you suspected me of an affair with that peroxide blonde at Blackpool? You used to open my letters then and seal them up again."

Rose blushed hotly. "Why, Joe Carey! How dare you suggest such a thing! I never did—"

Joe waved his arms complacently. "Yes, you did, Rose, but you didn't think I knew it! This is not the time for arguing, Rose. Do you think you could open this letter neatly?"

She nodded, without meeting his eyes, which were full of dry amusement. "I'll need some boiling water."

With the aid of a steaming kettle, she had the envelope open in a few minutes. Joe extracted the folded half-sheet of notepaper which it contained.

Dear Sir (began the note),

We are apprised by your solicitors that you will arrive here within a few days and regret we will not be present to receive you. Since the disappearance of our master, Sir Mortimer, strange things have been happening in and about this house, and we frankly do not care to remain in it any longer. We regret the inconvenience you will be caused by the lack of servants, and trust that our places will soon be satisfactorily filled. We realise, of course, that by leaving without notice we are forfeiting a month's wages, but are agreed that no other step is possible. If you will not regard it as an impertinence, we would wish to warn you that there is something very odd about this house.

Yours respectfully,

John Hobbs, Martha Cole, Sophy Harding.

When he had finished reading the brief letter aloud, Joe looked up with a grin. "I'll bet the butler wrote it," he said. "The scholarly language is a bit above the level of Martha Cole, who sounds like a cook, or Sophy Harding, whom I imagine to be an apple-cheeked—and unsophisticated—housemaid.

Diana uttered a sudden exclamation. "Joe! Do you think—"

Rose had been smitten with the same idea. "The parts are made for us!" she declared. "I can play the cook to perfection; Diana can be the apple-cheeked housemaid and you can be the scholarly John Hobbs!"

Joe stroked his chin doubtfully. "Perhaps Malcolm Channing knows his cousin's servants," he pointed out.

"The paper said he had been abroad for a long time," protested Diana. "And servants never stay a long time nowadays."

"It's our only chance," urged Rose. "He can't turn his cook, housemaid and butler out of doors."

"O.K.," said Joe laconically, putting the letter in his pocket. "But if we land ourselves in a worse mess that ever, don't say I didn't warn you. Rose, you stay here beside the fire while Diana and I forage in the kitchen for props."

Rose didn't relish being left alone, but she forced herself to smile bravely and agree.

In the kitchen, Joe took Diana's arm and whispered hurriedly in her ear. "I didn't want to say so in front of Rose," he said, "but someone cut the wire while I was talking on the telephone to Sir Mortimer's solicitor. We weren't cut off by the Exchange— the line suddenly went dead in the middle of a sentence. I'm certain it was cut."

Diana looked at him anxiously. "Then you think there really is a danger?"

"I don't know. I'm deuced glad this fellow Channing is turning up. Perhaps when the blighters who cut the wire see the car arriving, they'll think better of it and make themselves scarce. But I don't know. I've a hunch we're in for—fireworks."

His forehead was creased by a worried frown. "This much is certain, we're going to get out of here first thing in the morning. With the coming of dawn, we go."

Diana giggled. "What a shock for Mr. Malcolm Channing when he wakes up and finds the servants gone and the house empty!" she said. "I hope he can make coffee and boil eggs!"

"We'll let him worry about that!" declared Joe.

Within fifteen minutes the Careys and Diana were made up for the parts they were to play. They were all experienced troupers and almost uncannily clever at improvising costumes. Joe had an old dress-suit in his bag and a pair of false side-whiskers completed his disguise. Diana found a cap and apron in the kitchen which, worn over a dark dress, made her an exceedingly attractive—if not quite unsophisticated—housemaid. Rose looked as though she had been bending over a kitchen range for at least twenty years of her life. At the last moment Joe held a dress rehearsal.

"We'll do," he decided at last. "After all, it's for one performance only. When the curtain rises the following morning, we exit—rapidly!"

Almost at once their cue came. Peering out of the window, Joe saw powerful head-lights coming along the road and swing into the drive. A new note mingled with the wild noises of the storm; the crushing of gravel on the drive as a large car purred up to the door.

Looking into the living-room to make sure that everything was in order, Joe swore suddenly. Their wet clothes were still draped artistically along the mantlepiece! Rose was just in time to strip them down and scamper to the kitchen with them when the bell rang.

Joe coughed nervously, shot his cuffs and proceeded majestically to the front door, opening it with a stately dignity which might well have provoked a pang of envy in the bosom of the real John Hobbs. Diana faltered a pace or two behind them. Rose's head peered furtively from the shelter of the half-closed kitchen door.

On the porch stood a tall man with broad shoulders who was carrying a suitcase in one hand. Young; he could not have been more than twenty-six or seven. He had a good nose and mouth and his blue eyes were handsome and friendly, but his jaw, smooth, wide and massive, while endowing his face with character, was too dominant a feature for good looks. When he smiled, as he did now, he was exceedingly attractive. His face was bronzed almost to the colour of mahogany.

Stepping in briskly, he placed his suitcase on the floor. "I'm Malcolm Channing," he said. "I suppose you're Hobbs?"

Joe bowed stiffly.

"I've left my car in front," Channing continued. "It can stay there all night. I'm too fagged to put it in the garage."

His eyes travelled past Joe, came to rest on Diana and lit up with admiration. For a moment he stood staring at her almost rudely, then he turned to Joe.

"I say," he said brusquely. "It wasn't necessary to rouse the whole household, you know. I'm not as inconsiderate as all that. I'm only sorry I had to get you out of bed at this hour, but I wanted to be here as soon as possible."

"We thought you might like something to eat, sir."

"No." Channing shook his head. "I won't trouble you to that extent. I should like a drink, though. I've had a cold drive."

Joe inclined himself from the waist respectfully. "There is a whisky-and-soda in the living-room, sir," he replied, with a faint gleam in his eyes. "I'll bring a glass." With a wave of his hand, he indicated the living-room door.

"Thanks." Channing cast another admiring glance at Diana, then went into the living-room.

"Leave my suitcase there for the present," he added. "You can take it up when you show me my room."

Diana and Joe went into the kitchen. Joe found a clean glass and hurried through to the living-room with it, then returned and closed the kitchen door carefully.

"Well, girls," he said. "What do you think of the new master?"

"A good-looking, but rather chinny young man," pronounced Rose.

"He looks rather a decent sort," declared Diana. "I feel heartily ashamed of the deception we're practising on him. Can't we make a clean breast of the whole affair and trust him not to make trouble for us?"

Joe looked doubtful. "Do you think it would be safe?"

"I think we should," said Diana. "He looks as though he'd take it in the proper spirit."

"Rose?"

Rose shrugged her shoulders. "Just as you think. I don't mind."

"Very well, then, we will." He hesitated. "Not that I like the job."

"I'll do it," offered Diana.

"No," protested Joe. "It's up to me."

"Don't be silly," retorted Diana. "After all, isn't he more likely to see the joke if I tell him? Men aren't usually awkward over trifles when they're approached by a girl. Besides, I can turn on the tears if he's inclined to be harsh."

"O.K., said Joe. "Beauty before brains. My tears would only get us all three months hard!"

Framing a tactful little speech in her mind, Diana went to the door of the living-room. Feeling suddenly very bashful, she knocked timidly. There was answer and she knocked again.

The door opened and Channing stood on the threshold. His eyes lit up when he saw her and he moved forward as though hypnotised. With a queer little sigh, he put out his arms and drew her to him, holding her in a firm embrace. His lips found hers and lingered on them, long and ardently.

For a moments Diana was lost in the bliss of the first real kiss she had ever experienced. Then she tore herself from his grasp, her eyes flaming with indignation.

"You cad!" she cried. "You utter cad!"

There was a resounding smack as the palm of her hand struck his face, then she turned and ran down the hall to the kitchen.

CHAPTER 4

"The rotter!" exclaimed Rose indignantly, when Diana bolted into the kitchen and told her friends what had happened. "I'd like to give him a piece of my mind."

Joe's face was grim. "I'm going in there to knock his block off!" he declared. "If he thinks he can insult you like that, Diana. He's making the mistake of a lifetime. I'll tear him apart, the lousy cad!"

He started for the door, but Diana caught his arm and held him back. "You're a sweet thing, Joe," she said affectionately. "But he's head and shoulders taller than you. He could give you three or four stones in weight."

"That's right," agreed Rose. "I'm proud of you for thinking of it, Joe. I didn't think you had it in you. But what's the use of you getting pounded to a jelly by that big egg, even if he has kissed Diana? A kiss wears off quicker than a black eye."

Joe rubbed his chin reflectively. "There's something in that," he admitted.

"What beasts some men are," said Diana bitterly. "Because he thought I was a servant he imagined he could go as far as he liked. I suppose he thinks I should be flattered by his attentions. Ugh!" She rubbed her lips vigorously.

"And yet he didn't look a bad sort," murmured Rose.

Diana caught the older woman's eye and blushed. It was true that she had been attracted at first sight by Malcolm Channing's appearance. He had looked so strong and clean and manly. Oh, well!

"You can't always judge by appearances," she said.

"I gather we continue to deceive this gentleman?" put in Joe.

"We certainly do," agreed Rose. "And what's more, I hope

the guys that got his cousin get him. He'll be no loss."

"Shouldn't we tell him about the man who was skulking in the garden?" suggested Diana. "And the warning note?"

"Let him find out for himself," retorted Joe. "We'll lock ourselves in a couple of bedrooms upstairs, then if the fireworks start, we'll be out of the way. Let Channing play Guy Fawkes."

Diana looked doubtful. "What if he gets hurt?" she faltered.

"It'll serve him right!" snapped Rose.

The bell from the living-room rang at that moment. Joe started up to answer it, then checked himself.

"Let him ring," he said. "We're going to bed. Holy Moses! It's after one. There ought to be trade union hours for servants!"

The back stairs started in a corridor leading from the kitchen door. They turned out the kitchen light and tiptoed noiselessly up the stairs. As silently as mice they flitted along the first-floor landing and opened a door at random. Joe switched on a light which revealed a large bedroom, in the centre of which stood a double bed made up ready for occupancy with a thick eiderdown spread over the blankets and sheets.

Rose sank down on it with a sigh. "This is heaven!" she said, closing her eyes.

"You two bunk together here for the night," remarked Joe. "I'll go and sleep in the next room."

"No, you don't!" retorted Rose, springing to her feet again. "You don't leave me, Joe Carey! Not on your life! There's no saying what might happen before the night's over."

Joe sighed. "Alright," he agreed wearily. "We'll all park in here. It means sitting up for the rest of the night, or course, but that's a detail."

"That's the worst idea you've had so far," said Diana. "I'm one little girl who wants a few hours sleep before the coming of the dawn. You two can stay here and protect each other from bogies, but I'm going next door. And let me tell you, the fireworks that waken me will be record-breakers for noise!"

"Are you sure you'll be alright?" sked Joe uncertainly.

"Quite sure. If I should need help, I'll knock on the wall." She went to the door. "Good night," she said.

The next moment she was gone. They heard her opening a door and turning on a light.

"We shouldn't have let her go," said Rose. "I don't like her being alone. There's something sinister about this house."

"Oh, Diana's alright. She's a plucky kid," replied Joe, but his tone, too, was doubtful.

The room next door was similar to the one in which Diana had left the Careys. She locked the door, switched off the light and laid herself on the bed without undressing. It was a relief to relax. She pulled the quilt over her, closed her eyes and tried to compose herself to sleep. Perhaps she was too tired to sleep, or perhaps her mind was too occupied with the peculiar happenings of the past hour or so—at all events, sleep evaded her. In a few minutes her eyes flickered open and she raised herself on one elbow.

She was thinking of Malcolm Channing. Thinking of him half resentfully, half regretfully. She resented the insult he had offered her. It was a caddish thing to do even if he thought she was a servant—or rather, especially if he thought she was servant. And yet, he didn't look the sort of man who would take a mean advantage of a defenceless girl—a housemaid in his cousin's employment. That kiss… It still burned on her lips. At the time it had seemed that her very soul was being drawn from her body. For an ecstatic moment she had yielded blissfully in his arms.

Diana sighed. It would have been so wonderful to be kissed like that if they had known each other for a time and were in love. But under the circumstances in which it had been given, it had been a caddish insult. They had met for the first time and he had regarded her as merely a pretty housemaid, to be kissed and forgotten. Well, he should have kissed her lightly, so that she, too, might forget. That kiss would linger in her memory forever. It seemed that it had bruised her heart.

"I hate him!" she murmured resentfully. "I hate him!"

But her tone lacked conviction. She knew in her innermost heart that she was hurt rather than offended. Sleep was no nearer, so she slipped out of bed and padded softly to the window. The storm had abated and a pale glimmer of moonlight relieved the darkness of the garden.

Suddenly she peered out into the night, her eyes focused on the dark, vague outline of a bush on the lawn. Surely it had moved slightly—or something had stirred within it!

She had not been mistaken. For a moment a white patch showed above the bush, like a handkerchief—or a pale face! It disappeared again, then the branches stirred once more and a dim shape slipped away into the night.

The sight frightened her. Her own breathing began to sound loudly in her ears. She could hear her heart pounding like the blows of a sledgehammer. The room seemed to be filled with the noise of it. She felt a sudden impulse to run from the room, but her feet would not move. They felt numb and heavy as lead. Her scalp prickled, as though with the touch of icy fingers. Her eyes were riveted, wide and staring, on the dark shape of the bush where the sinister figure had been lurking.

"This won't do! She rebuked herself. "I'm letting my nerves get the better of me."

Going back to bed, she sat down and tried to compose herself. Should she go into the next room and tell Joe and Rose what she had seen? Throw in the sponge and stay with them for the rest of the night?

No, she couldn't do that. For one thing, Rose was frightened enough, already, without being scared afresh. For another, she couldn't go back on her words and confess that she herself was frightened. Frightened? For an awful minute she had known stark terror until her brain had calmed her jangled nerves!

Let them sleep if they can, she decided. But—please God!— let the dawn come soon!

A stair creaked and she was at the bedroom door in a flash, listening with an ear pressed close to one of the panels. She heard footsteps on the landing and someone trying the doorhandle of the room in which the Careys were sleeping. Then the footsteps passed on, to halt again outside her own room, and fingers fumbled with the handle of her door. She held her breath, but after a brief pause the person outside moved on. Instinct told her that it was Channing. Surely it could be nobody else. He was probably cursing inwardly the servants who had gone to bed and left him to choose a bedroom for himself.

The footsteps stopped at the third door in the corridor, then she heard Channing—if Channing it was—moving about in the room beyond. A pair of shoes were dropped noisily on the floor, then bedsprings creaked. Evidently Channing, too, was content to go to bed with his clothes on!

Diana tiptoed back and sat again on the edge of the bed, now awake beyond all hope. Minutes passed while she sat there, immobile as an image of stone. The house was quiet with that awe-inspiring hush which comes with the still, small hours of the morning. The subdued whine of the dying wind sounded like a funeral dirge. Occasionally a fitful spasm of rain spattered the windowpane with drops as though a giant, tired of his play, were tossing abroad his last handfuls of water.

A clock downstairs mournfully chimed half-past one.

She was stretching herself with a yawn when a faint sound

made her sit up rigidly, her muscles tensed, listening intently. It came again, low and muffled, but this time there was no mistaking it.

Someone was breaking into the house!

Before she could decide how to act, she heard a creaking of bedsprings from the room in which Channing had retired, his muffled footsteps on the floor, then his door opening gently. He padded along the corridor and down the stairs.

It was obvious that he had also heard the intruder, but he had no reason to suspect the menace that awaited him below. If she had only warned him! About the man who had been listening at the French windows; the threatening note; the severed telephone wire; the man who had been lurking, a few minutes ago, behind a bush in the garden! Channing was going downstairs to God knew what lurking danger!

Without hesitation she slipped across the room, unlocked the door, and hurried out to the landing, depressed the switch that flooded the stairs with light and ran down headlong.

She was too late!

Already the mysterious intruder and Channing had met. As she reached the ground floor, she heard a shot fired in the direction of the kitchen, then sounds of a furious struggle. There was a thud as the kitchen table went over; a tinkle of glass; the crash of broken crockery!

To and fro two determined men were battling, smashing everything flimsy which came in their way. Diana heard the grunts and gasps which follow the sharp impact of fist upon flesh; the wheezing of a choking man with an adversary's thumb on his windpipe.

Disregarding personal danger, she ran to the kitchen and turned on the light. As she did so, Channing tripped over a capsized chair and fell backwards heavily. The man he had been fighting backed away, a blunt-nosed automatic gleaming evilly in his hand.

The newcomer was short and burly. He wore a dark grey suit which was spattered with blood. More blood streamed from his pulped nose. With muttered curse he spat out a tooth through bruised, puffy lips.

Channing, too, had suffered damage in the fight. One of his eyes was closed and rapidly colouring. His jacket was ripped from the neck to the small of his back, and the buttons from it were scattered over the floor. He picked himself up slowly, keeping a wary eye on the other man.

"Who the devil are you?" he demanded. "And what's the meaning of this?"

The other levelled his automatic significantly. "Don't move," he said. "I've got you covered. Name's Channing, eh?"

"That's right, Malcolm Channing. And let me tell you—"

The short burly man waved his arm irritably.

"That'll keep," he snapped. "My name's Bellow, Mister Channing. Detective-Sergeant Bellow, of Scotland Yard. And I arrest you for the murder of your cousin, Sir Mortimer Channing!"

CHAPTER 5

The kitchen was like a shambles. The floor was carpeted in splintered wood and shattered crockery and glass. In a daze, Diana stooped and picked up a single broken plate and placed it mechanically on the dresser. The eyes of the short, burly man flickered in her direction as she advanced into the room, but he kept his weapon trained unswervingly on Channing.

"I arrest you for the murder of Sir Mortimer Channing," he repeated in a cold harsh tone.

Malcolm Channing laughed oddly and passed a bruised hand over his damp forehead, brushing back his disordered hair.

"What utter rot!" he retorted. "Why, I wasn't even in the country when he disappeared!"

"That'll keep!" said the man with the automatic grimly. "The less you say now the better!"

Channing laughed again. "You haven't warned me that anything I say will be taken down and used in evidence against me. Isn't that usual?"

The others eyes glowed angrily. "I don't want any more of your lip," he snapped.

His eyes roved about the room—but the automatic did not waver, and his finger was crooked threateningly against the trigger. With his free hand he pointed to one of the overturned kitchen chairs.

"Pick that up," he growled, "and sit down." He watched suspiciously while Channing complied.

"Put your hands behind you and between the back spokes of the chair," he said, when Channing was seated. "That's right."

Producing a set of handcuffs, he tossed them to Diana. "Just click these over his wrists, miss," he said. "They'll lock automatically."

Diana obeyed, moving mechanically, as though she were sleepwalking. There was something unreal about the whole scene.

"I say!" protested Channing. "This is a damned uncomfortable position!"

The other man chuckled. "You'll be more uncomfortable before I've finished," he retorted. "I'm not taking any chances of your escaping."

Kneeling down with his automatic close at hand on the floor beside him, he drew Channing's ankles back and hitched the toecaps of his shoes to a crossbar beneath the seat of the chair. With another set of handcuffs, he fastened them there securely. With his arms behind him and his legs from the knee downward doubled under him, Channing was trussed as securely and uncomfortably as possible!"

Straightening up, the short burly man glanced about the room.

"Where are the vegetables kept?" he asked Diana.

The girl stared at him. The question seemed so out of place, so absurd.

"Don't stand there looking at me!" he snapped. "Fetch a potato, or a small onion!"

She delved into a cupboard and produced a medium-sized potato, liberally coated with mud. He took it from her and turned to Channing. "Open your mouth!" he commanded.

"I'm hanged if I will!" hissed Channing through his teeth.

"Open your mouth!"

"You go to hell!"

Drawing back his fist, the short, burly man drove it with considerable force into the pit of his captive's stomach. Channing collapsed with a groan—his face ashen-grey, his head lolling to one side.

The man who called himself 'Detective Sergeant Bellow, of Scotland Yard' prised apart the unconscious man's jaws and inserted the potato. Producing a large coloured handkerchief, he folded it and bound it across Channing's mouth, tying it at the back of his head.

Diana caught his arm and shook it savagely. "You brute!" she cried. "There was no need to do that to him!"

The man thrust his bullet-shaped head forward, his chin jutting out belligerently, his lips curled back from his teeth, his eyes narrowing unpleasantly.

"Think not?" he sneered. "Well let me tell you, I don't want any interference from you. This fellow's a murderer—a lousy murderer, d'you hear?—and I'll treat him as I see fit. Watch your step, see, or I'll run you in for obstructing an officer in the execution of his duty!"

There was no mistaking the menace in his eyes and in the deep growl of his voice. Diana backed away in sudden fright. He followed her swiftly and caught her arm.

"Now we'll take a look round upstairs, you and I," he said. "Lead the way, sister, and mind your step."

They went out of the kitchen, she in advance, he following with one hand on her wrist, and in the other, the long, blue-nosed automatic. At the head of the first flight of stairs the man noticed a door. He opened it, revealing an empty cupboard. Nodding his head significantly, he turned to Diana.

"Where are the other servants?" he demanded.

There was no need for the girl to answer, for the door of the bedroom of which her companions had taken possession opened and Joe and Rose appeared on the threshold. Rose was holding her husband's arm with both hands. Her face was like a mask of ivory-coloured wax with fright.

"What's up?" asked Joe the moment his eyes fell on Diana. "I heard a noise, but Rose wouldn't let me out of her sight. It sounded as though someone was being kill—"

He drew his breath sharply as his eyes, travelling beyond Diana, rested on the man who stood a pace behind her. He was not a reassuring sight, with his blood-splashed suit, swelling nose, encrusted with blood, and bruised lips.

Rose, peeping over Joe's shoulder, uttered a scream and shrank back.

"Keep that woman quiet!" snarled the man with the automatic.

"Hush, darling, hush. Making a noise won't help a bit," whispered Joe to his wife. Squaring his shoulders manfully, he glared at the other man. "Who the dickens are you, anyway?"

"Detective Sergeant Bellow of Scotland Yard."

Joe breathed more easily. "That's a relief! I thought you were—"

The other curled his lip scornfully. "Never mind who or what you thought I was. Step lively; walk down the corridor and stop when I tell you."

Rose drew back, dragging at Joe's arm. "Joe, I don't like this! I'm afraid of that man!"

"Shut up!" snapped the short, burly man.

Joe glared at him. "Even if you are a detective," he retorted, "you can't speak to my wife like that!"

"I can't, eh!" He came forward slowly, menacingly, and jabbed the nose of the automatic against Joe's ribs. "Listen and learn something. I'm in charge here, and what I say goes. When I tell you to walk, you walk—and do it quick!" His eyes glowered on Rose. "If you want this man of yours to keep his whole skin, keep your trap shut—tight! Now—walk!"

Without another word, Joe and Rose stumbled along the corridor in front of him. They reached the cupboard and their captor threw the door open and motioned them inside.

"It's a tight fit," he chuckled sardonically. "But a loving couple like you won't mind that!"

"Look here—" began Joe hotly.

There was an unpleasant light in the other's eyes and his finger tightened on the trigger of his automatic. "Inside!"

There was no mistaking the threat in his tone. They huddled together in the cupboard. The door slammed upon them. Their captor locked it and put the key in his pocket.

"Pity there was just room for two," he leered at Diana. "I'll have to find somewhere else for you."

She shrank from him, her eyes flooded with fear and suspicion.

"You're not a detective!" she declared suddenly. "You're a—"

"A crook?" he grinned. "Taken you a long time to get wise, hasn't it? If you'd had your wits about you, you'd have known from the start that I wasn't no Scotland Yard man."

He was surprised to see the relief which shone in her eyes.

"Then it was all a fraud?" she breathed shakily. "Mr. Channing isn't a—a murderer?"

He laughed derisively. "So that's the way the land lies? In love with him, are you?"

Her cheeks flamed. "I'm not!" she declared vehemently. "I'm not!"

"Oh, no, I guess not!" he mocked. "Say, sister, you wouldn't be so delighted to find out that Channing's as innocent as a newborn babe if you didn't love him. Gosh, though, you're a fast worker, aren't you? Or did you know him before?"

"You're quite wrong, I tell you!" snapped Diana indignantly.

"Well, I've got not time to argue," responded her captor. "Now, where am I going to stow you?"

His eyes travelled along the corridor, resting in turn on each of the doors which flanked it.

"What a lot of trouble you folks would have saved yourselves and me if you'd only got out when I warned you," he growled.

"Then it was you who left the note on the doorstep?"

He nodded. "Yes, it was me. H'm. I guess I'd better tie you up and leave you in one of the bedrooms for the present."

Diana's brain was working rapidly. "Look!" she cried suddenly, pointing to the head of the stairs.

The man wheeled rapidly with his automatic levelled and peered in the direction her finger indicated.

"What?" he grunted. "I don't see anything."

"A face!" she gasped. "Looking up at us!"

Cautiously the man with the automatic crept to the head of the stairs and looked down. Diana placed her knee in the small of his back and pushed, exerting all the force of which she was capable. He lost his balance and fell forward, throwing up his arms with a wild yell. Thump! Thump! Thump! His heavy body rolled over and over down the stairs.

Diana ran swiftly into one of the bedrooms. She opened the window and looked out. A drainpipe hugged the wall a foot from the windowsill. She slipped through the window and climbed down into the garden.

CHAPTER 6

Stooping close to the ground, Diana ran for the shelter of a mass of foliage which loomed up on the lawn a few yards from where she had reached the ground. The wind had died, but a cold rain continued to fall and the low, rambling house behind her looked ghostly in the dripping mist. Buried in the heart of a thick bush, she shivered with cold, for the drenched leaves were icy against her face and dripped frigid globules of water down her neck.

Climbing through the window she had dimly heard a horrible shout of wrath from the depths of the house which had chilled her blood and made her realise that to fall again into the hands of the man she had sent hurtling down the stairs would be disastrous. Now she looked up at the window through which she had climbed and saw the pale blur of his face looking from side to side, looking for her.

While the white face was framed in the window she kept very still, hoping that the dense leaves about her would conceal her. Shortly she sighed with relief, for he drew in his head and slammed down the window.

A few moments later the front door opened and he appeared on the porch and peered about him. He was so close now that she could see the cruel, enraged expression on his broad, flat face, but his eyes roved over her hiding-place and passed on, looking further afield into the velvet blackness of the night. He walked forward to where the dim shape of Channing's car stood and submitted the interior to a searching scrutiny.

At last, he turned away, and, looking down the gravel drive, uttered a low, shrill whistle. It was answered from a short distance away. He whistled again and approaching footsteps crunched on the gravel. In a few moments another man came out of the gloom, picking his way fastidiously among the puddles that dotted the drive.

The newcomer was an elderly man of medium height and slim build, with a neatly-trimmed iron-grey beard and a close-clipped moustache. His appearance surprised Diana for he was dressed in the sober garb of a professional man—a doctor, or lawyer, possibly—and was quite finicking in the way he minced along, taking care that the muddy drive did not defile his patent leather shoes.

A wing collar…fawn coat…pearl grey fedora…rolled umbrella…such details of his attire as the grey mist permitted Diana to see suggested an afternoon round of calls on respectable patients rather than a nocturnal adventure in a rain-soaked garden.

"O.K., Mr. Chard," said the short, burly man laconically. "The coast is clear."

"For heaven's sake don't use my name here," snapped Chard irritably. "I've told you that before, Mike. I'm too well-known to take risks like that." He glanced about him nervously. "Are you quite sure—"

"Sure, I'm sure," growled Mike. "I've got this fellow Channing trussed up and gagged and two of the fools who breezed in earlier are locked in a cupboard upstairs."

"Two of them?" repeated Chard with a swift glance at Mike. "What about the other?"

"She got away," replied Mike shamefacedly, "but—"

"You fool! You fool!" hissed Chard. "She'll have the whole countryside down on us!"

"Not on your life. She's only a girl. How far do you think she'll get on a night like this? Say, we'll be out of here before she can possibly raise an alarm." He waved an arm toward the house. "Let's go inside, boss. I'm soaked through already."

"And do you think I'm not?" retorted Chard. They went into the house and closed the door.

Diana slipped out of hiding, trembling with the cold, and ran down the drive towards the gates. Suddenly she stopped in her tracks and dived in among the trees which flanked the drive. She had just seen the shape of a man detach itself from the shadows by the gate and look up the drive! He heart missed a beat, but to her relief the man did not come toward her. He stood between the gates for a moment, then stepped back into the shadows.

She had intended to run out into the lane and along it in search of a house of some sort from which she might summon help. Now her plan underwent revision. Running softly among the trees she made her way to the high wall which surrounded the garden. It was too new and smooth to offer a foothold, but in one place a tree, with several conveniently placed branches, leant close to it. With the agility of one in perfect physical trim, she climbed up until she was high enough to put one leg over the wall. About to climb over and drop down on the other side, she noticed another man—a dark coated, slouch-hatted figure, motionless and strangely frightening—leaning against the wall a few yards away. She investigated two other parts of the wall, with similar results. Every twenty yards stood a still, terrifying figure. The place was surrounded!

Something sinister was afoot; something more terrible than her wildest fears. Rose had been right. What could she do? The question seemed to mock her. There was nothing, apparently, which she could do. Scarcely daring to breath, she crept back to the house and tiptoed close to the lighted French windows of the big living-room on the ground floor. A faint murmur of sound came to her—someone was speaking. She put her ear close to the broken pane and listened.

Mike was speaking in an incredulous tone: "Surely even Von Blon won't try it on a night like this, boss? It would be suicide!"

The thin, precise voice of Mr. Chard answered him: "Von Blon will try anything. He hasn't the faintest trace of nerves. I doubt if he knows what fear means. Besides, his ship is the latest and finest that Germany has produced. Even a storm like this will be child's play to him."

"I wouldn't want to be him!" There was a shiver in the short, burly man's voice.

"Mark my words, Mike, by three o'clock Von Blon will be here."

"If you say so—but say—"

"Well?"

"Ain't it dangerous for him to come"—Mike hesitated—"so soon after Sir Mortimer's—er—ah—disappearance?"

"There is a danger, yes," Chard agreed. "But it must be taken. We are desperately in need of this consignment and there is nowhere else to which we could have it delivered. But didn't you tell me that the police stopped nosing about here days ago?"

"That's right, boss, they did. And I've been working ever since, scaring the servants off the premises. Just when I had succeeded, these three fools, the two women and the man, had to blunder in, then Malcolm Channing arrived to make the party complete—but that's all right. I've settled their hash. We've got the house to ourselves. There ain't a soul we need worry about for miles."

"Except the girl got away!" retorted Chard.

"Aw, we can count her out. I'll bet she's sitting under a tree right now crying her eyes out with the rain trickling down her spine. Women are soft, boss."

There was brief pause, then: "Say, boss—" Mike spoke uncertainly.

"Well?"

"What do you reckon happened to Sir Mortimer?"

"The day after he disappeared, I received a note purporting

to come from him," replied Chard. "It said that for imperative reasons of his own he was forced to disappear for a time and that I must collect the next consignment myself. On the other hand—"

"Yes?"

"He disappeared ten days ago. The day after Von Blon delivered the last consignment. He disappeared, Mike, without passing on the consignment to me."

"Then you think he did the dirty? Double-crossed the gang?"

"The consignment was worth five thousand pounds. Sir Mortimer has not been more than one step ahead of his creditors for years. Figure it out for yourself!

"I guess you're right. He made a getaway with the stuff."

Chard's quiet voice spoke again: "There's always a chance that he didn't cheat us. Perhaps there's another reason for his disappearance. He had a finger in more than one pie, you know. Before Von Blon arrives we'll find out."

"How?"

"By finding the stuff, if it's still in the house. If it is, it's hidden in the room. It wouldn't be anywhere else where he couldn't have it constantly under his eye and where the servants might stumble on it. We're ging to tear this room apart, if necessary, and find it if it's here. It might be hidden in that clock for instance, or disguised among the books in the bookcase."

"You mean we're going to smash up the happy home?"

"Yes," said Chard grimly. "That's exactly what I do mean. Five thousand pounds' worth of the stuff is at stake, Mike!"

"Five thousand! Hold on a minute while I get an axe!"

Listening at the window, Diana heard the man called Mike lumbering heavily from the room. Then Chard rose to his feet and moved about, examining the furniture and other effects of the room.

"He was a cute devil…" she heard him mutter. "I wonder where he hid it?"

CHAPTER 7

Diana was in a state of utter bewilderment. 'Five thousand pounds' worth of stuff,' Chard had said. Five thousand pounds! It was a staggering sum to one like Diana, who knew no greater wealth than a single week's salary at a time.

Flattened against the French windows, with her ear to the broken pane, she wondered what could possibly be the nature of 'the stuff'. Chard had said that it might be hidden in the clock, or among the books in the bookcase. That meant that it must be contained in quite a small parcel. Could it be precious stones? Were Chard and the missing Sir Mortimer associated with a gang of jewel smugglers—or jewel thieves? She could imagine nothing else which could be worth so much in such small bulk.

The noise of the living-room door opening and shutting attracted her attention. Mike had returned.

"I found a saw and an axe, boss!" he exclaimed with a tone of gloating in his voice. The destruction he was to wreak in Sir Mortimer Channing's luxuriously-furnished living-room evidently delighted him.

"We won't use them—yet," responded Chard. "We'll examine the smaller objects first, and if we don't find what we're looking for among them we'll take the table and chairs to pieces. You might investigate the contents of the bookcase, Mike."

There was a rumbling noise as the short, burly man emptied one of the shelves by the simple method of scooping its contents to the floor Diana carefully slipped her hand through the broken glass panel of the French window and pulled the curtain aside slightly.

She saw Chard fumbling with the clock, which he had removed from the mantlepiece to the table, while Mike examined the books on the floor, turning them over with his feet and kicking them aside one by one as they were proved to contain nothing more valuable than reading matter.

Shelf after shelf he emptied in this intensely practical manner and then he proceeded to take the bookcase itself to pieces. Chard, having proved the innocence of the clock, started sounding the floor of the room for loose boards.

They would be busy, Diana decided, for a good half-hour at least.

She was soaked through and her clothes were cold to the touch. But she was too excited now to feel uncomfortable. Noiselessly she slipped away from her peephole and made her way to the rear of the house. Finding the scullery window which Joe had broken an hour or two ago when they had first entered the house—it seemed countless hours!—she climbed in. A crashing noise from the front of the house informed her that Chard and his henchman were warming to their work.

In the kitchen she found Malcolm Channing, still trussed securely to the chair. She untied the handkerchief which covered his mouth and, inserting her fingers gingerly, extracted the potato which Mike had stuffed in as a gag.

The room was in pitch darkness, but Channing had no doubts regarding the identity of his benefactor.

"Thanks, awfully," he croaked hoarsely. "You've just about saved my life. There must have been half a ton of earth on that potato, and I've absorbed the lot. Ugh! I'll never eat another potato as long as I live!"

"Another man has arrived!" she whispered.

Instantly he was on the alert. "Have you any idea who he is?" he demanded tensely.

"The other man called him 'Chard'."

"Chard! Are you sure?"

"Quite sure."

"A middle-aged man…rather skinny…wears a beard…looks eminently respectable?"

"Yes. That's him."

"Great!" Channing's voice was jubilant. "I never thought he'd come himself. This is wonderful news!"

"They're searching the living-room for a parcel worth five thousand pounds," Diana whispered.

"Let 'em search! They won't find it."

"They were talking about a third man who is evidently coming here tonight with a consignment of some sort."

"That'll be Von Blon," said Channing.

"Yes, that was the name they mentioned."

"Are they sure he will come?"

"Yes. Chard said that the storm wouldn't stop him."

Her hand was resting on Channing's shoulder and she felt a slight shiver pass through him.

"I wouldn't be in Von Blon's shoes on a night like this," he said, unconsciously repeating the sentiment which Mike had expressed a few minutes before.

"Is there anything I can do to help you?" asked Diana.

Channing thought for a minute.

"It would take hours to file through these confounded hand-cuffs," he replied. "So, I don't see how you can help me to get free. You can take a message to someone for me, though, if you will."

"Of course, I will."

"You're a well-plucked 'un," he murmured admiringly. "We must get to know each other better after I've straightened out this tangle."

Diana stiffened at that. She had forgotten, in the excitement of recent events, the kiss which he had given her. Now she remembered it and her resentment returned.

"What is the message?" she asked coldly. "And to whom am I to deliver it?"

He did not notice her change of voice. "The grounds of this house are surrounded by men," he said.

"I saw them," she told him, shivering at thought of the fright their lurking shapes had given her.

"Bad staff work, that," said Channing, sternly. "They were told to keep out of sight. However, that can't be helped. Chard didn't see them or he wouldn't be here. I want you to go to the gate and tell the man who is stationed there—Pearson his name is—that—"

"Just a minute," whispered Diana. "Before we go any further, I want to know that I'm not stepping out of the frying-pan into the fire. I know that Chard and the other man are crooks, but I don't know anything about you. For all I know, you and your men may be members of a rival gang!"

Channing uttered a low chuckle. "You've got your head screwed on properly," he said. "No, we're not a rival gang. As a matter of fact—"

So engrossed were they that they had not heard the slither of creeping footsteps in the passage outside. To their dismay the kitchen light was turned on suddenly and they heard a low, malicious laugh from the doorway.

Diana wheeled, her eyes blinking in the bright light.

The short, burly man stood on the threshold, his small, dark eyes gleaming malevolently, his automatic levelled threateningly. He was an unpleasant sight, with his scowling brow, battered features, puffy lips which were slightly parted revealing the gap made by the absence of the tooth which Channing had knocked out, and torn and bloodstained clothing.

"'Scuse me butting in," he sneered. "Sorry to interrupt a friendly little chat." His ugly little eyes travelled to Channing's face. "So, the place is surrounded by your pals, is it? That's useful information for the boss. But I'm afraid the little lady won't be delivering any messages. I got other plans for her."

He advanced towards Diana, who backed away at his approach.

"Did me nicely, last time I had my paws on you, didn't ya?" he growled. "But I thought you wouldn't get very far. Couldn't stay away from me, eh? Well, you come along with me, sister. We'll find a cupboard or something where you'll be safe and snug for a while. Can't have you roaming about the place any longer. The boss doesn't like it."

While he spoke, his free hand snaked out and encircled her wrist. She tugged back and at the same time struck with all her might at his face. The blow stung him and his face became purple with fury.

"Damn you!" he snarled. "You little vixen!"

Drawing back his arm he swung his automatic aloft with the intention of clubbing her on the head with it. His back was towards Channing, and at that moment Channing acted. He was still manacled to the chair, but he lunched himself forward, chair and all, at the broad back of Diana's captor. His head made forcible contact with the base of Mike's spine.

The blow knocked the short, burly man off his balance. The automatic came down harmlessly and dropped from his fingers, clattering across the floor. Diana wrenched herself free and dived for it.

Mike righted himself and wheeled round with an angry bellow. Diana levelled the automatic at him.

"Stay where you are," she commanded steadily, "and put up your hands."

He checked himself and an ugly light came into his eyes. "You can't get away with this, sister," he snarled. "It'll on be worse for you later."

"I'll chance that," retorted Diana. "Put up your hands."

Without complying he drew a little nearer to her.

"Be sensible," he urged. "Give me the gun and I promise not to hurt you."

She backed away, still pointing the weapon. "Don't come any nearer or I'll shoot! She warned him.

Mike advanced another step, his beady eyes on her face. "You wouldn't have the nerve to shoot, sister," he said. "Besides, the gun ain't loaded."

With every word he was edging his way a little closer to her. Now he was crouching slightly, like a wild beast preparing to spring.

"Shoot!" roared Channing suddenly from the floor. "He'll have you if you don't!"

Shutting her eyes convulsively Diana pulled the trigger.

With an expression of wild-eyed amazement, Mike clapped his left hand to the fleshy part of his right arm and staggered back. A stream of crimson trickled between his fingers!

CHAPTER 8

A string of horrible curses issued from Mike's bruised lips. Diana swayed as a wave of nausea almost overwhelmed her at sight of the blood which stained the sleeve of his jacket and dripped from his fingertips to the floor. For a moment she was afraid that she would faint, but she managed to pull herself together.

"Mike!" It was Chard calling in a strained, nervous tone.

"Answer him!" hissed Channing from the floor. "Tell him you're alright."

"I'm alright, boss," shouted Mike with a scowl at the automatic in Diana's hand.

"I heard a shot," responded Chard, still calling from the living-room.

"You tripped and your gun went off," prompted Channing.

Mike muttered something but dried up abruptly as a hard look came into Diana's eyes.

"I tripped and me gun went off," he cried hastily.

Chard seemed satisfied with that. He asked no more questions and they could hear him moving about in the living-room once more.

"What next?" whispered Diana.

Malcolm Channing was lying humped up on the floor with the chair to which he was handcuffed on top of him.

"Give me a hand up," he replied. "This is the most infernally uncomfortable position I've ever experienced. Keep an eye on your friend, though."

Diana edged towards Channing, keeping the automatic levelled at Mike. When the chair was righted, Channing breathed a sigh of relief.

"If the Spanish Inquisitors had known what can be done with handcuffs and a chair, they'd have scrapped all their other implements of torture," he said.

"For the love of Pete, don't keep me standing here all day," grumbled Mike. "I'm bleeding like a pig."

"A most appropriate way for you to bleed," responded Channing heartlessly. "Give our friend Chard a shout and tell him to come here. Tell him you've found what he's looking for."

Mike did as he was told and a few moments later Chard appeared in the doorway. He started with horror as the sight which met his eyes.

"Stand over there beside your colleague," Channing instructed. To Diana he added: "Don't shoot unless he tries and tricks."

"My dear sir!" protested Chard. "My dear sir! I'm afraid you've made a mistake. Please allow me to explain—"

"If you can explain what you're doing in this house you're pretty good!" retorted Channing.

"Nothing could be simpler," purred Chard. "My good friend Sir Mortimer Channing, deputized me to—er—to obtain for him an—er—parcel which he forgot to take with him when he left the house."

"Containing a clean collar and his toothbrush?" mocked Channing. "That's lie number one! We'll hear the rest later. Stand over there beside your confederate!"

"But, my dear sir—"

"Did you hear me?"

"Yes. Yes. Very well."

Chard's eyes never wavered from the automatic in Diana's hand while he sidled across the room.

"Do be careful, my dear young lady," he quavered. "Such weapons are dangerous. You never know when they may go off."

"It won't go off as long as you do as you are told," said Channing. "Search your colleague's pockets and find the key of these handcuffs."

Chard opened his mouth to speak, though better of it and began to fumble nervously in Mike's pockets. Mike cursed suddenly as Chard's bungling fingers hurt his injured arm. "Look in the upper lefthand waistcoat pocket," he growled.

Much agitated, Chard fumbled in the pocket indicated and produced a small brass key. Under Diana's watchful eyes, he unlocked the handcuffs that shackled Channing's wrists and ankles to the chair. Channing rose with a wince and took one or two limping steps.

"Ye gods!" he exclaimed, wiping the beaded perspiration from his forehead. "That was torture!"

He relieved Diana of the automatic and eyed their captives grimly.

"For the love of Gawd!" snarled Mike suddenly. "Are you going to let me bleed to death?" His right sleeve was stained crimson from the shoulder to the elbow, and the blood rolling down his arm and dripping from his fingers had made a pool upon the floor.

"I'm willing," retorted Channing. "But it would be a shame to cheat the gallows of such promising raw material." He returned to Diana. "Do you suppose you could bandage his arm?" he asked.

"I'll try," she said.

Finding a pair of scissors, she slit the injured man's jacket and shirt from cuff to shoulder, exposing the wound. The bullet had drilled a neat hole through the fleshy part of the arm and the wound was by no means as serious as the amount of spilled blood suggested. The blood was already congealing. Rummaging in a cupboard, Diana found a clean sheet which she tore into strips and used to bind up the arm. When the dressing was completed, Channing motioned Mike to a chair.

"I think we can't do better than give you a dose of your own medicine," he said.

Under his supervision Diana handcuffed the wounded man to the chair, taking care not to hurt the injured arm. Far from appreciating her tenderness, Mike was volubly profane during the operation until Channing, with an unpleasant light in his eyes, ordered him to be quiet. Mike wisely subsided.

Leaving him there, the others went through to the living-room, Channing shepherding Chard, with the nose of the automatic at the base of his spine. The room looked as though a wild bull had been loose in it. Books lay everywhere in wild profusion; two legs had been sawn off the table; the upholstery of several chairs had been slit, and the stuffing strewn in heaps upon the floor; hardly an article of furniture had escaped in a whole condition.

Malcolm Channing's blue eyes softened as they rested on the half-empty bottle of whiskey which stood on the mantlepiece. He turned to Diana. In the excitement she had forgotten that she was soaked to the skin; now she was shivering and her teeth were chattering.

"You need a stiff glass of whiskey," he told her. "Do you mind bringing me a glass—two glasses, rather?"

She brought them and he poured two liberal quantities. Diana shuddered at the taste of her first sip but he made her drain it to the last drop and she was grateful when she felt the glow which suffused and enlivened her whole being.

Channing found a box of cigars among the wreckage of the smashed table and lit it with a rapt look on his face. He exhaled a cloud of fragrant smoke and his blue eyes twinkled at Diana through the steel-grey haze.

"I needed this, partner," he said.

Glancing at the clock, he turned to Chard.

"It is ten minutes to three," he said. "Von Blon will be here shortly. I don't know what the usual arrangement is, but I expect Sir Mortimer had a code of signals. A certain signal would mean that the coast was clear and that it was safe to drop the consignment. Another would warn Von Blon to steer clear. Am I right?"

Chard returned his gaze blankly. "I don't know what you mean," he replied.

"That's a stupid lie," said Channing.

"I assure you—"

"Don't please. You're going to tell me that you've never heard of Von Blon and that you don't know what he brings from Germany every ten days."

"That is entirely true," responded Chard. "This is all Greek to me. Who is Von Blon, Mr. Channing?"

Diana came forward and stared hard at him. "Why, you wretched little liar!" she exclaimed.

"Look here, Chard," said Channing steadily. "All this pretence is useless. You aren't deceiving me for a moment."

Chard glared at him without replying.

"What method of signals did Sir Mortimer use?" asked Channing.

"I refuse to tell you!" snapped Chard.

"That's better! Defence instead of prevarication. But you will tell me, Chard. I promise you that."

"You can't make me," hissed Chard.

"I can't? We'll see about that."

The big man handed the automatic to Diana. "Keep him covered while I'm gone," he said. "I shan't be a minute."

He was as good as his word. In a few moments he returned with a coil of stout cord. Lifting Chard in his arms as though he were a baby, he threw him on the couch which stood against the wall opposite the fire and proceeded to bind him hand and foot until he could not move anything but his head. When that was accomplished, he sat on the couch beside the prostrate man and gazed sternly into his eyes.

"You're a priceless swine, you know, Chard," he said. "You've lived for years in luxury on the profits from the hellish traffic you and my cousin and Von Blon have been conducting together. Prominent member of your church, aren't you?—and a bit of a philanthropist?—but you've made a good few thousand a year by damning the souls of fellow human beings."

"You can't prove it," said Chard.

Malcolm Channing nodded. "As you say, I can't prove it. That would be awkward if I were Scotland Yard, Chard. I would be powerless to punish you. But I'm not Scotland Yard. I'm merely a big-game hunter of sorts on a holiday—and I've chosen to spend my holiday hunting you. I'm not the law, so abstract justice doesn't worry me. I don't have to prove it, Chard. I'm judge and jury—and executioner. And I find you guilty!"

Fumbling in one of his pockets he produced a flat leather case. Opening it he extracted a gleaming hypodermic syringe and two tiny vials of colourless liquid.

"If I was Scotland Yard," he continued, "I should be forced to warn you that anything you said would be taken down and used in evidence against you. And if you refused to speak, I should be powerless to make you. Unfortunately for you, I'm not Scotland Yard. A few days ago, I told a friend of mine, a scientist, about you, Chard. He holds strong views about your profitable hobby. If he had his way, men like you would be wiped out—like the rats they are. He gave me this"—he held up one of the vials "—this, Chard, which contains a virulent poison, only recently discovered. One drop of it injected into your arm would paralyse your nerve-centres and kill you within a few minutes. And the beauty of it is, Chard, that no one would ever be able to say what killed you. There is no known method of discovering the presence of this poison in a dead body. It completely loses its identity within a remarkably short time."

Chard was staring at Channing with the terrified expression of a rabbit helpless in the hypnotic power of a snake. His forehead was moist with perspiration.

Channing's expression was grim and relentless.

Diana, looking on, was bewildered by the unreality of the scene. She was vaguely frightened, too. Something was happening which filled her with a sense of awe.

"Chard," said Malcolm Channing, in a low, tense voice, "Von Blon will be here soon. What are those signals?"

"I won't tell you!" screamed Chard.

Channing stood up and walked to the fireplace. The bound man's eye followed him with an expression of stark terror. Laying the leather case on the mantlepiece, Channing dipped the needlepoint of the hypodermic syringe into one of the vials and depressed and released the plunger, filling the syringe with liquid. He walked back to the couch where the frightened man lay and leant over him.

"Chard," he said, "Von Blon will hover about for a few minutes, then if no signal is given, he will go back to where he came from. Don't be a fool, Chard. You have only one chance for your life. What is the signal for the delivery of the consignment? And is there any signal which will make him land in the grounds of the house?"

"I won't tell you!" hissed Chard, through white, quivering lips. "I won't tell you!"

His eyes roved wildly to the syringe in Channing's hand. "You wouldn't dare kill me!" he shrieked.

Diana heard a subdued hum which seemed to come from a great distance. Channing went to the French windows and threw them wide open. The hum came nearer, deepened in tone and gained in volume, became louder, louder. It sounded like pebbles being thrown in rapid succession on the tight skin of a drum. High above the whisper of the dying wind and the 'drip-drip' of the thinning rain it clamoured, swelling into a roar like the beating of great wings.

"Your last chance, Chard," said Channing sternly.

The bound man squirmed, but the cord which pinioned him had been tied by an expert hand.

"You devil!" he whimpered.

Channing took his captive's wrist and inserted the needle of the hypodermic syringe under the skin.

Diana caught his arm with a startled cry. "You can't!" she protested. "You can't!"

His face grim and set, Malcolm Channing pressed the plunger, injecting the fluid into Chard's veins. The bound man uttered a shrill scream, then lapsed into unconsciousness.

CHAPTER 9

The whisky, quick!" snapped Channing. "I've got to bring him out of this faint."

"You devil!" breathed Diana. "You've killed him in cold blood!"

His blue eyes hardened and seemed to bore into her brain. "The whiskey!" he reiterated harshly.

She brought him the bottle. He moistened Chard's lips with the liquor and allowed a few drops to trickle down his throat.

Above the house beat a steady drumming, a monotonous roar...

Chard's eyes opened and he looked up weakly at Channing, who was bending over him. With the return to consciousness, terror took fresh hold of the helpless man. He shrieked aloud with fear at the fate which would be his in a few—pitifully few—minutes.

Channing put a firm hand over his mouth. "You've got one chance, Chard," he said. "In this bottle"—he held up the remaining one of the two vials—"is the antidote to the poison. But it must be administered quickly."

"For the love of God," pleaded Chard helplessly.

"The signals! What are the signals?"

The bound man hesitated.

"You'll die if you don't tell me," hissed Channing. "Can't you feel your body stiffening already, Chard? That's the nerve paralysis starting. It begins at your toes and the tips of your fingers, gradually working through your body. When it reaches your heart, you'll die! Can't you feel it, Chard? That awful numbed sensation?"

Chard could feel it. His eyes betrayed the fact. They were wide and staring. His face streamed with perspiration.

"I'll tell you!" he gasped. "Only—for God's sake—don't let me die! The sundial on the back lawn—it has a large white cement base…underneath the dial are…concealed lights… worked by twisting the pointer…two flashes means…'deliver the consignment'…"

"What is the signal to make Von Blon land?" demanded Channing.

"Turn on the light…and leave it on," whispered Chard weakly.

Channing nodded with satisfaction and strode towards the French windows. The drumming noise still beat upon the air above the house.

"The antidote!" cried Chard piteously.

"You don't need it! The stuff I injected into your veins was water—ordinary tap water!"

Chard's eyes widened. "But the numbed sensation…I could feel it! You're lying to me!"

"Auto-suggestion! I told you that you would begin to feel numbed and fear did the rest."

Channing vanished into the garden. After a moment's hesitation, Diana followed him. She found him standing by the sundial at the rear of the house looking up at the sky. Tilting her head backward she saw a dark shape, like a huge bird, circling the house.

"Von Blon in his Fokker!" said Channing.

He turned and began to investigate the sundial. It stood on a round cement base, fully twenty feet in diameter. He ran his fingers round the underside of the dial and uttered a sharp exclamation; he had found a groove in which was set a circle of electric light bulbs.

Seizing the pointer, he twisted it as hard as he could. It shifted suddenly to a new position on the dial. Instantly the whole area of the cement base was flooded with light. The aeroplane continued to circle above for a few moments, then the hum lessened and it banked and began to descend.

"He's coming down!" exclaimed Channing. "Run to the gate and tell Pearson to draw his men in nearer. Tell them to keep in cover until I signal—I don't want Von Blon to see them until it's too late."

With one backward glance at the huge shape which was swinging earthward, Diana turned and ran toward the gates. When she returned a little later the Fokker had come down on the long stretch of grass behind the house and Malcolm Channing was walking toward it.

A guttural voice, charged with suspicion, shouted from the aeroplane: "Wer ist da?"

Without replying Channing continued to advance.

Suddenly a blinding gleam of light from the Fokker cut the darkness and Channing was revealed with an automatic in his hand. He wheeled at once and ran back. Reaching Diana, he dragged her with him to the shelter of an angle of the house.

"Duck down!" he muttered. "The blighter's certain to have some sort of firearms."

The beam from the Fokker's searchlight travelled over the house, investigating corners and angles. Von Blon was more than suspicious—and he was ready for trouble. A squat, dark object appeared in the light.

"A machinegun!" breathed Channing. "The blighter's got a—"

He broke off sharply as a sudden 'crack!' sounded from among the trees to the left of the house. There was a tinkle of glass and the Fokker's searchlight went out.

"Good work!" Channing exclaimed approvingly. "One of my men," he added, "—sniper—crack shot at Bisley. Hope he's got enough sense to take cover quickly, though."

Almost before the words were out of his mouth, Von Blon in the Fokker had swung his machinegun on its pivot. With a staccato stutter, it poured a stream of leaden death into the clump of trees from which the shot had come. They could hear the thud of the bullets against the trunks of the trees and the cracking and spattering of flying twigs which were clipped from the branches. There was nothing to tell whether the sniper had been hit, however—they learned later that he had flattened himself on the ground and escaped the hail of death which screamed over him.

There was a sound from the side of the house and a man came running out.

"Chard!" exclaimed Channing hoarsely. "How the dickens did he get free? Oh, the fool! The fool!"

Diana closed her eyes convulsively for Chard was running across the grass toward the Fokker waving his arms and shouting at the pitch of his voice. The machinegun swung round and stammered out its angry message. The bullets, humming like hornets through the air, flattened themselves against the walls of the house, shattered windows and chipped the stonework.

Chard spun round and fell backward to lie motionless on the grass.

Diana, fighting back the waves of nausea which had overwhelmed her, opened her eyes. "Is he…" she faltered.

Malcolm Channing nodded soberly. "He must be riddled with bullets," he replied. "Poor devil!"

The girl trembled from head to foot. Channing put his arm round her and held her in a close, comforting embrace.

There was a roar as the mighty engine of the Fokker quickened again into life. The 'plane ran forward and swung upward, missing by mere feet the roof of the house. With a shrill wail of humming wires and stays it mounted higher into the air, its propeller whirring like mammoth wings.

Three sharp cracks sounded from the trees where the sniper had again brought his repeating rifle into action. One bullet hit a telephone wire and there was a resonant 'twang'. The others buried themselves in the Fokker. The engine faltered and missed a beat.

"By the Lord Harry!" exclaimed Channing. "He's got her!"

The Fokker lurched and swayed like a wounded bird, then swerving, swung its nose earthward and hurtled down. It hit the turf with a crash and buried its nose deep in the earth, throwing up a fountain of soil and small stones. An explosion followed and the wrecked machine burst into flames. Red and orange tongues of fire shot up into the air and licked hungrily at the fuselage.

Within moments the aeroplane was a red-hot tangle of twisted metal and blazing wood.

CHAPTER 10

They were sitting in the living-room; a quiet, awed little group of people; Diana, Malcolm Channing and Detective Inspector Pearson of Scotland Yard. Mike was there, too—handcuffed and glowering. Through the windows they could still see the white-hot glow of the burning wreckage of Von Blon's Fokker. The hungry flames had consumed to a cinder all that was mortal of Von Blon and his funeral pyre was now a skeleton of twisted metal. On the lawn, covered by a white sheet, lay the machinegun-riddled body of Simon Chard.

"Poor devil!" said Malcolm Channing suddenly. "Poor devil!" He was thinking of Von Blon and the others knew it. They too could not help shuddering at the thought of the aviator's terrible death.

Diana shivered. "To die like that!" she whispered. "In the midst of a blazing inferno."

Detective Inspector Pearson moved awkwardly in his chair. "Horrible to think of, miss," he said. "And yet it was a fine death in a way. A man's death. Von Blon was a famous flying ace during the war. One of Richtofer's Circus, the pick of the German flying fighters. He would have wished to go out that way—burning to glory with the 'plane he loved. If he had fallen into our hands, it would have meant at least five years imprisonment. Prison would have been Hades for a man like Von Blon. Perhaps he's better dead."

"But what were they doing; Von Blon and Chard, and Sir Mortimer?" asked the girl. "What was the traffic they were carrying on?"

Pearson glanced at Malcolm Channing. "Perhaps you'll tell her, sir?"

Channing nodded. "They were smuggling drugs—cocaine and heroin," he said.

The room was lit only by the firelight and the grey and rose half-light of the dawn. Diana, looking at Channing, who was sitting in the shadow, saw that his jaw was set and his eyes were hard and steely.

"Of all the hellish commodities that were ever brought or sold, or bartered, cocaine is the worst," he said. "It can truthfully be said of the syndicate composed of Chard, Von Blon and my cousin that they dealt in human souls and thrived and battened on the destruction of the health and happiness of their fellow beings. The addicts who bought the foul stuff from them would have committed any crime, any beastliness, while under its influence, and were little better than raving lunatics when deprived of it. Cocaine robs the senses, degenerates the mind; makes a beast of a man. Worse than a beast—deprived of cocaine, the chronic addict is a weak, despicable thing who will grovel in the gutter for a pinch of 'snow'."

He turned fiercely on Mike, who shrank back in his chair.

"You worked for them! You lived on their filthy money! You know what cocaine does to a man! Did you ever try it?"

Mike shook his head. "God forbid!" he said.

Malcolm Channing mopped his forehead.

"You have heard of Philip Marble?" he asked Diana.

The name was familiar. Diana could hardly repress a shudder when she remembered in what connection she had heard it. "The murd…" she faltered.

"Yes, the murderer," agreed Channing bitterly. "He was hung a month ago for shooting his guardian. He was my friend at Oxford—the best friend anyone ever had. I was big-game hunting in Africa when I heard of his trial. I took the first boat home and landed at Southampton three days before the morning on which he was hung. Through the courtesy of the Home Secretary, I managed to see him in prison. It was a shocking experience. He was no more than a skeleton, with shrunken cheeks and staring eyes. They were allowing him drugs to keep him quiet—it wasn't worth while trying to cure him when he was to die in three days. He told me what had brought him there—cocaine. He had been an addict for two years. A 'friend' had started him on the habit. Got him to try it 'just once' as a new experience. He tried it again—and again. It got a grip of him. Every penny he could lay his hands on went to buy the filthy stuff. Eventually, he was at his wits' ends how to obtain more. His guardian had some funds in trust for him which were payable at his—the guardian's—discretion. Philip went to him and demanded money. Knowing only too well what Philip wanted it for, the old man refused. Philip begged and pleaded, went down on his knees for money, but the guardian stuck to his guns. Not a penny would he part with to be spent on cocaine. Philip went crazy and threatened him with a gun. Somehow—God knows how—it went off. The old man was killed instantly—Philip, my friend, was a murderer. And yet, at one time—before he started using drugs—he was the kindest and best fellow I ever knew. You know the rest. The hangman's rope got him—but it only finished the work cocaine started!"

With a large linen handkerchief, he wiped his brow again. "He was pitifully glad to see me when I went to him in prison and he told me the whole story. Not only that, he said he was the only one of hundreds of cases in London of lives ruined by the drug habit. I was startled. 'But what skunk supplies the stuff?' I asked. He smiled. It was easy to obtain. He knew a score of peddlers of heroin and cocaine—you only needed money. 'Where does it come from?' I asked. 'Abroad,' he replied. 'Germany, chiefly. It's smuggled in by a syndicate. There's a fortune in it.'

He looked at me queerly. 'I'll tell you this,' he said. 'I believe I know the name of one man in that syndicate—and that man is Mortimer Channing.'

"I was staggered. I hurled questions at him, but either he wouldn't or couldn't tell me more. Afterwards, on thinking it over, I went to Scotland Yard. They confirmed the fact that there was a syndicate at work, smuggling drugs, but they hadn't the faintest clue to the identity of its members. I offered my services to help in running down the gang, on condition that I was allowed to work my own way. After some parley, they agreed.

"I lay low—hushed up the news of my return from Africa—and kept an eye on my cousin, Sir Mortimer Channing. Gradually I learned things. I connected him with Chard, who was a partner in an old established firm of solicitors with offices in Holborn. Chard I connected with another man, a known criminal, who was the intermediary between the syndicate and the peddlers. Eleven days ago, I was watching through a telescope from a tree a quarter of a mile away when Von Blon dropped a parcel of drugs from his Fokker in the grounds of this house.

"The following evening, when my cousin set out to walk to the nearest village where one of Chard's messengers was to meet him to collect the parcel, I was waiting in a car with two assistants. We had been spying on him all day. We drove up as Mortimer came out of the gates. He was surprised to see me, naturally, for he had not known that I was in England, but I explained that I had just arrived home. I offered him a lift, and when he was in the car my two assistants overpowered and chloroformed him. The parcel of drugs in his possession was evidence enough to convict him, but I wanted to account for Chard and Von Blon as well.

"He refused to answer questions, so I was forced to keep him hidden away—quite illegally—in the hope that the others would show their hand when the next consignment was due, as it was, early this morning. I forged a note, purporting to come from my cousin, and sent it to Chard. The rest you know."

There was a lengthy silence, then Inspector Pearson rose to his feet. He crossed the room and jerked Mike up.

"I'll take this fellow along now, sir," he said. "And we'll collect your cousin at the place you told me. I'll withdraw my men now—you won't need them any longer. I'll see that a couple of policemen are sent up from Norwich in the morning to keep Nosy Parkers from swarming over the grounds. Good night, sir." He cast an admiring glance in Diana's direction. "Good night, miss."

Diana and Malcolm Channing were left alone together. Suddenly Diana sprang to her feet with a cry.

"Good heavens!" she exclaimed. "Joe and Rose!—I forgot all about them—they've been locked in a cupboard upstairs for hours!"

"Joe and Rose!" repeated Channing with a frown. "Oh, yes, the butler and the cook. Poor blighters! We'd better release them at once."

They hurried upstairs and unlocked the door of the cupboard on the first floor where the Carey's had been shut up by Mike over two hours before. They found Joe and Rose wrapped in each other's arms, huddled together at the bottom of the cupboard fast asleep!

CHAPTER 11

D iana turned over in bed and her eyes flickered open. The morning sun, streaming in the windows, dazed and hurt her eyeballs. She dropped her eyelids over them again and buried her head under the bedclothes.

Someone was shaking her shoulder. "Diana, get up! It's seven o'clock…we've got to get out of here!"

It was Rose speaking. With a sigh, Diana opened her eyes again and blinked about her. Then she sat up in bed; memory returned in a flood. Last night—good heavens!—could all that have happened last night?

Except for her shoes she was fully dressed. She had tumbled into bed with her clothes on at four o'clock, utterly exhausted. She turned tired eyes on Rose. "I remember now," she said. "We let you and Joe out of the cupboard—"

"That infernal cupboard!" exclaimed Rose. "It was like a coffin. I was never so uncomfortable in my life, until, by some miracle, I fell asleep."

"When we woke you, you both simply tottered to the bedroom next door and slumped on the bed, dead to the world!"

"No wonder!" declared Rose fervently. "I'd have slept the clock round, only Joe wouldn't let me. He wants to get out of here as quickly as possible and I don't blame him."

"I staggered in here," Diana went on, "and dropped on the bed like a log and Mr. Channing—"

"He's snoring his head off in there," Rose interjected, nodding in the direction of the third bedroom. "But let's cut out the conversation now, Diana. If we hang about here for another hour or two, we'll have a lot of explaining to do. Don't forget we broke into the house in the first place."

Diana sat on the edge of the bed and ran a pocket comb through her thick golden waves. "So much has happened since then that I'd forgotten all about Joe's burglary," she said. "Are the Scotland Yard men gone?"

"I didn't even know they were here," retorted Rose. "You forget Joe and I spent half the night in that confounded cupboard. But there's no one about now. There's a tangle of blackened metal on the lawn at the rear, though, and the grass for yards about is scorched to nothing. What on earth happened last night, anyway?"

"A lot of things!" said Diana fervently. She slipped her neat little feet into her muddy shoes. "I'll tell you the whole story later, but for heaven's sake let's have some breakfast now. I'm starving!"

"Well, who isn't?" retorted Rose.

They went downstairs and found that Joe had prepared ham and eggs, toast and coffee. He had also gathered together their three suitcases, so that they would be ready to start off immediately they had finished breakfast. All that had been wrong with the car the previous night, he had discovered, was a lack of petrol. He had remedied that by 'borrowing' two gallons of petrol from Malcolm Channing's saloon Bentley, and the little two-seater was ready for the road.

"Don't you think we should let Mr. Channing know we're going? Suggested Diana timorously.

The other two stared at her.

"What, and have to explain that we aren't his cousin's servants—that we deliberately broke in last night?" demanded Joe.

"And ate his food and drank his whisky," added Rose.

"It seems rather shabby to walk out without a word," said Diana.

"We're lucky to be able to!" replied Joe. "It isn't easy walking out of prison without considerable fuss!"

"Have you forgotten what Mister Channing did last night?"

asked Rose pointedly. "Because he thought you were only a housemaid, he kissed you. After an insult like that—"

Diana's blue eyes hardened. "Yes, you're right," she agreed. "He doesn't deserve any consideration."

And yet, when the others were ready for the road, they found her in the kitchen, setting a second batch of breakfast on a tray.

"Who's that for?" asked Rose suspiciously.

Diana had the grace to blush. "It doesn't seem right to leave him without any breakfast," she explained hastily. "He may not be able to cook."

Rose shook her head and threw up her hands expressively. Without waiting for further comment, Diana hurried upstairs and placed the tray on the mat outside Channing's bedroom door. She knocked twice hastily, then ran downstairs.

Her companions were waiting for her at the front door. Joe fumbled in one of his pockets and produced the letter addressed to Channing which they had found on the living-room mantlepiece when they first entered the house. He went into the living-room and replaced it in a conspicuous position. Diana giggled at that. She was picturing Channing's face when he found the house empty, the servants gone, and a note of resignation awaiting him, dated the previous day!

The little two-seater made up for its dereliction the previous night by running sweetly and smoothly all the way to Norwich. They found lodgings for the week, then went to the theatre and met some other members of the cast of 'All for Love'.

There were large headlines in the papers the following morning:

INTERNATIONAL DRUG RING SMASHED

GERMAN FLYER PERISHES IN WRECKAGE OF BLAZING 'PLANE

LONDON SOLICITOR SLAIN BY ACCOMPLICE

SIR MORTIMER CHANNING IN CUSTODY

SCOTLAND YARD MAKES MANY ARRESTS

WHOLESALE ROUND-UP OF WEST END DRUG PEDDLERS.

Columns of closely-set type described the events of the small hours of Sunday morning at The Grove, Norfolk. Sir Mortimer Channing, it was stated, was in prison awaiting trial with a large number of the syndicate's underlings. Malcolm Channing's name was not mentioned (he preferred the credit for the whole affair to be ceded to Scotland Yard).

Diana thought of Channing frequently during the next few days. Thought of him wistfully, regretfully. He had seemed so entirely her ideal of young manhood. She had been immensely attracted to him at first sight—but he had spoiled it all by treating her like a forward barmaid, to be kissed at will and forgotten. Had he forgotten? She knew that she could never forget.

On the last night of their week at the Norwich Theatre, Joe came to the dressing room which Rose and Diana shared, just before the performance was due to begin.

"Channing's in the stalls!" he declared. "I peeped through the curtain just now to see how the house was filling up and I saw him. Not only that—the stage manager told me that the chap sitting with him is one of the local police inspectors!"

They looked at each other apprehensively.

"Now we're in for it!" said Rose gloomily. "We'll be arrested after the show!"

"What can they do to us?" asked Diana anxiously. "After all, we didn't do anything so very bad."

"Breaking and entering, stealing a quantity of food and whisky, impersonating the servants, stealing two gallons of petrol," Joe ticked off the list of their crimes on his fingers.

Diana turned quite pale. She had heard of a man—a starving man—who had been sent to jail for a month for stealing a single loaf!

"We should have left money to pay for everything, but I forgot," said Joe. "Even if we had, I suppose the charges would stand."

"What can we do?" gasped Diana.

Joe shrugged his shoulders. "Go on with the show for the present," he replied. "And face the music when it comes. After all, I was to blame. Even if they send me to prison, you girls will probably escape with a caution."

"Not on your life!" said Diana firmly. "We'll share and share alike!"

During her first appearance, she could not keep her eyes from straying to the stalls where Malcolm Channing sat with the grim-faced inspector of police, and as she left the stage she was horrified to see Channing leave his seat and make for one of the exits. A few moments later she was alone in her dressing room when the doorkeeper presented Channing's card. In a still, small voice, she told him to show in the gentleman.

Malcolm Channing came in and closed the door. He stood with his back to it, looking at her with an odd little smile.

"Well, what did you mean by it?" he asked suddenly.

"Mean by what?" she faltered.

"By leaving your job without notice," he retorted with twinkling eyes.

A wave of relief flooded over her. "Then you aren't going to arrest us?"

"Arrest you? You deserve a medal! You were wonderful that night. But what on earth made you run away in the morning?"

She hesitated. "Well, we had made so free with everything—"

"Including my heart?" Channing grinned at her confusion. "When I was awakened by someone knocking at my door and found a breakfast tray on the matt, I was mildly surprised," he went on. "It seemed an odd hour for breakfast after a strenuous night. But when I dressed and came downstairs to find you gone, I was completely bewildered. And the note on the mantlepiece—well, I didn't know what to make of it."

"We thought it would puzzle you," said Diana mischievously.

"It did. Of course, I quickly found out that the three 'servants' who greeted me on my arrival at the house weren't my cousin's servants. Since then, I'd been living in an empty world. You were gone without a word and I hadn't the faintest idea how to find you."

Diana was silent.

"It was Milton who found you in the end—Inspector Milton, of the Norwich police," he continued. "I sent out a description of all three of you and he recognised it. He sent for me to come here tonight and see the show. The moment you came on stage a load was lifted from my heart—since then I've been living in a new world. I've been longing so terribly to find you again."

He took her hand, but she drew it away.

"Do you remember what happened—that night—when I knocked on the living-room door just after you arrived—you opened the door, and—and—"

"I kissed you!" he said fervently. "Do I remember? That kiss has kept me going these last terrible days, when I thought I had lost you forever."

"It was an insult, that kiss," she replied quietly.

Taking her gently by the shoulders, he turned her round to face him."

"You are quite wrong," he said sternly. "I had been hunting in Africa for over a year—in darkest Africa, where the heat dries the marrow in your bones and makes leather of your tongue. Then a month of hell, when all I could think of was the dope traffic, that made swine of decent men. You came to me, the living embodiment of all the dreams which had sustained me through the physical hardships of Africa, and the mental agony of the last month. You stood there at the door, with your eyes shining like beacons and the light gleaming on your hair. I kissed you; it was inevitable that I should. If death had been the reward for kissing you, still I would have kissed you!"

"If only I'd known!" she breathed.

He walked to the door and opened it.

"Milton!" he called.

The grim-faced inspector appeared in the doorway.

"Yes, sir?"

"Have you your handcuffs?"

The inspector fumbled for, and found, the linked bracelets of brass,

Channing returned to Diana's side with them dangling from his hand.

"What are you going to do?" she asked.

"I'm going to arrest you after all."

He slipped one of the bracelets over her slender wrist and locked the other to his own.

"I think," he said, "a life sentence will meet the case!"

A strong arm went round Diana's waist and a hand under her chin tilted her lips upward to meet his.

Joe and Rose appeared in the doorway and looked in cautiously.

"Joe!" exclaimed Rose. "Good heavens, Joe! He's kissing her again!"

THE END